SLOTH

THE DAMNING BOOK 4

KATIE MAY

EXPRESSO PUBLISHING, LLC

To my amazing, incredible readers. Super sorry about the cliffhanger in the last book. I'll try to avoid them from now on (laughs evilly). Or will I?

Oh, and also to my mom because I promised I'd dedicate this one to her. Just...don't read the sex scenes. Please? Actually, pretend that there are no sex scenes whatsoever and that your daughter isn't writing about multiple men banging one woman. I think we can all live much happier that way.

CONTENTS

When Z wins the Damning—a competition that pits the best assassins against each other—her world is overturned. Suddenly, she's forced to be the assassin for the exact kings she wishes to kill.

Fortunately, she has the seven princes to help her with the tasks ahead, each prince one of the seven supernatural species descended from the Seven Deadly Sins... and her fated mates. There's a prophecy surrounding the seven princes that they'll either save the world or destroy it. They despise their parents and their inhumane treatment of humans.

At the end of the first book, Z had been poisoned by a competitor of the Damning named Zack at the order of Aaliyah. Her mates are completely unaware that she was poisoned...and that the poison is slowly killing her.

The kings assign seven tasks, seven games, Z has to complete to prove her loyalty. Despite her hatred for them, a spell administered by the mage king prohibits her from harming any member of the royal family.

She completes the first task, assigned by the mermaid king. In the process, Dair kills his evil older brother, Tavvy, who'd attempted to rape and kill Z. Just before he dies, Tavvy tells Dair that he and the rest of the Z's mates weren't born—they appeared out of thin air.

Meanwhile, a mysterious female named Aaliyah is sending extinct supernatural creatures after Z, including a gorgon, kraken, and fae. She instructs her monsters not to kill Z, but to bring her to Aaliyah alive.

At the end of book two, Z discovers that Jax, her vampire mate, has gone missing.

The kings assign Z her next task—find Jax and return him to the capital in five days. If she fails, she dies. If she succeeds, the kings will have a special reward waiting for her. The kings force Axel, their former assassin, and T, a member of the Alphabet Resistance who has been taken prisoner, to accompany them. Dair, who has finally confessed the truth about his father's torment to Z and the others, remains behind to recover.

While in the Vampire Kingdom, the inn they are staying at is lit on fire, and Z is kidnapped and brought to the Bloody Carnival—a macabre event where vampires and other nightmares prey on humans. She meets a young boy, Miles, who she instantly feels protective of.

Killian, Lupe, Devlin, and Axel search for Z, while Jax and Ryland continue their quest for Jax. Dair, back at the capital, uses a spell to bring him to the others.

During the confrontation at the Bloody Carnival, Miles is killed, a fact that devastates Z. Axel agrees to search for Miles's younger sister while Z and the other freed humans bury the bodies.

The gang—now including Dair—finally catches up to Ryland and Bash, who announce that Aaliyah has been keeping Jax prisoner. Through her connection with Jax, Z knows he's been forced to feed on blood regularly, losing himself to the bloodlust and madness.

Aaliyah arrives with her pet gargoyles and Jax and tells the group that she's Z's sister and a demon. A fight ensues. During the battle, Jax is stabbed and killed, and Aaliyah disappears before anyone can stop her. Z, in her grief, pours white light into Jax, bringing him back to life. In the process, the poison coursing through Z's system catches up to her and she collapses.

Meanwhile, Axel finds Miles's sister and discovers she's the first nightmare-human hybrid to exist.

T reveals to have been the one to give Z's location up to the human traffickers at the Bloody Carnival in exchange for S's—his brother and Z's ex-boyfriend—soul. At the end of book three, S is alive and well and demanding to know Z's whereabouts.

CHARACTERS:

Z — Member of the Alphabet Resistance that advocates for human rights, assassin, mate to the seven princes, and winner of The Damning. She is poisoned at the end of book one

Dair — Z's mate, mermaid, and descended from Envy. Like all mermaids, he's forced to live as a mermaid for twelve hours a day and a human the other twelve. His father constantly cuts his legs off, grows them back, and then cuts them off again each night.

Devlin — Z's mate, genie, and descended from Greed. He has a soul trapped in his lamp that he accidentally lost. He's Z's childhood sweetheart.

Killian — Z's mate, incubus, and descended from Lust. As a child, he was forced to watch his father rape and kill his nanny. Currently a virgin.

Lupe — Z's mate, shifter, and descended from Wrath. His father implemented the first human concentration camps. He prefers to fight with words rather than violence.

Ryland — Z's mate, shadow, and descended from Pride. He hides his face in his shadows to hide his hideous facial scarring. He was the first to know all of the princes were mates with Z.

Jax — Z's mate, vampire, and descended from Gluttony. He's facing madness because he refuses to drink human blood and is only coherent around Z. Currently engaged to Atta. He was kidnapped by Aaliyah at the end of book two but is rescued in book three.

Bash — Z's mate, mage, and descended from Sloth. He distrusts the mate bond and the lack of free will, so he struggles with his affections for Z.

Atta — Shifter and descended from Wrath. She's Lupe's younger sister and the mate to Mali, but is currently engaged to Jax.

Mali — Vampire and descended from Gluttony. She's Z's best friend who unwittingly betrayed her, leading to the death of the mage, Diego. Mate to Zack (now dead) and Atta.

Diego — Mage and descended from Sloth. Z's best friend and mate to HH. He was murdered by Zack protecting Z after Mali betrayed them.

T — Z's friend from the Alphabet Resistance and brother of S.

S — Z's deceased ex-boyfriend who was killed by shifters and T's brother. It's discovered that Devlin had his soul inside of his lamp until he lost it. T makes a deal with human traffickers to retrieve his soul, thus bringing him back to life.

B — Leader of the Alphabet Resistance.

A — Z's former mentor before he died.

Aaliyah — Main antagonist of the series who wants to capture Z for reasons unknown. She reveals herself to be Z's sister and a demon at the end of book three.

Zack — Mage and evil assassin who killed Diego and poisoned Z. He was Mali's mate, but now he's dead.

Axel — Shadow and ex-assassin of the kingdoms.

PROLOGUE

T

He was here.

Alive.

In front of me.

I couldn't help but note the minuscule changes from when I last saw him. For starters, his hair was slightly longer, grazing his chin in brown waves interwoven with darker red streaks. The change was so menial that I probably wouldn't have noticed if I didn't carry around a picture of my brother, taken two days before his accident.

Two days before he went on a mission with Z and never returned.

She'd told me that he'd been ripped apart by shifters, that she watched it happen, but that wasn't the truth. At least it wasn't completely the truth.

Somehow, some way, my brother's soul found its way into Devlin Genie's lamp. The Prince of Genies had been carrying my brother's soul around for years, and we'd been none the wiser.

What happened when those shifters attacked? What

deal did my brother make with the fucking prince, Z's fated mate and lover?

I stared into his eyes, so much like my own, but his expression was guarded. I would've almost described it as wary before deciding that didn't quite encapsulate it.

Confused.

Yes, my brother was most definitely confused.

He stared around the tiny shack we'd found ourselves in. It was the only location I could find at such short notice, nothing but four walls of distressed wooden boards, a crumbling roof, and squares where there were once windows, the ground beneath them littered with shards of broken glass.

I knew the princes and Z wouldn't have realized I'd left yet. No doubt, they would be searching for me, if not now, then later. I was supposed to be their prisoner, their slave, but I'd be damned if I let them chain me again. Not after I'd gotten my brother back.

I'd traded my soul for his.

Once again, guilt swamped me when I thought about what I did. Giving up Z's location to that trafficker...

I told myself over and over again that her mates wouldn't let anything happen to her, that she was no doubt safe and in their arms, but even those comforting thoughts couldn't negate the guilt and worry. For all I knew, she was still trapped in one of those sick human carnivals so popular in the Vampire Kingdom.

Or dead.

"T," S said slowly. His forehead creased. "Where are we? Where's Z?"

A lump formed in my throat, and no matter how

many times I tried to swallow it away, it remained. It wasn't painful or anything, but it sat there, just sat there, and I felt as if I was suffocating.

My brother's face lightened when he said her name, the love in his eyes plain to see, even as his features twisted and contorted.

So how the fuck did I shatter his heart—the heart that only just started beating again mere minutes before—by telling him Z had moved on with seven other men? Seven other men...who happened to be the feared princes of the land. That one of them was the same man who'd broken her heart as a teenager, the first person she'd ever loved.

"S," I began cautiously, gauging his reaction carefully. "What do you remember?"

Do you remember dying?

The shifters attacking?

Devlin?

His face remained placid, except for the slightest tightening of the skin around his eyes. He absently scratched at the back of his neck.

"I don't..." His nose wrinkled. "I don't remember." Shaking his head from side to side, he frowned and speared me with an intense look. "But where's Z? I need to see her!" When I didn't immediately answer, at a loss for what to say, he lunged forward and gripped both of my shoulders. "Where the fuck is my girlfriend?"

Oh shit.

ONE

BASH

What the fuck are we going to do?

I stared at Z's face, serene in sleep. Some of the worry lines that had grown more prominent over the last few weeks had abated entirely. In sleep, there was no heavy weight resting on my mate's shoulders, pushing her into the ground.

Thunderous anger cascaded through me at the thought of Zack, the asshole assassin from the Damning who'd poisoned my mate. He was dead now, but apparently, we still couldn't escape him.

My mouth felt unbearably dry as I rested my hands above Z's chest and sent a burst of healing magic into her system. Her mouth parted, a tiny gasp escaping her, as she arched her back. Her beautiful features were etched in pain, her blonde brows furrowed.

"I know, baby. I know," I whispered, feeling as if my heart was being torn in two.

Because while there was fear and agony...there was also guilt. A lot of fucking guilt.

I'd been an asshole to Z when I discovered the truth about the mating bond. A real dick. I knew she didn't love me the way she did the others, and I had no one to blame but myself. My love was toxic, a burden I wished no person had to bear, but now that I couldn't even offer Z the chance to experience it, I felt oddly bereft. Empty. Devoid of anything remotely human.

"How is she?" Devlin strode into the room we'd rented out in the nearest inn, just on the outskirts of the Vampire Kingdom. His olive complexion was waxy and pale, and his dark brown curls were wildly disheveled.

It'd been hours since we arrived, since I confessed the truth to my brothers about Z's condition—a secret I'd been carrying for far too long. They were angry at first, as they rightfully should've been, but that anger quickly transformed into worry for our girl. Lupe and Killian went to the local library to do research, though I had no idea what they were looking up. It was impossible for me to determine the exact type of poison used, and her symptoms could be attributed to nearly a hundred different combinations. Either way, they felt the need to do something, anything, besides sitting here and twiddling their thumbs.

I understood that. I did.

Dair was sleeping in the room next door, his body still recovering from his father's torture a few days prior. Ryland was trying to calm a distressed Jax—yet another problem to add to our list of fucking problems. Problem, problem, problem, problem.

I was really beginning to hate that word.

Because Z, my perfect, angelic mate, was somehow

able to bring Jax back to life. We had no idea how that was possible, but whatever transpired between the two of them somehow exacerbated the poison running rampant through her bloodstream. The amount of power she'd wielded...

It had broken her.

And by default, it broke my already crazy vampire brother too.

The brief coherence he'd found had shattered until he was back to the rambling, drooling, fearful man he'd become after he accidentally killed Sasha many years ago.

"Bash!" Devlin snapped, pulling me out of my thoughts. His lips pursed as he glared at me, and I realized I'd never responded to his question.

"She's the same," I admitted with a heavy sigh. I was running on empty, but I wouldn't stop, couldn't stop, not until Z's eyes opened. Until she graced me with one of her cocky grins that only curled up a corner of her lips.

"I can't lose her," Devlin whispered hoarsely. "I can't."

"I know." I brushed a hand through my blond hair. "I'm doing everything I can—"

"Well, that's not good enough!" His words made me flinch, though I tried to hide it. I failed, apparently, because his eyes immediately softened, some of the tension draining from his taut shoulders. "Look, I'm sorry. I know you're doing everything you can—"

"I am," I said firmly, interrupting him as I turned away to face Z once more. "You're not the only one who cares about her, Dev."

You're not the only one who loves her.

But those were words I would never say out loud, never admit to my brothers or the sleeping girl in front of me. Those words held power, immense power, and I knew my life would be irrevocably altered the second I uttered them.

"You're right." He dragged a hand down his face, his tongue snaking out to lick his upper lip. "I know you're right. But fuck..."

"Fuck is right," I murmured.

Frowning, I stared once more at Z's sleeping face. Z. Zara. Susan. Gabriella. So many names were associated with this tiny slip of a girl, but which one was *hers*? Was she cold and crass like Z? Sweet and bubbly like Zara? The girl next door finding love for the first time like Susan? Or was she still that innocent girl, trying to hold on to her family and friends like Gabriella?

"We need to talk about what Aaliyah said," Devlin interjected softly. He brushed his knuckles against Z's face, and she stirred, almost as if she was seeking out the genie's warmth unconsciously. My heart battered my ribs, each beat getting deafeningly louder as I peeled my gaze away from hers and towards her tiny hand hanging off the bed. So pale. So still. So...lifeless.

Maybe that was what was fucking me up. Z always seemed to be larger than life, a presence capable of lighting up any room. It was physically painful to see her like this, as if someone had stuck a thousand knives in my chest and were dragging them downwards, across all of the sensitive organs present.

"I don't trust that bitch further than I can throw her,"

I muttered, unwilling to peel my gaze away from Z's fingers. Did they twitch? My gaze narrowed as I willed them to move, to do anything but lie there limp and docile.

"She said she was Z's sister," Devlin pointed out, and I knew he was talking more to himself than to me. Out of my periphery, I watched as he absently scratched at his stubbled chin. "But Z doesn't have a sister. I would know."

Jealousy unfurled in my chest, the feeling reminiscent of a wilting rose with black, drooping petals and a thorny stem. There was nothing beautiful or serene about this particular flower.

I would never admit to anyone how jealous I was of Devlin's relationship with Z. He knew her before any of us did. He *loved* her, and in return, he had her love. A selfish part of me wanted her to myself even now. What would that be like? To have Z's undivided attention and love?

Immediately as I thought that, I swept it away, brushing it beneath the proverbial rug.

Z never picked between my brothers and me, and she didn't have a favorite. To claim that her love and attention were divided was wrong and untrue. She loved fiercely and passionately, willing to go to the ends of the earth if you were one of those few people fortunate enough to be loved by her.

And maybe, with time, one of those people would be me.

"What the fuck are we going to do, Dev?" I queried, dropping my face into my hands. My stomach was a tangled nest of emotions and sensations. It felt like lumps of coal had taken up residence there, each one heavier than the last. "We have two days to find the cure and head to the capital with Jax. If we don't..." I didn't even bother articulating the ending of that thought. It was too horrible to consider.

"We'll figure something out," Devlin said resolutely. "We always do."

"But—"

His head whipped in my direction, his violet eyes narrowing as his power flared around him. "No buts."

"And you're sure wishing on your lamp won't help?" I pressed. Genies were the only nightmares who weren't able to use their own powers without a conduit, so to speak. They needed someone to wish on their lamp in order to use their magic. But as Devlin had told us numerous times, he couldn't cure Z. The poison coursing through her was magical in nature, no doubt a product of a powerful mage and not a natural ailment of the body. As such, his genie powers couldn't cure her.

We'd tried.

We'd all fucking tried.

Not even my magic could save her life. It was almost as if my powers bounced off of her, ricocheting from her skin like she was made of titanium.

What the fuck did Zack give her?

"Aaliyah knows," I whispered, swallowing around a lump in my throat. "She knows how to save Z. I don't trust her, but we don't have any other option. Maybe we should—"

"No." Devlin shook his head dogmatically. "No,

we're not bringing Z to that bitch. It's what she wants, and we still don't know what for."

"But if it's that or losing Z..." I squeezed my eyelids shut, though that did little to dispel the horrific images that bombarded me. Losing Z was unimaginable. It couldn't fucking happen.

As if reading my thoughts, Devlin said, "That won't happen." He placed a hand on my shoulder, for once looking anything but immaculate in his suit, his buttons undone and tie removed. There was even a stain on the collar of his shirt that hadn't been there prior. "We'll find a way to save Z and get back to the capital." His face hardened with steely determination. "I refuse to accept any other alternative."

Where would a crazy as fuck vampire hide?

Moving with the shadows, I stealthily ventured around the corner of the inn, glancing in both directions in search of Jax.

He'd left the room in a hurry, muttering beneath his breath about his blood no longer tingling. His words had instantly concerned me, though I refused to show how much to my already volatile brothers.

Vampire blood tingled when they came in contact with their mate. To hear that Jax's no longer did that...

Something happened to my brother when he died and came back to life. I didn't know what it was for sure, but I knew the only thing that could potentially save him was Z.

And with Z indisposed, that burden fell on me.

I swallowed, my throat burning with emotion, as I thought about the way I'd left my sweet assassin mate. My little dove. She looked so still sleeping in the uncomfortable bed of the inn. Angelic almost, with her golden hair cascading around her pillow like liquid amber.

When would she wake up?

I refused to believe that her condition was permanent. Absolutely refused.

"Jax!" I bellowed, not bothering to remain quiet as I moved towards the thicket of trees at the edge of the property. The forest looked as if it went on for miles and miles, nothing but skeletal branches as far as the eye could see. "Jaxon!"

"Fairy blood. The blood sparkles. Why doesn't it sparkle? Why? Why? Why?"

I followed the voice farther into the trees, past a stump and towards the tallest oak in the forest. Crouching down, I met Jax's blood-red eyes as he struggled to control his vampire form.

My brother was sitting beneath the tree, his legs pulled up to his chest and his arms wrapped around them as he rocked. His light brown hair was pushed away from his face, and sweat beaded on his forehead.

"Jax," I said gently, cautiously, as if attempting to corner a wounded animal. "Are you okay, man?" It was a stupid question, and I felt like a complete imbecile the second I asked it. Of course he was not okay. He'd died, for fuck's sake, and had come back to life. Not only that, but Z, the love of his existence, was dying with no cure in sight.

Not dying, I reminded myself firmly. I needed to believe that, or else something inside of me would fracture.

I allowed the shadows surrounding me to disperse, revealing my scarred face to him.

"Jax..."

"My blood doesn't tingle," he said, his urgency evident in every taut line of his face and the way his body trembled. "It doesn't tingle."

"Okay. Okay." Keeping my movements slow, giving him ample opportunity to pull away, I placed my hand on his shoulder, giving it a soft squeeze. "Do you want to... talk about it?"

"It doesn't tingle because she's not there," Jax continued, his hand snapping upwards to grip my wrist. I could feel my brows furrow in concern.

"What do you mean?"

"She's not there." He shook his head from side to side rapidly, his grip tightening on my wrist. "Not there. Not there. Not there."

"What do you mean?" I demanded, knowing that I needed him to be coherent for one goddamn minute of his life in order for me to understand. I had a feeling that what he had to say was immensely important. Maybe the key to solving this entire fucked-up mess.

Trembling, Jax released my hand and brought a single finger to his own forehead.

And then, with his voice nothing but a hushed murmur, nearly lost in the ruffle of tree branches overhead and the occasional squeak of animals, he said, "She's *here*."

"In your head?" My heart raced, danced, tangoed, never slowing down, never stopping, always racing.

Did something happen when Z healed Jax? I supposed it could make sense. After all, she'd collapsed the second she finished. Maybe the poison hadn't been what made her drop to the ground. Maybe it had been—

"And here." He pointed at my own forehead, and my confusion only amplified. He then gesticulated wildly towards the inn, where I knew my other brothers to be. "And there."

"Jax, I don't understand—"

"We keep her here," he continued earnestly, his eyes ensnaring my own and beseeching me to understand. Suffice to say, I had no idea what the fuck he was rambling about.

"I don't—"

His eyes lit up suddenly, sparkling with an inner radiance, and for a brief moment, I didn't see any of the lunacy I'd grown accustomed to. Clarity emanated from his gaze as the red gradually faded away. He cocked his head curiously to the side as he stared down at his arms. For a moment, he was silent, his face creased with confusion, as if he couldn't understand where he was and how he'd gotten there.

I waited with bated breath for him to speak, not daring to say anything and send him spiraling back into another one of his fits.

"My blood..." His frown deepened. "It tingles again."

"Jax, man, I have no idea what you mean by that." My shadows coiled around me in agitation, brushing against my cheeks and arms and whispering to me like long-lost friends. I knew only my eyes were visible through the inky darkness, and it was them Jax focused on.

"Z," he said softly, his words causing me to straighten in alarm. Panic momentarily stole the breath from my lungs before his next words soothed my frayed nerves. "I think she's awake."

THREE

Z

Everything hurt.

My head throbbed painfully, as if someone had taken a sledgehammer to my skull, and my skin felt dry and itchy. Even my stomach tightened and twisted uncontrollably, and I just knew I was going to vomit. I felt disgusting, like the feeling you got when you traveled for a long period of time in a stuffy vehicle. Sweat plastered my hair to my forehead as I shifted on the uncomfortable bed, a moan leaving my parted lips.

I was distantly aware of muffled voices reaching me, as if from a distance.

"We'll find a way to save Z and get back to the capital." Devlin. I would recognize the husky tenor of my first love anywhere. He said something else, but his words were lost to the rapid *thump-thump-thump* of my heart.

I wearily blinked open my eyes, only to immediately shut them when I was assaulted by blinding artificial light. I didn't recognize the room I was in, but if I had to guess, I would've said we were at an inn.

Another moan escaped me, and I felt someone grip my hand, squeezing tightly.

"You'll be okay, baby. I promise," Bash whispered, his voice meant for my ears alone.

Baby?

Despite the pain I was in, a part of me perked up at the term of endearment. I would've been the first to admit that my relationship with Bash, out of all my mates, was the most fragile. Tenuous at best. But he was here with me now, stroking my sweaty hair away from my face and whispering in my ear.

"Bash..." I murmured groggily, and he stilled, his hand tightening around mine.

"Baby?" His voice was a breath of air, and I instinctively turned my face in his direction. When I reopened my eyes, I met a pair of emerald green ones framed by thick lashes. His lips were a hairsbreadth away from my own as he leaned towards me.

"Bash," I repeated.

Time seemed to still, my bright blue eyes locked on his green ones. I swore even our hearts were beating in tandem. I knew something significant was transpiring between us, but I didn't know how to put it into words. It was one of those cheesy as fuck moments that you read about in romance novels, when the woman and man stared into each other's eyes deeply, emotions running rampant between them like a taut wire sparking. His pupils dilated, his lips parted, and—

"Z!" Devlin's voice broke through the moment like a bullet shot out of a gun. Bash pulled away abruptly, his customary scowl firmly back in place, as Devlin moved to join me at the bed.

For once, there was no arrogance marring his handsome features, only worry and a relief so strong and staggering, it took my breath away.

"Oh, thank fuck," he breathed. He looked as if he wanted to grab me from the bed and pull me into his arms, but before he could do that, I began to cough. And cough, and cough, and cough. It felt as if I were losing my lungs, each one scratching at my throat until it was raw and bleeding. I twisted my face away, sitting up in bed, and abruptly vomited onto the distressed wooden floorboards of the room we were staying in.

"I'm sorry. I'm sorry," I said as another cough shook my body. Tears burned my eyes as a wave of blistering, red-hot pain washed over me.

"Don't you dare fucking apologize." Bash's voice was choked, heady with emotion. "You're sick, Z. Very fucking sick."

"Why didn't you tell us about the poison?" Devlin demanded, his harsh words belying the gentleness of his hand on my back, stroking my blonde hair.

"Because..." I struggled to control the pain. The last thing I wanted to do was whimper and scare the shit out of my mates. I could tell they were already terrified, their bodies held stiff and tension emitting from their pores. "I didn't want you to worry."

"So you were just going to fucking die?" Devlin snapped, still stroking my back. "We could've helped you, Z. We could've—"

"You couldn't have done shit!" I protested immediately. "Between the kings' trials and Jax's disappearance, not to mention the appearance of that psycho bitch and her monsters—"

"We could've done something," Devlin said, interrupting my rant. He removed his hand from my back and moved to stand in front of me, kneeling down until I was forced to meet his penetrating violet stare. I'd always loved his eyes. The purple color was darker near the pupil before expanding outwards in streaks that were significantly lighter. When he used his powers, his eyes seemed to illuminate as if a candle were lit beneath the surface. It was ethereal and beautiful, just like the man himself.

He cupped both of my cheeks tenderly, his eyes tracking a single tear that cascaded down my cheek. I hadn't even realized it had fallen, but there it was. That damn, traitorous tear.

Behind me, I felt a cold washcloth on my neck, brushing the sweat from my sticky skin, and Bash all but thrust a glass of ice-cold water into my hands. I took a few sips, my stomach instantly lurching and rebelling against the liquid, before handing the cup back to him and reclining in the bed. Bash fluffed a pillow up behind me, providing me something comfortable to lean against.

My mates. Taking care of me. Loving me.

My heart lodged in my throat.

"You don't always have to be strong. Sometimes, it's okay to fall apart. Sometimes, it's okay to rely on your mates," Devlin told me.

His words were very nearly my undoing.

Because I *knew* he was right, I honestly did, but it

was hard to eradicate years of believing I had to do every-thing on my own. That my survival was determined by me and only me. I didn't know how to phrase that to Devlin, how to make him understand, so I settled on whispering, "I know that."

"Do you?"

Fortunately, I was saved from answering by the door to my room being pushed open, Ryland and Jax running inside. At least I assumed it was both of them. I only saw Jax, but a hulking shadow followed closely behind him, sticking to the walls.

"Z!" Jax's eyes, wild with fear, met mine as he lunged forward. He would've probably collapsed on top of me if it hadn't been for Ryland materializing between us.

"She's sick!" he snapped, his tone taut with worry and tension. "You need to be gentle."

Jax's expression hardened, almost as if he was prepared to fight Ryland in order to get to me, but one glance over the shadow's shoulder had his face crumpling.

I searched his eyes warily, half expecting to see his usual madness, but surprisingly, he appeared coherent.

"We were so fucking worried." Jax took a step around Ryland, his eyes still fixed on me. Slowly, he lowered himself to his knees and placed his head on my lap. His voice was muffled from where his lips rested against my upper thigh, but I could still understand him clearly as he muttered, "The voices are quiet now."

"Jax..." Trembling, I brushed my fingers through his light brown hair. Even that small touch took too much energy. But I couldn't stop.

I'd seen Jax *die*. I'd held his broken, bleeding body in my arms as the life drained from his vibrant eyes. The fissure inside of my chest had transformed from a mere crack to a canyon, and I'd known that the only bridge capable of breaching the distance would be my mate's survival. I'd refused to accept anything else as an alternative.

I remembered my power entering his body, filling him up and breathing life back into him. I had no idea how that was even possible, but it'd happened. And then, his eyes had opened, spearing me with a look so full of love and awe that I would've died a very happy assassin.

Yet somehow, I was still here. Tired, yes. Sick, yes. Hurting, yes.

But alive.

How was that possible? I was certain death would claim me, but I'd been willing to embraced the Grim Reaper if it meant my mates living.

Almost as if Ryland were privy to my thoughts, he whispered, "How is this possible?" A shadowy hand curled around my cheek as his ice-blue eyes ensnared my own. They were wide with terror as they penetrated my very soul. "How are you awake?"

"I told you," Jax interjected before anyone could answer. He didn't lift his head from my lap, but his voice was loud enough for the others to hear. "We're keeping her here. For now."

"I don't understand," Devlin said, sounding irritated by the prospect. If I weren't in such agony, I would've cracked a smile. There wasn't a lot that could ruffle my genie, but him being in the dark about something important, especially something concerning me, had that effect.

"It's the mating bond," Jax explained patiently. Finally, he lifted his head and met each of our gazes, one after the other. "I realized it when I was with…" His face twisted with pain before he quickly smoothed out his expression. "When I was with Aaliyah. The mating bond between us…it's more than we could ever imagine."

"What the fuck do you mean?" Devlin snapped. Before Jax could answer, the genie turned towards Bash. "Go grab Dair and call Lupe and Killian."

Bash turned towards me, seemingly reluctant to leave, before clenching his jaw and nodding briskly. My eyes followed him until the door swung shut behind him.

It took about ten minutes for the rest of my mates to arrive. Dair, apparently, had been resting in the room next door, since Bash hadn't allowed him to sleep in the same bed as me. My handsome mermaid immediately wheeled himself beside my bed and gripped my hand, refusing to release me, even when the others arrived.

Killian chastely kissed my forehead, his eyes wordlessly saying everything he didn't speak out loud. Unlike the others, he didn't shy away from expressing his relief at seeing me alive and somewhat well. Tears fell down his cheeks as he tangled a hand in my blonde hair and pressed his forehead to mine.

Lupe was just as needy as the others, if not more so. Without preamble, the growly bear shifter climbed onto the bed and spread his muscular legs out on either side of me. I leaned back into his warm embrace, and his strong arm banded around my stomach. With anyone else, I imagined the position would've felt restrictive and uncomfortable, but not with Lupe. Never with Lupe. I could tell he needed the connection more than anyone. His eyes flashed repeatedly as he struggled to control his wrath, struggled to not give into the sin that coursed through him.

Almost absently, I brought his hand up to my mouth and kissed his palm. His large fingers were calloused, though I knew my shifter was a lover, not a fighter. He preferred to settle his disputes with words and diplomacy instead of senseless violence. Still, there were times that he gave into his wrath and absolutely destroyed everyone and everything in the immediate proximity. It was hard for any of my nightmares to escape the sins they were born into.

"I'm okay," I assured him, though I spoke loud enough for the others to hear as well.

As if to directly contradict my words, a cough rattled my body, blood spitting from my mouth and landing on the white bedspread. All eyes fell on the splatter of red liquid as flames entered my cheeks.

"Oh shit," I murmured, trying for a smile. "Hopefully, they have good maid service here."

No one even cracked a smile. Damn. Tough crowd.

"Baby..." Bash began, and my heart hammered once more at that word. I wouldn't admit it to anyone, but I kind of liked being his baby.

"You're sick, Z. Very, very sick," Devlin said, picking up where we left off before the others arrived. He turned towards Jax, who was still crouched beside the bed, his head resting on his forearms and peering up at me. "Now, what did you mean earlier? About the mate bond?"

Jax licked his upper lip, keeping his gaze trained on me as he considered where to start. I couldn't help but note that he spoke slower than a normal person, almost as if he were testing each word before he said it. I wondered if it had to do with the vampire insanity that plagued him for years, as if a part of him had forgotten how to function normally. I knew that there were only two things that could help him—drinking blood and being around me.

"When I was with Aaliyah," he began softly, and another flash of pain shadowed his eyes. I knew my vampire lover had faced unspeakable horrors when he was with that bitch. I didn't know the extent of it and I almost didn't dare ask, but I knew it haunted him. Guilt distorted his face as he struggled for words. Taking a deep breath, he began again. "When I was with Aaliyah, I was lost to the madness. First, it was my normal madness—the type I get when I don't drink blood. But then...but then I was driven by bloodlust. It was all I could focus on, all I could think about. Blood. Blood. Blood. Blood."

All of my mates went still at Jax's story, and I knew that they, too, experienced guilt over what happened. Misplaced guilt, obviously, since they'd had no control over what that sadistic bitch did to him, but guilt all the same.

"Anyway." Jax cleared his throat, as if uncomfortable with all the pitying looks. I didn't entirely blame him. "The only times I was cognizant was when I was with Z."

"When you were with Z?" Killian repeated,

scratching absently at his tattooed neck. "What do you mean?"

"When you hallucinated Z?" Lupe asked for clarification, his low voice a rumble that reverberated through me.

Jax shook his head. "No, when she visited me."

All eyes turned to stare at me. I could even feel Lupe's gaze pressing down on my scalp from where he towered over me on the bed. I wiggled, feeling confused and anxious in equal measure.

What the fuck was Jax talking about?

The only times I'd "visited" him were in my dreams, where—

Holy fuck.

"You mean those were real?" I whispered hoarsely, every muscle in my body locking tight and then spasming as horror infiltrated my system.

Devlin's eyebrows knitted together. "What was real?"

"Dreams," I responded vaguely, gesturing with my hand towards my head as if that could somehow explain everything. I licked my upper lip anxiously. "I had these dreams about Jax. These horrible, horrible dreams..." A weight filled with poison and lead dropped in my chest.

"They weren't dreams." Jax shook his head sadly. "You were there, Z. I don't know how to explain it, but you were with me."

"Oh god."

My heart rattled in my chest as I recalled everything I'd seen, everything I'd thought was nothing more than a horrible dream.

Jax, broken and bleeding and staring at me with hate filled eyes.

His body strewn on a cross, blood dripping from the numerous wounds on his body.

His mouth painted red with blood as he fed on human after human.

And then his body connecting with mine as we devoured one another. As ecstasy ripped me apart and then stitched me back together.

Heat flushed through me at that last thought, and if the banked fire in his eyes was any indication, he recalled that exact same memory.

"Why didn't you tell us about the dreams?" Bash demanded in irritation.

"Just another thing she kept from us," Devlin muttered, and my heart cracked directly down the center. I knew my secrets had hurt my mates—Devlin especially, who still feared he would never regain my trust—and that they might never trust me again. I couldn't even blame them.

Secret after secret was piling up on me, on all of us, like dirt covering a wooden coffin six feet below ground.

"Devlin," I began placatingly, but he simply unleashed the hurricane force of his glare on me before immediately turning away.

"Not now, Z," he snapped, his hands clenching. He couldn't even fucking look at me, and that hurt more than I cared to admit.

"So this bond..." Killian pressed, flashing me a tentative, understanding smile. I returned it gratefully. Trust my sweet incubus to know when I needed to change the subject.

"I believe it's what's keeping Z alive and conscious. At least for now," Jax confessed. "When I was with Aaliyah, I believe the bond allowed Z's soul to visit me. So while her body remained here with you, her soul traveled to where I was. It would explain why Aaliyah never saw her or even sensed her—because Z wasn't actually there."

"But I was physical," I pointed out, the words rubbing against my throat and causing me to cough once more. Lupe growled sharply, his large paw moving to my back to rub up and down. Once I got myself under control, I hurried on. "I had a tangible body when I was with you. At least it seemed as if I did in my dreams."

"Because you're my mate," Jax said simply, in a tone that left no room for argument. And maybe...

Maybe that was explanation enough.

"And that bond between us...?" Killian continued.

"I don't know for sure." Jax said, our eyes meeting and a bolt of ice slashing through my chest. "But I believe that we're keeping her soul tethered to her body. When she was unconscious, I felt...empty. As if I were missing a crucial piece of myself. Did anyone else feel that way?" Jax twisted his head to encompass all of the men in the room. When they nodded, seeming to understand what he meant, he continued, "I believe that's because Z's soul was slowly leaving her body. But between the seven of us, we were able to keep it inside. I don't know if I'm making any fucking sense—"

"You're making complete sense," Devlin said, interrupting Jax's explanation. His violet eyes flickered towards my face before immediately turning away. His face hardened, his lips slashing into a grim line. "But how long can this last?"

Surprisingly, it wasn't Jax who answered, but Lupe. My shifter tightened his arms around my stomach and placed his chin on my hair. The slightest bit of pain erupted in my stomach, but I didn't dare voice that out loud. Lupe would lose his shit if he realized he'd hurt me, even if it was unintentional.

"Not long," he growled. "I did a lot of research on mates when we first met Z" —I couldn't help but smile at the thought, knowing my shifter loved to research everything there was to know about the world— "and I remember reading a section about the bond between soulmates. There wasn't a lot of information, mainly because I didn't know it was important at the time, but I believe Z will begin to draw on our own souls to feed her own. And when that happens, it'll mean that she'll only have a day or two, at most."

"And we only have a day or two to make it back to the capital," Dair pointed out.

"So we go back to the capital, present Jax, and then find a cure," I decided. When all of them opened their mouths to protest, I spoke gently, attempting to tamp their anger. "It's the only thing I can think to do. We have no idea what this poison even is or how to cure it. So we get home—"

"You won't last that long!" Bash bellowed, straightening from where he was indolently reclined against the wall. He pointed an accusatory finger at my face. "If you would've trusted us to help you sooner—"

"Don't act like you didn't already know!" I snapped. "You told me yourself that you knew—"

"Because I wanted you to feel comfortable telling us yourself—"

"So don't go thinking—"

"Enough!" Lupe's roar caused my hair to blow around my face, and when I turned my attention down to his tree trunk arms, I found that coarse brown hair had sprouted as his bear made an appearance.

"Lupe's right," Dair said. "Fighting will get us nowhere."

"But we need to do something!" I exclaimed in exasperation.

"How about you guys find the cure?" a deceptively calm and cheery voice said from the doorway. We were all so distracted with each other that we hadn't even realized that someone had portaled into the room with us. Devlin and Bash moved to stand protectively in front of us, protecting me from view, and Lupe growled. His growl abruptly cut off when he realized who was with us.

Atta, Lupe's sister and Princess of the Shifters, smiled and waggled her fingers.

"Attie? What the hell are you doing here?" Dair demanded, rolling his wheelchair until he was beside Devlin.

"I followed you, dumbass." Atta rolled her eyes, tossing a perfect orange curl behind her ear. She nodded towards Dair's tablet. "You didn't turn off the tracking feature."

"Why would you—"

"Because I want to help," Atta interjected. She turned towards me, and to my confusion, guilt entered her pretty features, darkening her face. "I know what's wrong with Z. And..." She took a deep breath, her shoulders reaching her ears before falling. "And I know how to cure her."

FOUR

My grip on my sister's wrist wasn't rough as I dragged her down the hall, towards the second room we'd rented for the night. None of my brothers would hurt her, but I knew that with their tempers so high and frayed, it was best to get Atta away from them. Not that I was much better.

She didn't complain as she followed along behind me, her head lowered and her vibrant hair cascading around her face to conceal her features.

When we finally reached the room, I didn't hesitate to push it open and all but barge inside. Atta followed behind me, though reluctantly, her feet dragging against the garish green carpeting.

"Lupe, I can explain…"

"What the fuck were you thinking, Atta?" I bellowed, spinning around to face her. My sister blanched, her skin turning as pale as moonlight, but she didn't say a single word to defend herself. How could she, after what she'd done?

She'd known for days about Z's condition. And more than that, she knew how to cure her.

"I screwed up, I know that, but if you would just listen—"

"Listen to what?" I shoved my large hand into my hair, the brown strands no doubt sticking up in all directions. "That you were willing to let my mate die?"

"I never would've let it come to that," Atta insisted firmly, wrapping her arms around her chest and dropping her gaze to her slipper-clad feet. "I just..."

When she trailed off, apparently unable to continue, I quirked an eyebrow and pressed, "You just?"

"I just needed to make sure Mali was all right," she confessed at last, her words running together in her desperation to make me understand, make me see. But how could I? My sister, my closest friend, had let my mate suffer for days. I wasn't saying that I'd forgiven Z for keeping this a secret from the others and me, but in her mind, there was no cure, no way to save herself. She'd chosen to suffer in silence, only so we wouldn't bear the brunt of her burden.

But Atta?

This entire time, she knew exactly how to save Z, and she chose to remain silent. She could fire off all of the excuses she wanted, but it didn't change the fact that betrayal carved open my chest, slicing at my sensitive heart until it wept red, sticky blood.

"I don't want to hear your excuse." I focused on something over her shoulder, as it pained me to stare directly into her eyes.

Wrath percolated in my stomach, demanding an

outlet. I wanted to rage, scream, attack. Break everything inside of this room until the carpeting was covered in glass and wood.

But instead of doing any of that, I thought of my sweet, precious mate and her bright eyes staring back at me. Gradually, my temper abated until my bear was no longer clawing at my brain, demanding to be set free.

"I was doing what I needed to do for Mali," Atta hissed through gritted teeth, her hands clenching and unclenching repeatedly by her sides. "I had no idea what would've happened if that bitch Aaliyah discovered she told me the truth about Z. I couldn't risk—"

"So you've been meeting with Mali?" I glared at my sister, who at least had the decency to look sheepish. "The woman who betrayed her best friend?"

"She didn't know what was going to happen," Atta protested immediately. Weakly though, as if she didn't quite believe it herself.

Mali's second mate, Zack, was the man who'd poisoned Z in the first place. Not only that, but he killed one of Z's best friends, Diego.

All because of Mali.

All because the stupid girl believed his false words and lured Z and Diego straight to him.

"She loved him," Atta continued softly, and I scoffed.

"Zack was a monster. No one is capable of loving him." I shook my head to banish some of the mounting anger that always seemed to arise when I thought of the cold-hearted assassin. "But enough about Zack and Mali and Aaliyah. Tell me what you know."

Atta tentatively smoothed a hand down her golden

dress, the color that represented all shifters, as her green eyes flashed with pain. Maybe it was my tone of voice, since I never usually raised it with her, or maybe it was the stiffness of my posture.

Either way, she knew that something between us had been altered irrevocably.

Taking another deep breath, she whispered, "It's a poison common in the Mage Kingdom."

"Obviously." Fuck, did I really think she could help? That she would suddenly procure the answer to all of our problems in a vial?

"It's commonly used for their executions," she continued, watching my reaction carefully. At her words, I froze, my spine straightening.

"I've heard about that," I murmured in fear, my mind spinning a mile a minute and my heart racing. "It's one of the most potent spells in the entire world. Apparently, it's created by generations of mage kings. As soon as one ascends to the throne, he adds a tiny bit of his power and blood to the potion, making it even more potent."

Fuck! No wonder Bash couldn't heal her and Dev couldn't wish away the poison. It was literally centuries of magic combined.

"Exactly," Atta said with a decisive head bob. "But I was also told that they keep a cure nearby. Apparently, one of the kings came into contact with the poison a few hundred or so years ago, and since then, they always keep a vial of the cure on standby."

I'd heard that rumor too, but I hadn't even begun to believe that the poison in Z's veins was that. How the fuck did Aaliyah get her hands on something like that?

"Atta." I moved so I was directly in front of my little sister and placed my hands on her shoulders. I was so large and she was so small, she appeared delicate and breakable beneath my much larger hands. She didn't flinch as she would've done with my father. She knew that I would never hurt her. "Thank you."

"I can't even begin to explain how sorry I am for keeping this from you," Atta admitted softly, tears filling her mossy green eyes. "But I hope we can move past this, brother."

"I..." Hesitating, I bit down on my lower lip. I knew Z would want me to forgive her, and I knew I would, but not yet. "I need time."

Her face fell, but she didn't try to stop me as I stepped around her towards the door. I needed to go to my brothers and Z and tell them the news. Bash should have more information about the poison and cure. If my estimation was correct, the ride to the mage kingdom should take less than a day. That would give us a few hours to find the cure before we had to travel back to the capital, located in the center of all the kingdoms.

We could do it.

We had to.

Just before I left, though, I hesitated, looking over my shoulder to spear my little sister with a soft look.

"Thank you, Attie," I whispered, and her answering smile was glorious.

"Go save your mate, brother," she said. And just before the door swung shut, I could've sworn she added, "While I go save mine."

FIVE

AXEL

For some reason, the little girl was afraid of me.

It was completely ridiculous. I wasn't even carrying around my favorite machetes, creatively named Mary and Larry. Mary was a little shyer than her brother, more subdued. Her kills were always quicker too, due to her sharp nature. Now Larry, on the other hand...

He liked to take his time. Make his victims bleed and hurt.

Larry likey when they hurty.

Was it weird to talk about your weapons as if they were your children instead of inanimate objects? Probably. I blamed it on my lack of sleep the last few nights.

Oh, and the fact that I murdered people almost daily, earning myself the nickname of the Butcher. You couldn't be what I was without losing tiny pieces of yourself, and consequently your mind, in the process.

"I'm not going to hurt you," I told the little hybrid for the one millionth time. Well, one million and one times.

"Go away, butt face!" she bellowed, and though her tiny voice quivered with fear, her face, when it popped over the top of the sofa, was hard.

The girl, whose name I still didn't know, was the younger sister of Miles, the teenage boy Z met and befriended at the vampire carnival. When he died, Z had made me promise to find his little sister and take care of her.

I didn't know why Z trusted me, maybe she didn't know about Larry and Mary, but I was determined not to let her down.

At least not yet.

I knew that would happen eventually, though, when we returned to the capital.

Unease slithered in my stomach, but I forced it away as I peered at the little girl and attempted to make my voice calm and soothing.

The strange, strange little girl who, somehow, had both mage and human DNA inside of her. A hybrid. The first of her kind.

Something fiercely protective entered me.

I knew without a shadow of doubt that this tiny human would be hunted and killed if anyone discovered what she was. For so long, humans and nightmares had been living side by side, with no sign of harmony in sight. But this girl? She was proof that change was upon us. That nightmares and humans *could* live as one. That breeding between our two species, which had once been deemed impossible, could actually occur.

"I'm not going to hurt you," I said again, holding my hands up and forcing a smile on my lips. Since I didn't usually smile, unless I was embracing Mary while Larry jealously looked on, it probably came out all weird. I was pretty sure only one side of my mouth quirked upwards and my eyes started blinking rapidly.

Dammit.

"Where's my brother?" the teeny tiny human continued, once again popping her head up from behind the couch. The windmill she'd been living in with Miles was surprisingly well maintained. Only a few cobwebs rested on the highest wooden boards where they couldn't reach, and there was no dust in sight.

"What's your name, kid?" I asked, venturing a step forward. When a fire ball ripped by me, just barely missing my adorable face, my grin widened. She was definitely a little badass spitfire.

"I'm not a kid!" Her chestnut hair, streaked with red and gold, flew around her face as her brown eyes sparked green with her mage power.

"Look," I rolled my eyes and took another step closer, "I'm not gonna hurt you, Spitfire. I don't even have my lovers here with me today." I spread my arms to show that Mary and Larry were, in fact, absent.

She didn't need to know that I'd put a spell on them to make them the size of toothpicks and then shoved them in my pants, right next to my balls. They made them all tingly. My balls, I meant.

"How do I know that?" she demanded, and I had to give her credit—she may have been young, but she wasn't stupid.

She had every reason to fear me, and rightfully so. If

she knew who I was, the Butcher of the kingdom, she would cower and run.

But instead of confessing that to her, I simply let myself dematerialize into nothing but a shadow, the threat clear enough.

If I wanted to, if I intended on harming her, I could easily disappear and reappear seconds later behind her, a blade to her neck.

But I didn't hurt children. That was a line I would never cross, not after my own old man beat the shit out of me and my mom before meeting his...err...untimely demise.

Mary didn't like Daddy Dearest. And Larry liked to join in on the fun.

Hesitantly, her face betraying her nerves, the tiny girl scrambled to her feet, keeping her back against the wall so I couldn't sneak up behind her.

"Mary-Lynette," she stated at last, and I swear it was fate or some shit.

"I know someone named Mary," I said, smiling wistfully at the thought. Shaking my head, I focused back on the tiny human. "But, kid, there's a *lot* we need to talk about."

SIX

Z

The Mage Kingdom.

We were traveling to the Mage Kingdom.

I'd never been there before, not even on missions when I worked for the Alphabet Resistance, but I'd heard rumors about the kingdom that evoked the sin of sloth.

When Lupe told us about the potential cure, I'd thought my men would be ecstatic. And they were, at least at first.

But then they all looked at Bash, whose face had drained of color, and the whoops and cheers diminished until the room was silent.

"I haven't been there in years," Bash confessed, shakily running his fingers through his blond hair.

"The Mage Kingdom can't be as bad as the vampire one," I said, trying to joke, though my tummy tightened at the thought of all I'd endured at the hands of those sadistic bloodsuckers.

The pervy vamp I'd killed.

Miles's death.

What seemed like a lump of coal became lodged in my throat, and I attempted to clear it away.

"I wouldn't be too sure," Bash murmured, and when his eyes flickered in my direction, I saw something pained and haunted in his expression, something I had trouble articulating into words.

"I'm not going to run into your harem, am I?" I joked. It was common knowledge that a lot of powerful male mages had harems of women to give them pleasure. Those fuckers were too damn lazy to do anything themselves.

When Bash didn't immediately respond, I narrowed my eyes into slits. The thought of him with a harem of beautiful women made me a teeny tiny bit stabby.

Okay, a lot stabby.

Bash rolled his eyes in exasperation. "Of course not." He gave me a look like my question was ridiculous.

"But did you ever have one?" I pressed, turning my head to cough into my sleeve. All of my mates stared at me in concern, Lupe practically growling, but I ignored them. There was something immensely more important than my impending death. "Before me, I mean. Did you have a harem, Bash-hole?"

A cocky as fuck smirk danced on his lush lips. "So what if I did? Would that bother you, little mate?"

"Fuck off." I folded my arms over my chest and gave him a completely unimpressed look, like the thought of him with other women didn't cleave me in two.

I knew I was unsuccessful when his grin widened,

seemingly pleased with my show of possessiveness and jealousy.

"Do you truly want the answer to that?" Bash took a step closer, placing his arms on either side of me where I was caged in on Lupe's lap once again.

"Here we fucking go," Devlin murmured.

"I can sense the sexual tension," piped in Killian, but we ignored them.

"Fine." I held my chin up and met his dark green gaze. "Let me hear all about the women you fucked. Your perfect harem." His white teeth flashed when he smiled before immediately disappearing with my next words. "And I'll tell you all about the men *I* fucked. About the way they—"

Lupe growled harshly, and another one of my mate's made a disgruntled noise in the back of his throat. But I didn't look at them. My attention was fixed on Bash.

His eyes darkened, and his jaw clenched.

"Z..." he warned.

"What?" I asked innocently.

He leaned closer until his breath brushed against the shell of my ear, sending goosebumps skittering down my spine.

"Don't test me, woman. I'll spell the shit out of every one of those men. They won't have cocks left once I'm done with them."

I shouldn't have found his words as hot as I did. Even with the pain reverberating through me, tightening all of my muscles, I still found myself growing needy.

Damn. Why did that turn me on so much?

I filed that under "topics for therapy," right alongside my *stab first, ask questions later* tendencies.

"But I thought you were going to tell me about your harem," I pressed, cocking an eyebrow, and he glowered.

"You damn well know that I have no harem. That I never had a harem." He leaned away from my ear, only to immediately press his lips to mine. It wasn't quite a kiss, but it sure as shit felt like one. The heat he emitted sent waves of lust through me. "You're just fishing for compliments. What do you want me to say? That you're the only girl I dream about? The only girl I want? The only girl I—" He cut himself off quickly, backing away from me with a thunderous expression on his face.

"The only girl you what, Bash?" I queried, my voice uncharacteristically serious.

But instead of answering, my mage mate rolled his eyes and leaned back against the wall, folding his muscular arms over his chest.

"I need to plan out the trip to the Mage Kingdom," he said, changing the topic with an ease that left me staggering and lightheaded.

Or that could just be the poison.

Sometimes, my mental thoughts cracked me up.

"We need to leave within the hour," Devlin added.

"It's going to take most of the day to get there," Dair threw in. "And once we're there, we're only going to have a few hours to find the cure and administer it to Z." His blue eyes, as bright as the sea itself and just as inviting, met mine. "I don't fucking like this, guys."

"None of us do," Lupe growled out, his arms tightening around me until I felt blissfully trapped.

"But we have no other choice," I finished for all of them.

We had less than two days to find the cure and return to the capital. That left very little margin for error.

What could possibly go wrong?

Famous last words, Z. Famous last words.

ONLY AN HOUR LATER, WE WERE PACKED AND READY to go.

We chose to take one vehicle, and immediately, my idiotic mates began fighting over who would sit next to me. That conversation ended, though, when Dair wordlessly grabbed my wrist, guided me onto his lap, and then wheeled us both out of the inn and into the blistering hot midday sun.

My eyes greedily admired his strong, bulging biceps as he rolled us forward—all of that golden skin on display, the sinewy muscles...

"My eyes are up here," Dair said in mock horror.

"Shut up." I whacked his arm, my cheeks blazing at being caught blatantly ogling him. But then I decided, why the hell not? He was my mate, and if anyone deserved to stare at his impressive forearm porn, it was me.

Dair smirked at me, the look so unlike his usual despondent expression, and began to flex his muscles.

"I can't help but look at you," I confessed, deciding to be honest as my eyes trailed over him.

Dair was easily my golden prince, with honey-colored

hair, bright blue eyes a girl could get lost in, and broad shoulders leading down to a tapered waist. His golden skin, a product of all of his time in the sunlight, was flecked with the slightest splattering of freckles, somehow adding to his allure.

I didn't care that he was in a wheelchair because of his sadistic father and brothers.

My mermaid mate was so, so beautiful.

Perfect.

"I wish I could see myself the way you see me," he whispered hoarsely, his eyes lapping me up with the same feverish intensity as mine did him. "I wish you could see *yourself* the way I see you. The way all of your mates see you."

I snorted, the sound escaping before I could contain it. "A loudmouth, stabby, psycho chick?"

I knew I was being self-deprecating, but I didn't care. I also knew I was being extremely hypocritical. How the fuck was I supposed to convince my men they were deserving of the entire world if I didn't believe that about myself?

This was why we all came together, why our souls merged and became one. We were all broken, still learning to love ourselves, and somehow, we'd found each other in the dissonant chaos of our lives.

"You know what I see when I look at you?" Dair smoothed his hands up and down my arms, and I marveled at the differences in our skin tone. Mine was pale, almost too pale with my sickness, while his had a healthy, golden glow. His next words snapped my eyes back to his arresting face and those sea-blue eyes, brighter than any ocean or lake I'd ever seen. "I see someone who's strong but vulnerable. Someone who's terrified of appearing weak, even in front of the men she loves. I see a woman who has lost so many people, yet still manages to get out of bed every damn day. That takes strength, Z. A lot of fucking strength.

"There were times when I thought I would never open my eyes again," he continued. I was vaguely aware of my other mates exiting the inn and glancing in our direction before immediately moving to enter the car. "When I thought I wasn't strong enough to. But then you came into my life, and I realized that I don't always have to be strong. Sometimes, I can rely on other people." He speared me with a pointed look.

For years, Dair had been suffering in silence, unwilling to admit to anyone that his family had been torturing him. Was *still* torturing him. My heart ached when I thought of all he must've endured before he came clean to his brothers and me.

"Good advice," I whispered, lowering my gaze to his lips. His tongue snaked out to lick the top one, and goose-bumps pebbled on my arms.

"How about this?" He shifted my weight on his lap, his strong arms tightening on my stomach. "Every day, I'll list one of the many things that makes you amazing. Maybe it'll finally penetrate that pretty skull of yours." He knocked on my forehead gently, and I smirked, lowering myself into his arms so my head rested on his shoulder, facing his neck. His enticing, ocean scent surrounded me as he finally began to wheel us towards the car. I was honestly surprised Devlin had allowed us even that minute to talk. I could see my genie in the driver's seat of the vehicle, his face taut and lined with stress.

"Okay, deal." I kissed the column of his throat. "But I'll do the same for you. Starting with the fact that you're the kindest, most compassionate man I know."

He snorted. "So I'm the nice guy? You do know most nice guys end up in last place."

Lifting my head from his neck, I offered him a teasing smirk, allowing my hand to travel down his chest and to his cock. I rubbed him a few times through the material of his shorts until he was hard for me, a pained groan leaving his throat as his arms tightened around me.

"Guess what, baby?" I murmured in his ear, and his heart picked up speed at the pet name. "In my world, nice guys end up in first place."

DEVLIN

I was freaking the fuck out.

I tried not to let it show, but inside, I was a tangled nest of nerves and crippling fear.

What the fuck were we going to do?

I lived my entire life having a plan, always a plan. From sunup to sundown, my day was meticulously organized, but now, everything was changing. Spinning. Distorting. I couldn't even begin to wrap my head around it all.

Z was sick, dying even, and there was nothing I could do to save her except drive as fast as I could towards the Mage Kingdom. Fuck. Fuck. Fuck! I wasn't used to feeling so...helpless. It scratched incessantly at my skin, drawing blood, but all I could do was accept the pain.

Z sat in the backseat with Dair on one side of her and Jax on the other, his head in her lap. She stroked his light brown hair soothingly, though her eyes remained distant, already fixed out the window at the passing scenery. Bash, Killian, and Ryland were squished together in the back of the van, matching scowls on all of their faces as they stared intently at the back of Z's head. No doubt, they wanted to pull her into their arms, hold her tight, and never let her go. I knew, because I felt the exact same way.

"What should we expect when we reach the Mage Kingdom, Bash?" Lupe called from the front passenger seat. As the largest man of the group, it made complete sense that he would claim shotgun. He easily filled up two seats with his hulking muscles and towering frame. Even now, he had to duck his head slightly so he wouldn't hit his head on the roof.

I watched in the rearview mirror as Bash scratched absently at his cheek before dragging his hand down his face. I pulled my attention back to the road when he finally answered.

"It's not as bad as the Vampire Kingdom, if that's what you're asking," he settled on at last, and my hands tightened almost imperceptibly on the steering wheel until my knuckles were stark white. The Vampire Kingdom saw humans as nothing more than pets. Rodents. We'd had to put a collar and leash on Z, much to her anger, just to enter the inn without arousing suspicion. And then there was the Bloody Carnival...

Anger reverberated through me just at the thought of that disgusting organization. Miles, the kid Z had befriended, had died there. Died. A fucking kid.

I was determined more than ever to burn this entire fucking system to the ground. For so long, I'd been held captive in shackles constructed out of civility and duty, but I'd been reborn in rage. I'd make everyone pay for the crimes they committed or die trying.

"You're not giving us a lot to go on, Bash-hole," Z quipped with forced lightness, twisting her head slightly to meet his emerald gaze. The movement hurt her, I could see that immediately when her ashen face twisted into a grimace and her eyes turned half-mast. She tried to conceal her reaction, tried to hide it behind a wide smile, but I knew her better than I knew myself. We all did.

Immediately, Dair ran a hand up and down her leg soothingly, and Jax twisted in her lap, nuzzling his cheek against her upper thighs.

"I don't know what the fuck to expect," Bash snapped, sounding irritated. I wanted to snap at him for using that tone of voice with our mate, but then I realized that the ire wasn't directed at Z...but at himself. "I spent most of my time in the fucking castle, oblivious to the horrors going on in the real world. Is that what you wanted to hear, Z? That your pretty boy mate was a selfish prick who cared more about how many people he could fuck than who his father was killing?"

"Don't be an asshole," Z hissed, bristling, and Bash's face contorted into a hideous sneer.

"I'm just being honest." Ripping his gaze away from Z's face, he focused out the window, a tiny crease appearing between his brow. "Until I met you, I was no better than a lot of these nightmares. I didn't think anything about the way we treated humans because I didn't know any better. They're not slaves in our land, but their station in life isn't much better. We use them for labor, meaning everything we don't want to do." Another wry smile twisted up his lips. "After all, our sin is sloth."

Z huffed and folded her arms over her chest, scowling at nothing in particular. "You still don't have to be an asshole. And you," she directed her glare in my direction, "eyes on the road."

Bristling at being caught staring, I pulled my attention away from the rearview mirror and focused on the passing buildings as we drove farther and farther away from the Vampire Kingdom. Good fucking riddance.

"Look..." Bash sighed heavily, but I didn't dare pull my attention away to stare at him again. "I'm sorry. Apparently, being an asshole is just in my DNA."

"That's stupid," Z snapped, still fuming. "You're not born an asshole."

"I beg to differ, at least where my father's concerned," Dair murmured, and silence reigned. Guilt strangled me as I thought of all my mermaid brother had endured right under my nose. All the torture and pain and suffering...

We all hated our families, but none more than him, and for good reason.

After a moment of suffocating silence, I heard Z whisper something to the mermaid, too softly for me to hear. He replied to her, a smile evident in his muffled words. Probably declarations of love or some shit.

Surprisingly, I felt no jealousy. I knew Z loved me just as much as she cared for him. I once had her all to myself and I cherished our time together, but I was grateful my brothers had her now as well. They needed her light to counter the relentless and consuming darkness that trapped us all.

"Bash," Z began after a moment of silence. "I feel..." She trailed off, and I just knew she would be chewing on that plush lower lip of hers. "I sometimes feel like you say things to purposely hurt me and push me away. Is that true?"

"You're not pulling any of the punches, are you, my love?" Ryland queried, sounding way too amused.

Ignoring him, Bash gritted out, "What don't you like me talking about? How much of an asshole I am? How much of an asshole I *was*? Or all the women I fucked in my life?"

"You're doing it again!" Z shouted, sounding exasperated. "You're self-fucking-sabotaging."

"Don't pretend you know what goes through my head," he snapped.

"Don't pretend that you hate me as much as you say you do," she replied just as angrily.

"I never said I fucking hated you. What did I say about putting words in my mouth?"

"I don't—"

"Enough!" I shouted, my violet magic sparking through the van. "You're acting like fucking children."

"He started it," Z grumbled at the same time Bash protested, "She's the one who started it!"

"What did I tell you?" I exchanged a droll look with Lupe, who rolled his eyes. "Children. Both of them."

"Rude." Z pouted.

"I fucking hate you all," added Bash.

"More or less than you hate me?" Z quipped.

And here we go again...

But before they could partake in another verbal sparring match, Z began to cough. And cough. And cough. And fucking *cough.*

"Devlin!" Dair cried in alarm, and I cursed as I pulled the car to the side of the road, ignoring the cacophony of honks that followed. I spun around in my seat as soon as the car was in park to see Z leaning forward, coughing violently as Dair and Jax both held her between them.

Blood dripped down her chin.

"I don't feel good," she whimpered moments before her eyes rolled back in her head and she began to seize. Her body twitched erratically, her back arching as white foam appeared in her mouth.

"Get her on her side!" Bash bellowed from the back seat as he leaned forward, fear evident in his normally stormy green eyes.

"Wh-wh-a-t-t-t the fuck is happening?" Killian asked, his stutter even more pronounced in his desperation. "Are we too late?"

Z's shaking slowed, and her eyelashes fluttered shut. She was sprawled across Dair's and Jax's laps, her face paler than I ever remembered it being before. I could barely breathe, barely think, through the panic constricting my heart like a tightening serpent.

I wasn't able to get air back into my lungs until Dair pressed his fingers against her pulse and sagged in relief.

"She's alive. Fuck, she's alive."

My own heart raced, the sloshing of blood in my head so loud and deafening, I was afraid I would topple over at any second.

Losing Z...

I wouldn't survive that.

None of us would.

"We need to get to the Mage Kingdom. Now!" Bash said, his lips compressed into a thin line. His eyes flickered to Z's sleeping form, something indecipherable passing behind his verdant green eyes, before he forced his gaze away and slumped back in his seat. "We need the fucking cure."

"Lupe?" Ryland's strangled voice had my attention snapping his way, but his eyes weren't on me—they were fixed on the bear shifter beside me. "You need to calm the fuck down, man." The dark shadows around him tightened even further until they obscured his eyes, a clear sign of his agitation.

I turned towards Lupe in alarm, only to see that my brother was no longer in control. At least not all the way.

His fingers had transformed into keen claws that looked capable of slashing my head straight off my shoulders. Coarse fur sprouted on his arms, now twice the size they were before, and even more fur grew on his body as his bear struggled to break free. Fucking hell. The last thing we needed was an enormous grizzly wreaking havoc on our only mode of transportation.

Knowing I needed to appeal to his human nature before he lost himself completely, I attempted to reason with him. "Lupe, man, you need to calm down. Z needs you." He whipped his head in my direction, a growl escaping his throat as his eyes flashed yellow in the dim lighting of the van. I gritted my teeth together but continued on. "We need to get her to the Mage Kingdom. We can't do that if you become a motherfucking bear and destroy the vehicle. You understand?" I couldn't quite mask my irritation, but fuck it all to hell, we didn't have time for this.

"Think about Z," Dair threw in, his voice that soothing tone only he was capable of pulling off.

It was no doubt the repetition of Z's name that had his bear retreating and my brother taking its place. His face flushed red in shame as he stared down at his body, his clothes now ripped in some places from when he grew in size.

"Are you good?" I demanded, pulling the van back onto the highway. Lupe released a ragged sigh, running his fingers through his brown hair. His hand trembled slightly, though when he caught me staring, he lowered it to his lap.

"Yeah. I'm fine. My wrath...it's getting harder to control."

"I know." My jaw clenched together so tightly, I was honestly surprised I didn't break a tooth. "With Z the way she is... I just... I know." There was nothing more for me to say.

Lupe nodded curtly, schooling his expression again with a monumental amount of effort. "If anything were to happen to her..."

"Nothing will," Ryland broke in.

"I know that." Lupe didn't sound convinced. "But— Who the fuck is calling me?" He whipped his head in the direction of his tablet, which was now vibrating with an incoming call. My heart stuttered and got caught in my throat. I recognized the number displayed on the screen, and if Lupe's sharp inhale was any indication, he did too.

"Don't answer it," Killian warned shakily, but Lupe already had the phone pressed to his ear. The frown carved into his mouth was weary and grim, the crack in his personality as visible as it had ever been.

"Father," Lupe greeted, that one word cutting into me like a garrote. I couldn't hear what the sadistic bastard said on the other end of the phone, but Lupe's face drained of all color. His eyes flickered to Z in the backseat before focusing once more out the windshield. "I can't..." His jaw clenched, anger evident in every hard line of his body, but whatever his father said next had something shuttering in his eyes. "I understand." Pause. "Yes."

No goodbyes were exchanged as Lupe hung up the phone...and then abruptly tossed it against the dashboard with a roar of fury that stirred my hair.

"Fucking hell!" Bash hollered, but Lupe ignored him, looking ready to grab something else and break it as well. Considering the fact that the only other thing he could break was me, I tried to speak to him.

"What happened?"

"My father," Lupe bit out, his eyes flashing with acidic rage.

"What about the asshole?" Ryland asked icily.

"He wants me home. Now."

"Now?" Killian parroted.

"Fuck," added Dair.

Lupe clenched and unclenched his hands as he stared stormily out the window. His expression was thunderous. "He threatened Z."

"He..." Darkness permeated my soul, tainting something inside of me. "I'm going to kill the fucker."

"Get in line," muttered Ryland, and I had no doubt the shadow was serious. Ryland was silent, preferring to stick to the shadows than make his presence known, but I knew he was a formidable opponent. Passivity did not make him any less dangerous. He wouldn't hesitate to kill if it meant keeping his family safe. Keeping Z safe.

"Who the fuck do we hate more now?" Jax mused from where he plucked at Z's hair. He brought a strand of gold to his nose and inhaled deeply. His eyes, a strange combination of crazed and coherent, met mine. "The mermaid king or the shifter one?"

"Both?" Bash responded wryly.

"Then why don't we kill them." Jax spoke as if the answer should've been obvious, as if we were imbeciles for not thinking of that sooner.

"We can't just kill the ruling monarchs without expecting repercussions," Bash gritted out. "Besides, if we kill them and get caught, we'll be put into prison for the rest of our lives. Or killed. We can't protect Z and our kingdoms behind bars."

Instead of responding to Bash's reasoning, Jax dropped his attention back to Z, apparently done with conversation for the day.

"I have to go see my father," Lupe managed to grit out. I could tell it was taking every ounce of willpower for him not to bear out.

"Not alone." I met his gaze before focusing on the road once more. A few seconds later, we reached a tiny restaurant, and it was there I stopped, turning the car off and sitting in silence. Automatically, my eyes flew to Z, as they always did when she was with me. I needed to ensure with my own two eyes that she was okay, that she was alive.

I wouldn't be able to breathe normally until she was.

It was hard to fill my role as the unofficial leader of our group. All I wanted to do was cuddle up next to Z and show her how much I loved her. But I couldn't do that. Not yet. Not when there was a war brewing on the horizon and my sweet, perfect mate was at the center of it.

"Lupe and I will find a separate vehicle and go visit his father," I announced to the group, ignoring Lupe's wide-eyed stare and mounting protest. "No buts," I warned him firmly. I wanted more than anything to stay with Z, but I wouldn't—*couldn't* leave my brother unprotected, especially knowing what his father was capable of. Z would want me to go with and protect him, so that was what I would do. "The rest of you, take care of our girl."

"I don't fucking like this," Bash spat out. "Do you remember what happened the last time we split up?"

Death. Murder. Blood. Pain.

"Protect our girl," I told them severely, all but throwing myself out of the vehicle. As I moved to the backseat, Jax immediately got out, allowing me to slide in and lean over her. She looked serene in sleep. Peaceful, even. I might've believed she was simply sleeping, if there weren't a tiny wrinkle between her brows and the slightest downward tilt to her lips. At least my brothers had the sense to clean the blood from her face. I probably would've lost my damn mind if I saw it staining her perfect, porcelain skin.

My mate was in pain, and it fucking destroyed me. Obliterated me.

"I love you, baby," I whispered to her unconscious form, brushing a strand of her blonde hair behind her ear. Knowing what she would demand of me if she were conscious, I added, "And I'll look after the big idiot for you." I jabbed a finger in Lupe's direction, despite knowing she couldn't see me. "No harm will come to either of us. I promise you." I kissed her forehead, her cheeks, and then finally, her lips. Something salty merged with her usual flavor, and it took me a long moment to realize it was a tear—my tear.

This might be the last time I saw Z.

No! Don't think like that, Devlin. She'll be fine. She has to be fine.

"My turn," Lupe growled, all but throwing me out of the van to take my place. I wanted to punch him but quickly reined in the impulse. He couldn't control himself right now, and I knew that if I started something with him, he would explode completely.

The tension in his shoulders drained away as he stared at the woman we all loved more than life itself. He peppered kisses across her face, whispered that he loved her and would look after me, and then stepped back out.

Ryland, who'd moved to the driver's seat while we were preoccupied with Z, rolled down the window and leveled us with a fierce stare. For once, he wasn't hiding behind his shadows, his scars on clear display as his lips curled downwards.

"We'll protect her," he assured us softly. "She'll be safe."

"She damn well better be," Lupe growled out.

"Take care of yourselves," he continued, ignoring Lupe's interruption. "She'll have all of our asses the second she realizes you guys left to visit your sadistic father. Only trust one another."

"Done," we both agreed immediately.

Ryland nodded once more, his expression grave, before he slowly rolled up the tinted window, cutting off our view of him...and our view of Z.

Fuck, I couldn't breathe. I didn't think I would again.

A second later, the van was pulling away, leaving us alone in front of the restaurant.

Lupe couldn't stop pacing, his muscles rippling as his bear wrestled him for control.

"What the fuck did your father want?" I demanded. I was going to kill the sick bastard when I saw him...mostly because he took me away from Z when she needed me the most.

"I don't know." Lupe ran a hand through his brown hair, causing the strands to stick up in all directions in a disheveled mess. "He called and said to meet him in the capital in an hour's time. He said that if I was even a second late, he would 'slice the pretty assassin's neck.'" Anger emanated from his gaze, the same anger I knew was in my own.

Threatening Z...

He'd pay for that with his life.

"You know this is a trap, right?" I told him, and he nodded once, a simple bob of his head that said more than words ever could. There were years of pain in his gaze, pain that nothing could alleviate or abate. Pain caused from cruel words and unspeakable horrors I couldn't even begin to comprehend.

"I know," Lupe responded at last, already walking towards a car in the parking lot. He didn't hesitate to use his meaty fist to break open the window. Blood cascaded down his hand from the numerous cuts created by the glass, but he didn't seem to notice. Or if he did notice, he didn't fucking care. "But there's nothing I can do about it." He paused abruptly, straightening from his semi crouch to face me. The steely glint in his eyes gave me a pause, and instantly, I was on alert.

"What is it?"

"I don't care about the consequences anymore," Lupe told me, a darkness like I'd never seen before rolling across his expression. "When I see my father, I'm going to kill him. I'm going to rid the world of his stain once and for all."

Z

The mansion was a mismatch of architectural and decorative styles—from archaic with its stone blocks, stained glass windows, and torches protruding from the wall, to modern with sleek leather couches, a television hanging opposite them, and a glass coffee table on bright red carpeting.

I moved on silent feet to one of the couches, my eyes traveling around the room and taking in every detail with rapt focus. One glance out the window confirmed we were on some sort of cliff, the ocean frothing against the craggy, brown-gray rocks far below.

The floor plan, from what I could see, was open, the living room flowing seamlessly into a kitchen. But despite the modern appliances, it still appeared to be a castle from the before times. Old and dirty, but timeless. Elegant, even.

I glanced down at my bare feet, surprised by what I found myself wearing.

A...dress. An elegant dress that cascaded around my figure in ruffles and lace. It was a dark, verdant green that cinched at my waist, flaring outwards in a puffy skirt. My reflection revealed perfectly curled blonde hair that nearly reached my waist and the lightest application of makeup—pink lips, eyeshadow, and mascara that made my eyes pop. Tiny pearl earrings completed the ensemble.

"You look beautiful, Gabriella," a soft voice mused from behind me.

I spun, my heart lurching up my throat and becoming lodged there, to see none other than Aaliyah standing behind me.

She was even more beautiful up close, her skin flawless and glowing in the flickering candle flames. Orange-red hair cascaded down her shoulders in voluminous curls, a few of the strands held away from her arresting face by a barrette. She wore a red dress that slid off of her shoulders and fit her like a glove.

"What do you want?" I gritted out, my teeth clenched. "How did I get here?" I debated lunging forward and snapping her pale neck but decided against it. I had no idea where I was or how I'd gotten there. Knowing my luck, the second I killed the psycho bitch, her army of monsters would arrive and strike me down.

For now, I had to play this safe, and that meant refraining from slitting her throat with my fingernail.

A dangerous expression crossed Aaliyah's face, darkening her perfect features, even as she rolled her eyes and moved farther into the room. She gripped the hem of her dress with one hand, holding it just above her ankles, while her other hand trailed across the gray stone wall, her fingers digging into the grooves present.

"Don't you worry your pretty head, little sister," she

sang, incandescent anger tainting the laughter in her voice and turning it into something ugly. It was almost as if she couldn't decide if she was happy or wrathful, a conundrum that made her seem even more unhinged than ever before. "You're still with those...men." Her face twisted at that word, demoting her from beautiful to hideous in one second flat.

Fuck her. God, I wanted to kill her so bad, it was almost a physical ache. What she did to Jax...

But then her words penetrated my skull, and I strengthened almost imperceptibly.

"So this is a dream?" I reasoned, the fact bolstering my confidence. If it was just a dream, that meant I was still safe with my men. Well, not safe, per se, but I wasn't in hell with this bitch.

"Yes." Another twist of her ruby-red lips. Another annoyed glance in my direction. Another distasteful sneer aimed my way. "You can do so much better than those nightmares, you know. So, so much better."

"Why?" I quipped. "You want them for yourself?"

Memories of the way she'd treated my vampire lover played on a loop in my head. I didn't know the explicit details, but I knew with certainty that she'd tried to seduce him. Fortunately, Jax's love for me stopped her advances, even with the bloodlust plaguing his mind. Still, that didn't stop her from flirting with and touching him every change she got. It didn't stop her from placing a spell on him that forced him to give in to his sin, gluttony, and embrace the monster he tried so hard to contain.

For that alone, I would hate her forever.

Disgust curled back her upper lip, even as her eyes

danced with amusement. "I'm not interested in them like that. But thank you for offering, little sister."

Anger burned white-hot inside of me. "Then why do all of that to Jax? Why try to seduce him?"

"Because I needed to see if he was good enough for you," she responded immediately, earnestly, but the twinkle in her eyes made me think that I wasn't getting the full story. I didn't trust the murderous bitch any further than I could throw her. There was something wicked lurking just beneath her stunning exterior. Something dark, dangerous, and foreboding.

"Why am I here?" I hissed out, repeating my earlier question that she conveniently ignored.

I didn't expect her to answer me, so it was no surprise when she skillfully changed the subject once again. She continued to move farther and farther into the room, her hand moving from the wall to the top of the couch, her fingers caressing the leather.

"You heard the story about how the nightmares came to be, correct?" she questioned, her tone almost conversational. My brows furrowed, and I took an automatic step away from her.

"Yes. They're descended from the Seven Deadly Sins." That was textbook knowledge. Every human and nightmare alike were forced to study this before they were even out of diapers. It was that lineage that made nightmares supreme and untouchable. How could we lowly humans compete with spiritual entities?

"Did you know that the Seven Deadly Sins came to Earth after they fell in love with an angel named Gabrielle?" she continued, and my breath hitched. I could feel my heart racing beneath my rib cage, threatening to escape at any second. "It's funny how similar your names are." She flashed me a cunning smile, one that didn't quite reach her eyes. "Gabrielle. Gabriella. Funny coincidence."

"Where the fuck are you going with—?"

"But what the textbooks don't tell you, is that the world requires a balance. A light to every darkness. A night to every day. It's why the sun and moon constantly chase each other with no end in sight, trapped in a tango, a dance. An unrequited love story." Her gaze turned distant as she moved even closer to me. My back was flush against the wall, the open window directly beside me and leading down to the ocean far below. "The angel had a sister, a demon to be exact, but the fates prohibited the two of them from meeting. That didn't stop the demon from loving and protecting her sister from afar. When fate allowed the demon onto Earth with her own mates, she eagerly jumped at the opportunity. But unlike Gabrielle being mated to the Seven Deadly Sins, the demon was mated to the Seven Heavenly Virtues. You want to know how her story varies from Gabrielle's?"

I could barely breathe, barely hear. The only sound I was aware of was the hammering of my heart, the noise so deafening and consuming, I felt lightheaded. Dizzy. Nauseous. Bile crawled up my throat.

"How?" I croaked out.

Aaliyah grinned like the cat who ate the canary. "The demon killed her lovers, because she knew they would get in the way of her relationship with her sister. She chose her sister over her mates, as she would do time and time again." Her face was inches from mine, her eyes wide and slightly manic when they met my own. "I suppose you can say history is repeating itself."

"That's...that's a cute story," I managed to say. But the bravado I infused my words with was faked. Something cold and slimy settled on my skin like a disgusting layer of tar I couldn't scrub away.

"It is, isn't it?" She stared into my eyes another moment before turning away and continuing her aimless pacing. "Do you want to know how the story ends, Gabriella?"

"Don't call me that," I snapped, forcing my hands to stop shaking. "That's not my name."

She ignored me. "It ends with the demon getting exactly what she wants." She spun abruptly, spearing me with an indecipherable look that had every hair on my arms standing on end, saluting the world.

"And what exactly does she want?" I didn't dare breathe. Aaliyah was a ticking time bomb, and one wrong move would have her detonating, destroying everything in the immediate proximity.

A distressed, almost anguished expression marred her face as she moved to stand directly in front of me once again. Tears hung suspended on her thick lashes, as her brilliant green eyes turned hazy.

"She wants her family back," she whispered brokenly. And then, "Say hello to my next monster for me. I chose him especially for you."

Before I could demand more information, could piece together what exactly she meant, Aaliyah's hands were on my chest and she was pushing me...

Directly out the window and into the turbulent ocean far below.

I woke with a gasp being yanked from my lips. My hands were sweating, and my heart raced fiercely. Bright sunlight seeped through the open windows as I struggled to orient myself to my surroundings.

I was in the van still...but it was stopped. And from what I gathered, none of my mates were present either.

Panic momentarily stole the breath from my lungs until a rough hand clasped down on my shoulder, stilling me.

"Hey." Ryland's voice curled around me like heady smoke, and I squeezed my eyelids shut at the comfort and safety that immediately infiltrated my system, dissipating the fear and anxiety. "You're okay. You're safe."

"Where are the others?" I whispered, peeling my eyelids open all the way. His hand tightened slightly before he released me. A second later, his shadows coiled around me, their presence more comforting than menacing, and I found myself on a lap I couldn't see. His entire body was shrouded by his thick, heavy shadows.

"They're talking to a healer Bash knows," Ryland explained soothingly, his wispy hand brushing at a strand of my curly hair. "When you didn't wake up..." His voice hitched, almost as if he was replaying some unspeakable horror in his head, and I winced.

"How long was I out?"

"Too long," he responded tersely. "And then you

started muttering weird things..." His body shook beneath mine as featherlight kisses brushed the back of my neck. Goosebumps erupted on my skin before I could stop my body's visceral reaction to his touch.

Forcing myself to focus, I asked, "What things?"

"Aaliyah," he responded simply. "You said her name."

My dream returned to me with a vengeance, slamming into my mind and sending me toppling off a cliff—just as I'd done in my dream.

Before I could lose the memories of my mysterious encounter with her, because I truly believed she had somehow found a way to enter my dreams, I told Ryland everything that had happened, including the strange history lesson she gave me. Ryland listened without interruption, and the only indication he was distressed by my words was the tightening of his shadows on my arms and legs. They pushed down, cutting off my circulation, before immediately curling back in on himself.

Call me a kinky bitch, but a part of me really, really liked that.

"That's...interesting," he said after I finished my spiel.

"That's all you have to say?"

He buried his face in my hair, his shadows momentarily retreating to give me a glimpse of his dark brown skin. His hands tightened on my waist, smoothing across my stomach, before he dropped both of them to my thighs.

"Are we positive that this wasn't just a dream caused from your fever?" he pressed, but not as if he didn't believe me. If anything, it sounded as if he *did* believe me and was desperate for me to say something that would prove us both wrong.

"Positive. It felt real, Ry. I'm pretty sure Aaliyah entered my dreams somehow."

"That's not good, Z," he murmured, his voice laced with worry. His hands tightened on my thighs, and a sliver of lust embedded itself in my heart, despite everything going on. My breasts suddenly felt extremely heavy, my nipples aching.

"I know." His calloused finger lazily moved between my thighs, creating a pathway of fire through the material of my pants. When his thumb brushed against my pussy, I jolted, my entire body held tauter than a string on a bow.

"How long do you think the guys will be gone?" I whispered as he continued to pepper kisses up and down my neck.

"Long enough," Ryland murmured, dropping his hand beneath the waistband of my pants. I spread my legs even wider as he fingered the hem of my panties. After a moment, he shoved one finger inside and slid it through my juices.

My eyes rolled into the back of my head as he began to finger me in the back of the van, his entire hand resting inside my panties and his thumb rubbing against my sensitive clit. His other hand moved to cup my heavy breast, tugging at my nipple through my shirt and bra.

"Ryland..." I moaned, forgetting about the strange dream and the fall into the ocean that woke me up. I even forgot about the poison, my entire attention consumed by my shadow mate.

He moved his hand underneath my shirt, pushing it up around my shoulders. He then twisted my body so he could lower his head to my breast, sucking my nipple through the fabric of my bra and leaving wet spots in his wake.

His fingers moved faster and faster, pumping in and out of me as he continued to devour my tit like he was dying for a taste. He shoved down the cup of my bra, pushing my boob up even more, and sucked it entirely into his hot mouth.

I gripped his wrist with one hand, encouraging him to move his fingers even faster, while my other hand fisted in his dark hair. The shadows receded at my touch, revealing the mate I knew and loved. His obsidian hair and dark skin. The face mottled by vicious white lines. The eyes that peered back at me, emanating a sort of love you only ever read about in storybooks.

He released one breast and moved his attention to the other, shoving down the bra cup for that one as well and claiming my nipple. When his teeth clamped down on it, my hips shot off the seat, my impending orgasm on the horizon.

"Yes, Ryland. Yes," I praised as he pressed down on my clit. And then I was shattering, shaking, swearing as he continued to finger fuck me through my orgasm. When I finally came back down to earth, after traveling in circles around the sun, I claimed Ryland's lips in a desperate, frenzied kiss.

"How did you know that was what I needed?" I whispered as he lazily cupped both my breasts and gave them a squeeze. Somehow, he was able to distract me from everything that had just transpired in my dream. It felt so...ridiculous to worry about Aaliyah and her schemes when I was with my men.

"Because I know you," he responded simply, a smile dancing on his plush lips. A white scar sliced through his upper one, but it somehow enhanced his beauty. Ryland was stunning, there was no doubt about that. I never understood why he hid, but I wouldn't begrudge him something that made him feel more comfortable. "But you should probably fix your shirt. The guys and the healer will be here any second."

"Maybe I will if you stop fondling my tits," I teased as his thumbs ran over both of my nipples.

I was totally ready for round two. And three. And four and five.

"But they're just so pretty." He flashed me a roguish grin as he dipped his head and bit down on one. I gasped, threading my fingers through his hair, as desire percolated in my lower stomach, wetting my panties even more.

"Ryland..." I warned. "I need to fix my clothes. And hopefully, change my pants. A certain someone made me come inside my panties."

He grinned impishly at me, still not releasing my nipple from his teeth. I loved him like this, jovial and carefree, as if we didn't have a guillotine blade hanging over our heads. "Who was this fellow? Shall I beat him up?"

"Fellow? Who the fuck says fellow?"

"Um...the guy who just made you come in your pants." He finally released my poor, abused breast, frowned disgruntledly, and then helped me fix my bra and shirt. "Such a shame," he murmured with a dramatic head shake. "Such a damn shame."

I actually laughed out loud. "You're such a dork."

"Only when it—"

A loud squawk sounded from outside, cutting off whatever Ryland was going to say.

Immediately, he was on his knees, peering out the window, his muscles going rigid.

"Ry?" I asked, alarmed. I twisted around until I was able to grab a pair of knives I kept beneath the seat. The poison may have made me weak, but I wasn't an invalid. And if there was a threat coming, I would fight until my very last breath to protect myself and my men.

"Aaliyah said she sent another monster, didn't she?" Ryland asked grimly as his shadows flickered in and out of existence. I felt them coil around my body too, sheltering me from the impending threat.

"I didn't think..." I trailed off as I followed the direction of Ryland's gaze. It took me a moment to spot the creature flapping its huge, leathery wings in the distance. As of now, it was just a speck of gray in the sky, but I could see it rapidly approaching us, growing larger by the second.

"Is that...?" Alarm coated my voice as Ryland nodded gravely.

"That's a motherfucking dragon."

KILLIAN

Bash stopped the van in front of a desolate little hut a few miles away from the main road. Its mushroom roof poked through the boughs of trees, a strange combination of russet-red and pale gold. The house itself practically blended into the forest, constructed entirely of twigs and branches.

"Your healer lives here?" I inquired curiously, staring at the tiny, nondescript building in the middle of freaking nowhere. I scratched absently at the back of my neck as my eyes flickered to Z's sleeping face. She was so beautiful, it felt as if I couldn't look away, as if she were a blinding, all-consuming light somehow capable of chasing away the even darkest of shadows. You learned to crave the light, lose yourself in it, and you found that when it was absent, you had nothing but a gaping hole in your chest where your heart should be.

That was what she was—my light.

My heart.

"Paco is the best damn healer I've ever had the

displeasure of meeting," Bash confessed, though he didn't immediately get out of the van. Instead, he stared straight ahead, his blond brows furrowed and his emerald green eyes rife with pain and frustration. From where I was seated beside Z, I could only see his profile, but I knew my brother was deep in thought.

If I had to guess, that thought had to do with the sleeping blonde on my lap, her head resting dangerously close to my traitorous cock.

The fucker didn't get the memo that he couldn't lust after her until she was healed.

"Killian, Jax, and Dair...you guys come with me. Ryland, stay with Z," Bash instructed once the silence became too pronounced even for me. And I lived in the freaking silence.

"Why us?" Dair asked immediately, swiping at a strand of his blond hair in agitation.

Bash released a heavy sigh, his fingers once more tapping against the steering wheel. Ryland had driven the first few hours, but when Z started releasing distressed, pained noises in the back of the van, we feared he would crash in his haste to get to her. Bash had eventually taken over while Ryland hovered on the other side of her, his shadows repeatedly flickering in and out of existence as he struggled to control his growing anger and fear.

"Paco's powerful," Bash began by way of explanation. He moved to get out of the van, and after only a brief moment of hesitation, my eyes straying to Z's unconscious form, I followed. Jax began muttering under his breath the second he was away from Z, his arms wrapped around his waist and his eyes flicking in all directions without sticking on one thing in particular. Bash moved to help me with Dair and his wheelchair as he hurried to explain. "Paco might have a potion that can help, at least temporarily."

"Help?" Dair questioned once he was seated in his wheelchair. His forearms flexed as he began to roll himself up the cement. Fortunately, Paco had a driveway leading up to his shed instead of just plain dirt. And though it was cracked and crumbling, it was easier for Dair to wheel himself over than anything else would've been.

"With your legs." Bash nodded towards the mermaid prince, whose face went slack. Pain momentarily creased his features before he schooled his expression—a feat I knew took years of practice.

"What if I don't want help with that?" he retorted bitterly. "I've been in a wheelchair for many, many years. Just because I can't walk like you can, doesn't mean I'm—"

"Don't be an asshole," Bash bit out as he stormed towards the cottage, leaving Ryland and Z behind in the safety of the van. I wasn't worried about my mate. I knew Ryland would protect her with his life, as we all would. There was no one who was more important to any of us than that brave and perfect girl.

Dair's lips thinned before he eventually released a ragged sigh. "I'm sorry. I didn't mean to say that. I just..."

"Struggle," I finished for him, and when his eyes flickered my way in surprise, I blushed and ducked my head. "But if this Pablo can—"

"Paco," Bash corrected automatically.

"—help you, then shouldn't you let him try?" I tilted my head to the side curiously. I wasn't judging him. There was a lot I didn't understand, and Dair's torture at the hands of his brothers and father was one of them. I didn't understand how he felt, and I didn't think I ever would. If he wanted to remain in his wheelchair the rest of his life, proving to his family each and every day that they hadn't broken him, then he could and I would support his decision.

My brother seemed to hold this delusional mentality that his predicament somehow made him lesser than us, especially in Z's eyes. That couldn't be further from the truth. As an incubus, I could sense lust and love, and the affection wafting from Z was nearly smothering. But it was a good type of smothering, like wrapping yourself in a quilt after spending hours outside in a snowstorm. It didn't matter who she was with, she loved us all the same.

Loved us.

My heart still gave a rather girly flutter in my chest at the prospect of someone as incredible as Z loving and caring for someone like me. As quick as that thought came, I vanquished it. I was just as bad as Dair when it came to my own insecurities and self-loathing. How could I help my brothers if I struggled each and every day with my own turbulent mind?

Forcing myself to focus on the topic at hand, I turned towards Jax, who was staring intently at the tinted windows of the van, almost as if his gaze could penetrate the steel and see the slumbering girl inside.

"And him?" I bit down on my lower lip as I stared at the eccentric vampire. Like with Dair, I couldn't even begin to imagine what he'd been through with Aaliyah. "Do you think it could help with his blood madness?"

"It wouldn't hurt." Bash shrugged his shoulders, gently placing a hand on Jax's bicep to lead him in the direction of the hut. "Though I'm worried Paco's just going to tell him to feed. But fuck, maybe he'd be right—maybe it's time for Jax to embrace his nightmare and feed on blood the way he's supposed to. It can't be healthy to resist."

"He fed on blood when he was with Aaliyah," I pointed out, the only sound in the forest the crunching of leaves beneath our feet and the roll of Dair's tires. "But the second he was away from her, he fell right back into his madness."

"I think that has something to do with Z," Dair confessed. "He was coherent until she fell unconscious. And now that she's sick..."

"There might not be anything we can do to pull him out of this," Bash finished.

"You don't have to talk about me like I'm not here." Jax's voice was colder than I ever remembered it being, a slash of air that cracked open skin like a whip of fire. His sharp eyes swiveled in my direction, and I found myself tongue-tied, unable to speak around the man who had been my best friend for many, many years, even with his madness. "I know what you guys think, and I'm not mad. I'm not." He turned away from us, his gaze fixing firmly ahead as he shrugged himself out of Bash's grip.

"We're not saying—" I began diplomatically, but Jax cut me off.

"Yes, you are." His gaze turned vacant, and he quickened his pace so he was a few steps ahead of us all.

Silence settled between the four of us as we finally reached the entrance to the tiny hut, then Bash knocked on the wooden door. Like before, I couldn't hear anything besides our own hearts beating, so I focused on my other senses. I wasn't as skilled as using them as some of the other incubi, but through the closed door, I picked up a heady amount of...lust?

Was there someone with Paco?

The lust inflated significantly, usually a sign that the person had...um...completed, and then footsteps pounded against the floorboards.

"Whatcha want?" a snarly voice demanded as the door was thrown open, creaking on its rusty hinges.

I blinked at the tall man standing before me, unable to formulate any thoughts or words.

For starters, he was huge, his upper half practically bending in half, despite the hut being tall enough to fit two of me. He had peach-colored skin with dozens of intricate tattoos wrapped around his forearms and the hairiest chest I'd ever seen on a man before. His white hair was tied back in a long braid that touched his lower spine, though his beard was an untamed mess, caressing the middle of his pudgy belly.

And he was naked.

Completely and utterly naked.

I wanted to say that I wasn't a prude, but that wasn't true. I totally was a prude. I didn't like naked bodies, unless that naked body belonged to my beautiful mate.

And I definitely didn't like old guy penises. They

were...flabby. And strangely colored. And his was pointing straight at me.

"You brought Paco a present?" the man asked with a salacious sneer my direction. I blanched, trying to hide behind Bash's broad shoulders and pretend that there wasn't a withered and gray penis poking at my eyeball.

"Not for you, Paco," Bash said with a huff. "Can we come in?"

The man—Paco, apparently, who liked to speak in third person—actually pouted, his hand moving down his hairy chest to touch his...err...manhood. But instead of stroking himself like I thought he was going to do, he began to spin it like a windmill, the movement almost absentminded.

"Fine. Fine. Yer may come in." He had a thick accent that I couldn't place, but all thoughts of accents fled my mind when he spun on his heel to step back into his house and I saw his flabby ass.

"Is that...?" I began, my eyes widening in horror.

Dair turned green. "Bash, why the fuck did you bring us here? And why does that man have anal beads sticking out of his crack?"

"Paco is the best at what he does," Bash said, though he couldn't quite hide his grimace of disgust as we entered the healer's home.

To say this place was humble was an understatement if I ever heard one. Everything was constructed out of wood, almost as if he ventured out into the forest, cut down a few trees, and used the bark to make the home and furniture. The only color I could see was a leaf stuck to the wall, the green turning brown with decay.

Paco bent down when he reached what I believed to be a kitchen.

"Yer want something to drink?" he called, his ass in the air, which gave me an unwanted view of his sac. Was that a...was that a bump? On his sac? He should really get that looked at.

"We want to talk, Paco," Bash said, just barely containing his irritation.

"Paco waz buzy." His accent turned even more pronounced, changing all of the Ss into Zs.

Remembering the lust I felt before he entered, I searched the room for his partner. Instantly, I had a vision of a similarly tall woman with gray hair and a long beard leaning forward to put anal beads in his ass. In this horrible, disgusting vision, her breasts were so large, they scraped against the floor, and her entire body was covered from head to toe in coarse white hair like some sort of monster.

Bile raced up my throat, and I coughed to hide my reaction.

But alas, there was no woman. Only something that looked suspiciously like a pancake with a hole in it on his bed.

He couldn't...?

"I'm sorry for bothering you," Bash said cordially, his tone much kinder than I ever remembered it being with Z. I narrowed my eyes at him, but he ignored me, addressing the healer with earnest eyes. "But we were hoping you could help us with a few issues we have."

"Paco may be able to help." He scratched absently at his bearded chin before coming to a decision and nodding. He smiled at me. "Paco whip him with his cock and then help."

Wait...

The fuck?!

Dair snorted on laughter as I stared in wide-eyed terror at the giant of a man. Did he really just say...?

"You want to hit Killian with your cock?" Bash asked cautiously, like he was actually considering it.

"Just one slap," Paco insisted, once again twirling his cock in his fist. I was beginning to think he wasn't sexually pleasuring himself, he was winding himself up to penis bitch-slap me.

"No!" I protested immediately.

Bash took a step closer to me and hissed under his breath, "Do it for Z."

"I'm not allowing him to whack me with his cock!" I whispered-shouted.

"Just one little whack on the cheek," Bash insisted. "It's not like he's going to fuck you or anything."

My eyes turned even wider with horror.

"You don't think...?"

"Paco is getting impatient." Paco folded his arms over his chest and tapped his foot against the ground.

"Just bend down and take it like a man," Bash told me, but I was already shaking my head vehemently.

"Killian..." Dair twisted his head to give me a severe look. "We don't have a lot of time."

I grumbled under my breath, cursing out my brothers and life and Paco, as I squeezed my eyelids shut and leaned forward. I'd never been hit in the face with a penis before. Would it feel like a fish on my cheek? Not that I'd been hit with a wet fish either...

Boisterous laughter had my eyes snapping open.

Paco and Bash were holding their stomachs as they died of laughter. Even Dair was chuckling softly, though Jax remained stone-faced as he stared blindly out the only window looking back into the forest.

"Gullible little incubus." Paco clicked his tongue, still laughing, and moved to pat the top of my head condescendingly. It was then that I realized I was still leaning forward, putting my face only a few inches away from his cock, and I scrambled backwards with a...manly scream. Yup. Totally going with that. It wasn't a squeal at all. Men didn't squeal.

"What the...?" I glanced back and forth between Bash and Paco, my eyes narrowing into slits. "You tricked me!"

Bash offered me a sheepish smile. "Sorry, brother. I wasn't lying when I said Paco was...a strange mage. He does require payment, but that payment isn't whacking incubi with his cock." A bark of laughter escaped him unbidden, but when he noticed my thunderous expression, he quickly sobered. "He requires humiliation."

"Humiliation?" I practically screeched as I watched Paco amble towards a cauldron bubbling in the corner of the room. A wide grin split open his whiskered face as he turned back to us.

"Humiliation is Paco's secret ingredient," the crazy mage explained, his white braid swinging behind him. "Makes a delicious memory wiping potion."

"I really am sorry," Bash murmured to me, lowering

his voice so as not to be overheard by the healer. "I knew that we had to play along with whatever happened here. Last time I arrived, he made me dance around the living room while calling myself a pretty pony."

"Fuck you," I grumbled, and his eyebrows rose at my swear word. As a general rule, I didn't swear if I could help it. But I was freaking pissed at him for doing this to me. Granted, I knew my reaction had to be genuine or else Paco might not have helped us, but he still could've given me a heads-up. Obviously Dair knew, if his amused smirk was anything to go by.

Bash flashed me another guilty look before schooling his features and addressing Paco.

"Now that you've received your payment, can you help us?" Bash asked.

Paco straightened, wiping off his hands, before nodding once.

"Yes. Yes. Paco helps. Come." He gestured us forward, and just when I thought he was going to take us to some supersecret lab underneath his shed, he took one step to the right. Literally *one freaking step.* I found myself shoulder to shoulder with Jax and Bash as we clustered ourselves around Paco in the smallest corner of the living room.

"You like Paco's shop?" The healer turned bright eyes on to each of us, and unsure what the desired response was to this situation, I nodded.

"Yes. It's..." *Literally the corner of your house.* "Nice."

"Paco like nice." The healer winked at me, and I swore I felt myself die a little inside. Especially since with the way we were positioned, all he had to do was thrust his hips a tiny bit and his *thing* would be touching me.

"Killian likes...um...his mate," I stuttered out, mentally facepalming myself.

Paco's eyebrows touched his hairline. "Mate?"

"Our sick mate," Bash explained. "Which is why we're here."

"Sick mate?" I swore his eyebrows didn't move an inch from where they now rested at the top of his head, confusion permanently splayed across his face.

"She was poisoned," Dair explained, and his words turned the atmosphere somber. I didn't think any of us thought too closely about Z's condition. The thought of her not pulling through, of not opening up her beautiful eyes and spearing us all with a cocky look, of not surviving...

It was unfathomable.

Like, I literally couldn't wrap my head around a world without her in it.

Paco's eyes drifted to Dair as if noticing him for the first time. His lips, if it were even possible, turned thinner.

"You need Paco's help too, no?" Paco turned—I barely jumped out of the way before his dick could whip me—and began to sift through his cabinets. He muttered under his breath as he sifted through shelf after shelf of what appeared to be potions. Each one was in a translucent jar with no label, making me wonder how he knew what he was looking for.

"This help." Paco grabbed a jar on the top shelf and

all but threw it at Dair. The mermaid's eyes widened as he struggled to catch the glass container.

"What is it?" Dair made a face as he stared at the slimy, green substance.

"Help fix legs." Paco nodded towards Dair, and I watched my brother's face closely, his incredulous expression giving way to unreadability. "One spoonful every day. Not permanent. Will help," Paco instructed.

"I...eat it?" Dair's expression was carefully blank, and I wished desperately I could get him alone and ask him what he was thinking. I hated to see any of my brothers like this, but him most of all. He'd gone through hell, and I blamed myself every day for not noticing sooner how much pain he'd endured.

Paco gave Dair a droll look, as if questioning his mental stability, before he mimicked spooning soup from a bowl and swallowing it whole. There was a whole lot of tongue licking going on, and I shuddered in revulsion.

I took that as a resounding yes.

"Now, the poison," the old man continued. "Paco needs to know—"

Something roared in the distance, the noise nearly shattering my eardrums, and the earth began to shake erratically.

"What the...?" Bash murmured.

All four of us exchanged wide-eyed looks as one name passed our lips. One word. One letter.

Our entire lives tied up in it.

"Z."

TEN

BASH

I raced outside, my magic crackling in my hands. Green light emitted from my palms as I stopped to inspect the scene before me.

Z was awake, standing outside the van with Ryland beside her. Her head was tilted upwards, a look of utter horror etched onto her face. I followed the direction of her vision, a curse spilling from my lips at the monster nosediving for us.

A dragon.

A motherfucking dragon.

I'd never seen one before outside of the occasional history book. They were one of the species that had become extinct over time. But now it was here in the flesh, looking just as menacing and goddamn terrifying as one would expect a mythical creature to look.

Its scales were a verdant green, a few shades darker than my own magic. Its body was easily the length of the capital and the width of a small car. Dark horns erupted from the top of its head, directly over its pitch-black eyes, and its tail was covered in a number of pointy triangles.

Only one person had the power to bring extinct supernaturals back from the dead.

Aaliyah.

The bitch was attacking us again.

"Get her in the car!" I bellowed at Ryland as I stalked across the driveway. Z whipped her head in my direction, her stare indignant while her eyes spewed vitriol.

"Fuck off, Bash-hole." She had a dagger in each hand, and her legs were bent slightly as if waiting to pounce.

"I just want you to be safe!" It was hard to speak over the roaring reverberating across the sky from the rapidly approaching beast.

"And what better way to be safe is there than to save myself?" she retorted immediately, and I growled, wanting nothing more than to spank her ass into submission.

Instead of doing any of that, though, I moved to stand beside her. I could hear Killian speaking in hushed tones to Dair and Jaxon behind us, but I couldn't focus on what was being said. My attention was consumed by the monster bearing down on us.

"Does anyone know how to kill a dragon?" Ryland asked almost lazily, as if he were discussing the weather and not an immensely dangerous creature bearing towards us with death in its eyes. Because this monster totally wanted to eat us.

I didn't know about the others, but I would be a horrible dragon meal. Absolutely disgusting.

"Um...are we supposed to?" Killian's voice trembled

ever so slightly, but he stood firm, one of his hands resting on the hilt of a dagger in his waistband. Jax was beside him, standing slightly in front of Dair, who was staring into the jar Paco gave him with wide eyes, his expression inscrutable.

"If only Lupe were with us..." Z muttered, her brows furrowing together. Sweat beaded on her forehead as she swayed precariously to the side. I was there in a flash, placing one hand on her upper arm to hold her upright.

"Z..." I warned, my voice a rumbling growl. She was right—if Lupe and Devlin were here, you could bet your sweet ass that they would've forced Z back inside the van. But alas, they were gone, and it was up to me to be her knight in shining armor.

Though...

I was beginning to suspect she didn't need anyone to save her. If anything, our girl saved us way more than we saved her. If the look she threw me was any indication, the same thought had crossed her own mind.

I wasn't ashamed to admit that my girl was a badass. Some people seemed to believe that the men needed to do all the saving, but I didn't believe that. Sure, I wanted nothing more than to protect Z and hide her away from the world, but I knew she was more skilled at fighting than any of us. We were princes, for fuck's sake, while she was a skilled assassin with more kills under her belt than any of us could comprehend.

That didn't change the fact that she was fucking sick and looking weaker by the second.

If saving her life meant throwing her over my

shoulder and tying her to a tree, then that was what I'd do.

"I can fight," Z insisted. "I feel fine."

"Fucking liar," I snapped, and she bristled.

"Fuck you."

"Aww. You offering?" I tossed her a taunting smirk, but whatever retort rested on her pretty lips died the second the dragon flew lower into the clearing. This close, I could see its underbelly was a soft, milky color that was in direct contrast to its rippling green scales.

"The stomach," Z and I said at the exact same time. We also gave each other simultaneous death glares, so I called that winning. Totally couple goals.

"Aim for the stomach," Z elaborated, twirling a dagger around in her hands with an ease that left me baffled...and a bit horny, if I was being honest with myself. Though this was definitely not the time to be thinking with my cock.

"This should be fun," Ryland mused with a dark chuckle. His shadows wrapped tightly around him, hoisting him a few feet off the ground where he hovered. "I haven't had to kill anyone in a few months."

"Damn, Ry," Z scoffed. "Are you trying to make me horny before a fight?"

"Are you greedy for more, little dove? Did I not satisfy you when I fingered you to completion? Does the thought of me killing someone turn you on?" Amusement laced Ryland's tone.

"It does," Killian and Z responded at the same time, Kill's voice a screech as he felt her lust, while Z's remained calm and confident.

Wait? Fingered? Completion? What the fuck did I miss?

Leave to save your mate, and you miss out on everything, apparently.

Fuck them both.

I rolled my eyes at their banter, jerking my chin in the direction of the monster still circling overhead. I didn't understand why it wasn't attacking. Maybe it was waiting for—

"Guys." Jax's voice was soft, barely audible, but before I could respond to him, Z began to speak.

"What the fuck is the dragon doing?" Her nose crinkled as she squinted up at the monster.

"Guys."

"It doesn't want to kill you, Z," Ryland reminded her gently. "It wants to capture you."

"But it still doesn't explain why—"

"Guys!"

We all turned to look at Jax, but the vampire's gaze wasn't on it. It was fixed on the forest surrounding Paco's cottage...

And the dozen monsters surrounding us.

At first glance, I thought they were wolves or maybe oversized dogs. But when they took a step forward, their movements eerily synchronized, I realized they weren't dogs or wolves or anything I'd ever seen in the flesh before.

They were hellhounds.

Motherfucker.

Their fur was coarse and a dark, onyx black. It covered their slender bodies, patches of fur missing and giving them a savage, untamed look. Red eyes peered back at me, the malice in them unmistakable. The longer I stared, the more I began to believe that the flames of the Underworld itself lurked in their irises, the red shifting and contorting like fire.

"Welp…" Z licked her upper lip. "This just got more interesting."

"You don't fucking say," I sniped, my eyes shifting from the hellhounds to the dragon and then to the woman who'd become my entire fucking world. Cocking an eyebrow, I asked, "And I still can't convince you to run and hide?"

She gave me a droll look. "Maybe you should be the one hiding, Bash-hole. Heaven knows you don't know how to use the…" her eyes moved from the blade in the waistband of my pants to my cock, "stick you were given."

I rolled my eyes. "A sex joke at this time? Really? Real fucking mature."

"You love it."

I really do.

But before I could do something fucking ridiculous, like declare my undying love for her, the monsters charged. It was almost as if their minds were connected, as if they were waiting for some unseen force to give the command to pounce.

The dragon twisted in the air, coming straight towards us, as the hellhounds burst from the trees with malevolent growls.

Ryland curled the shadows further around his body, shooting up into the sky, and I watched as a blade materialized in his hand. I was forced to look away when a hellhound lunged at me, its fangs sharp and dripping saliva. I called on my power, growing it from a tiny orb to a brilliant ball of light, and threw it at the monster's face. It yelped in agony, my green fire licking at its fur and skin, until it fell to the ground in a charred and smoky mess. The whole exchange only lasted a few seconds before I was turning again, searching desperately for Z.

But I didn't have to worry. My girl moved like a shadow, ducking and dancing and weaving between the beasts. Her blades glinted in the sunlight as she sliced at one hellhound, ducking just in time as another one lunged over her head. She grinned manically, a fire entering her eyes, and threw one of her blades, landing it cleanly in the beast's stomach.

Satisfied that she could handle herself, I conjured up more flames and began to shoot the hellhounds at random. My eyes flickered towards my brothers fighting for their damn lives.

Killian was wielding his blade with a hesitancy that didn't surprise me. What did surprise me, however, was how good he appeared to be with the dagger, despite his limited training. With his sizeable bulk, it only took one stab to incapacitate a hellhound, and with the speed and flexibility associated with all incubi, he made the fight into a dance. With a little training, Killian could go from being an okay fighter to being a great one. Of that I had no doubt.

Z would probably come in her pants if she watched him fight now, that kinky shit.

Jax was also holding his own, zipping between the monsters with a burst of his vampire speed and lunging at their throats. His canines were extended, the tips dripping red, but he didn't appear to actually be drinking the blood of the beasts. Instead, he ripped at their throats, eliciting pained cries from the monsters, before darting away.

A shout dragged my attention towards the sky, just in time to see Ryland tumbling free from his shadows, falling towards the ground.

"Ryland!" Z screamed, and I called on my magic, forcing it forward so it caught him mid fall. His mouth dropped open as he stared at the cloud of green that had captured him, but he immediately snapped it shut when the dragon dived in his direction. I didn't know what the fuck happened, but it was obvious Ryland was weak. Even when he tried to call on the shadows, they burst to life and then immediately stuttered out.

I raced forward at the same time Z did, but before I could even think to use my magic, she was lunging forward, her blade extended. She jumped onto the green cloud I'd created for Ryland and used the momentum to jump even higher, slicing at the dragon's sensitive underbelly. The creature roared with agony, spinning in a wide circle, before hurrying back in Z's direction.

"Z!" I bellowed, racing forward. I shot rapid fireballs at the monster's belly, one after the other, but it didn't appear to do a damn thing. Sure, it hurt the little fucker, if his pained cries were any indication, but he didn't slow down. His clawed talon reached for Z—

Until it was immediately blasted away by a wall of water.

Dair appeared on the opposite side of me, standing

on two legs and a look of concentration on his face. I watched in fascination as he molded the water into a makeshift spear and solidified it until it appeared to be made from ice. And then he stabbed it into the dragon's chest.

Another roar left the magnificent creature's throat, and I felt a surge of anger ripple through my system. This monster...

It was innocent in this war. It had no idea what the fuck it was doing, only that it had to follow Aaliyah's bidding. And now we had to kill it, kill this glorious beast, or risk our mate's life.

I combined my magic with Dair's, throwing everything I had into killing the dragon. Hit after hit. Cut after cut.

"How the fuck is it still flying?" Dair demanded, his blue eyes glinting with his power.

"No fucking clue."

"Paco don't like intruders!" The long-haired mage appeared on the front porch of his house, his eyes filled with rage. He clapped his hands together, his magic cackling around him, before he shot it outwards in a sonic burst.

The remaining hellhounds whined before falling to the ground, one after the other in a domino effect. I had no idea if they were dead or simply unconscious, but I didn't care enough to ask.

When Paco's magic reached the dragon, the monster roared, writhing madly, before its black eyes fluttered shut and it fell from the sky.

Directly where Z was standing.

I screamed at her, but she easily rolled out of the way when the creature's ginormous body collapsed on the asphalt, cracking the road and sending me falling onto my ass.

Paco offered us a slanted smile, as if he hadn't just used magic even my own father wasn't capable of.

"Come inside." Paco crooked his finger in a come-hither gesture, his cock flapping madly in the breeze. "Paco helps."

Ryland materialized at my side, the shadows once more concealing him from view. But his pained grunt when he moved let me know he didn't get off scot-free.

Instead of questioning my brother, I nodded towards Paco ambling back into his house like he didn't have a dragon and a dozen hellhounds in his front yard.

"What the fuck is happening?" I queried, watching in my periphery as Z staggered to her feet, her face even paler than usual. Fear tightened my throat until even breathing felt impossible.

"I don't know." Ryland shook his head slowly. "But if your friend was able to wield that much magic...he might be able to help us save Z's life."

ELEVEN

LUPE

"**W**here the fuck are you going?" I hollered, barreling in the direction of my brothers.

"Language!" Killian chastised, but he was immediately shushed and reprimanded by Bash for giving away their location. Growling, I began to move faster, skirting a corner just as all six of my best friends ran out the door.

"This isn't funny!" I resisted the urge to pout like a petulant child. I wasn't one, despite what my father believed. I was ten, dammit, and it was about time I proved to both of my parents that I could be responsible and mature.

But I was getting really annoyed with my friends running away from me.

"It's a game!" Devlin called, his face peering around the corner of the hall. His violet eyes sparkled with mirth, but that only exacerbated my annoyance and rage.

"Games are for babies," I said with a huff of irritation, but I continued to prowl towards them.

"*Don't be an ass hat, Lupe!*" *Jax's head appeared around the corner next, his brown hair sticking up in all directions. Like me, Jax was a nerd at heart, preferring to spend his time face-first in a book. It made him horribly inept at talking to girls, especially Maggie, who we all knew he had a crush on. But Maggie was going to be my girlfriend. Jax could have Sasha, the daughter of that nice human maid.*

"*Don't call me an ass hat, ass hat!*" *I retorted bitterly. I quickened my pace, my legs already longer and wider than those of my brothers at my age.*

"*Then stop being an ass hat!*" *Jax snapped.*

"*Everyone, stop saying ass hat.*" *Bash's face appeared next, followed immediately by Killian's. Those two were inseparable. It made me a little bit jealous that they'd declared themselves best friends. We weren't allowed to pick favorites. I liked them all equally.*

"*Y-yeah!*" *Killian's stuttered with a decisive head bob. "Only ass hats say ass hats."*

Bash gave our friend a long look, his hand creeping up to pinch the bridge of his nose. "Dude."

Dair's head poked above all of the others, his blue eyes sparking and golden hair framing his cherubic face. Everyone always said that Dair was the prettiest of us all, a fact that we teased him mercilessly about. Who wanted to be the pretty boy? Girls didn't like pretty, they liked sexy men with muscles, which fortunately, meant me. Killian would probably be sexy when he got older, but as of now, his body was slender and lanky, his reddish-brown hair a little too long and flopping constantly in his eyes. It was a source of contention between him and his father. Mr.

Incubus wanted Killian to cut his hair, but Kill refused, preferring it long. He told me once that he wanted to grow it out and then donate it to humans who developed a sickness called cancer. I thought that idea was preposterous.

As if his parents would ever allow him to do that.

"What game are we even playing?" I folded my arms over my chest bitterly just as cold shadows caressed my neck. I spun in alarm, raising my hands to defend myself from the unseen foe, when Ryland's dark chuckle greeted me.

He was perched on the windowsill a few feet above the ground, his eyes flashing through the darkness that obscured his features from view. He smiled, the shadows lifting to reveal pearly white teeth, before they disappeared altogether. His smooth, unblemished face stared back at me.

"If you don't want to be 'it' anymore, I can do it," he offered with a nonchalant shrug. Indignation immediately filled me. I knew he didn't mean it as an insult, but it almost felt as if he was mocking me, as if he was saying that I couldn't handle being "it." I knew it was probably my wrath rearing its ugly head, but either way, I lifted my chin up stubbornly and gave him a fierce glare.

"I can do it."

Ryland's lips twitched, the only indication I'd done exactly what he wanted me to. Dammit.

"Tell me the game we're playing!" I demanded, annoyed at all of them. "Hide and seek or—"

"Lupe!" All of us stiffened at the familiar baritone voice, though I didn't think any of us had ever heard such rage before. It permeated my very soul, leaving ripples of apprehension throughout my body. Goosebumps emerged on my arms as I turned towards the figure barreling towards us from the end of the hall.

My father, followed by over a dozen attendants and guards, each of them with wide, terrified eyes, stalked towards me. Someone tried to speak to him, but the look he threw her was capable of frosting over glass.

I swallowed down the lump in my throat as I waited with bated breath for him to approach.

Despite his reputation, my father had never laid a hand on me. He didn't need to.

He had enough humans at his disposal to never run out of punching bags.

"Dad?" I cleared my throat as his vitriol filled eyes landed on me. "What's going on? Where's Mom?"

One of the attendants began shaking her head at me in warning, but before I could comment on it, Dad grabbed my arm and began to drag me down the hall after him. We passed my friends, all of whom stared at us with mouths agape, before they soon disappeared far behind us.

My shorter legs hurried to keep up with his brutal, demanding pace, but I didn't dare ask him to slow down. I'd never seen my dad so out of sorts before.

Normally, his facial hair was immaculately groomed, but today, it seemed even longer than I'd ever remembered it being. Dirty almost, like he hadn't showered in days. Strands of dark hair fell in front of his eyes, and that alone was a red flag. My dad always, always had his hair slicked back.

And his eyes...

Madness and desperation didn't even begin to encapsulate the emotions peeking out through them. They were wild and unhinged, angry and volatile. He was a ticking time bomb on a short fuse, and I just knew that whatever had occurred caused him to finally explode.

And everyone would pay the price.

Finally, when it felt like I couldn't take the suspense anymore, I managed to choke out, "What happened?"

"Your mother's dead," he gritted out, and the words felt like a wrecking ball destroying the very last piece of my soul. My mother wasn't the kindest woman in the world, but I knew she loved me in her own way. She was strict and forceful, bigoted and rude, but she cared about me in a way only a mother could. I hadn't seen her in a few months—she preferred to spend her time in the Shifter Kingdom while I remained at the capital—but she would write to me weekly. And now, she was...dead.

That word felt so final, so absolute. A part of me wanted to scoff at my father, to tell him that he had it wrong and my mother wasn't dead. How could she be, when we planned to meet next month and have dinner? When she promised to celebrate my birthday with me in a few months? I still had a card sitting on the nightstand beside my bed with her name on it for Mother's Day, one of the few human traditions that we kept when the Sins descended on this Earth.

Dead.

Dead.

Dead.

My legs wobbled underneath me, but before they could collapse completely, my father gripped my arm, yanking me upright.

"Don't fall apart on me, boy," he hissed, giving my arm a shake. "We have things to do."

I could barely get my next word out. It scratched at something raw and bloody in my throat. "What?"

And then my father smiled, and it was so disturbing and unhinged that I knew whatever remained of the man before my mother died had gone into that grave with her.

"Humans to kill."

"Lupe." Someone shook my shoulder. "Lupe, wake up. Lupe!"

I jolted awake, my heart racing a mile a minute as I struggled to orient myself to my surroundings. Realizing I was still in the stolen vehicle with Devlin driving, I rubbed a hand down my face and released a heavy sigh.

"Fuck. How long was I asleep?" I questioned, shifting in the uncomfortable leather seat in an attempt to stretch out my sore muscles.

Devlin barely took his eyes off the road as he answered. "Only a few hours. But you started thrashing, man. Bad dream?"

"Bad memory," I responded cagily, my words nothing more than a guttural growl as my bear struggled to break free. I didn't like talking about my dad any more than Devlin liked hearing about him. We all had our demons, but mine so happened to be one of the biggest dictators in fucking history.

Though I was sure my father and half the nightmare

population wouldn't agree with my assessment of the evil man.

"I thought your dad went back to the Shifter Kingdom," Devlin murmured as we began to drive through the twisting path of the mountain towards the capital building. "What is he doing back here?"

"I'm not sure," I responded warily. I didn't trust this one fucking bit.

Fuck, I should've been with Z, but instead, I was traipsing through the fucking capital without a word of reasoning.

Thoughts of my mate had a cold, icy fear slithering through my intestines. I knew my brothers would look after her with their lives, but that didn't stop the irrational terror from strangling my airways. I should've been with her too. Looking after her. Protecting her. It was my job as her mate to always provide for her. What if something happened while I was away? What if I didn't get to say goodbye to her? What if—

"She'll be fine," Devlin told me softly, removing one hand from the steering wheel to squeeze my shoulder. I wasn't surprised he knew exactly where my thoughts had taken me. No doubt, his were on the exact same airwave as mine.

"I don't like this," I said as we pulled to a stop in front of the capital building. Devlin's jaw clenched as he nodded once, putting the car into park and then turning off the ignition. For a moment, we simply sat in silence, staring up at the large building which had served as our home for the better part of our childhoods.

It sat in a valley created by the mountains, the stone

burnished in glittering gold. A dozen pillars held up a large balcony that blocked out the sunlight the closer to the entrance you ventured. There were hundreds of windows lining the perimeter of the building, each one displaying a copious amount of artificial lighting. A large body of water sat directly to the right of the mansion, and I spotted more than a few mermaids splashing about.

Anger darkened my vision at the thought of one of those mermaids being Dair's father, but I shoved that rage aside. For now, I had to remain levelheaded.

At least until I could figure out what the fuck my father wanted and get back to Z.

I exchanged a glance with Devlin, no words needing to be said, before we exited the car and stormed towards the front entrance.

The peach-colored walls were no doubt designed to give the room a cheerful atmosphere, but I knew better than anyone that the bright colors couldn't hide the darkness and blood staining every available surface. The Damning was held here every five years, and every five years, more bodies fell to the ground. Just thinking about the death and cranage that had occurred when Z won sent bile rushing up my throat.

All of those lives...

Most of them were murderers who deserved far worse fates, but some of them were innocent. The girls there for the Matching, for example, had no part to play in it. Yet their bodies were some of the many that littered the capital's halls and stained the carpeting bright red.

As if she felt me thinking of her, Mrs. Grinshaw, the organizer of the Matching and one of the palace's workers, hurried around the corner. Her gray hair was tidied back in a slick bun, and she wore a floral gown that cinched at her waist.

"Prince Devlin, Prince Lupe. You're here. Come." She turned on her heel without another word of greeting, stalking in the direction of the throne room.

I glanced at Devlin once more, his confusion mirroring my own, before hurrying after Grinshaw.

"What's going on?" Devlin straightened his spine, clasping his hands behind his back. Even without his crisp black suit on, he played the part of arrogant prince to perfection.

Grinshaw hesitated, almost as if she wanted to say more than she was allowed to, before simply stating, "I was instructed to bring you to the throne room."

Unease gripped my heart in an iron vise and squeezed until it felt like blood was sloshing around in my head. I couldn't ignore the tiny voice in my mind screaming that this was wrong, that it was dangerous, that I needed to turn in the opposite direction and run far, far away.

But my father had threatened Z. He knew what she was to me, to *us*, and he wouldn't hesitate to exploit those bonds for his own gain. She would be forced to travel back to the capital in less than two days, and if there was a trap waiting for her, I needed to know.

Grinshaw pushed open the door to the throne room, and we entered to complete fucking silence. Not a single breath of air punctuated it, causing my unease to amplify.

Six of the kings sat on their thrones staring down at

us. The only one absent was Ryland's father, the shadow king.

I could feel the power of their gazes as they pressed down on me, strangling my airways. The boy in me wanted to cower, but I held my chin up stubbornly and met my father's gaze.

"Father, what is this?"

This was more than a little concerning. It was fucking nauseating.

When we left to rescue Jax, all of the kings had returned to their respective kingdoms. What were they doing back? What the fuck was happening?

"We have a traitor in our midst," my father said lazily, rising from his seat. His yellow robes cascaded around his ankles as he moved. I'd always hated that fucking color. It looked like puke and piss mixed together. But as it was the official color of the shifters, so I had to wear the pu-iss color more than I cared to admit.

"You called me back here to discuss a traitor?" I scoffed in disbelief, though my heart was racing rapidly inside of my chest. I was half afraid it would develop arms and legs, burst through my rib cage, and then flop around on the floor like a dying fish.

I moved to readjust my reading glasses on my face before remembering I hadn't put them on. In all honesty, I had no idea where the fuck they'd gone.

My father snapped his fingers, and a moment later, a door on the opposite end of the throne room opened and two guards entered, dragging a familiar man between them.

Everything stopped. Paused. Tilted on its axis.

Devlin sucked in a sharp breath beside me, his eyes riveted on the figure held between the two guards.

"This traitor," my father's lips curled as he spat at the prisoner's feet, "has been accused of helping the resistance destroy us from the inside out. "

The resistance?

As in...the Alphabet Resistance?

"We had a plan to destroy their base of operation a second time, after they regrouped after our first attack," Dad continued, his upper lip peeling away in a sneer. "But when we arrived at the caves our spies told us about, we found the area completely deserted. It didn't take too long until we discovered that they'd been tipped off by this fucking bastard." He kicked at the prisoner's stomach, and the man wheezed, his face contorting in pain.

"W-what am I doing here?" I demanded, dragging my father's attention off the "traitor" and towards me. What the fuck would he do if he discovered the truth of Z's involvement in the resistance? No doubt, he would kill her. And me as well, despite our shared blood.

"You need to prove your loyalty to the kingdom and to me, your immortal king." A slanted, wicked grin pulled up his lips as my mind froze on the last two words of his statement. But I couldn't focus on that, not when my gaze was drawn to the broken man before me, his face mottled with bruises and scars but the defiant spark in his eyes unmistakable.

"And what would that be?" Devlin interjected, and another scowl pulled at Father's lips at being addressed by the genie prince.

"Torture the information we need out of him, the same way you did to that disgusting human."

T. He meant T, whom I was forced to hurt in order to spare his life.

I clamped my mouth shut to stop the flurry of insults that wanted to erupt. Bile swarmed in my lower stomach, but I kept my face carefully impassive.

A few things became painfully clear.

First, the kings, despite their haughty attitudes, still didn't know about Z's involvement in the Alphabet Resistance, which was probably the only thing keeping her alive.

Second, the kings had something to do with Aaliyah. I didn't know what, only what Jax had told me about the exchange he'd witnessed when he was her prisoner, but I didn't trust it for one goddamn second.

And third, this entire time, the shadow king had been a spy for the resistance.

Fuck.

Z

Everything hurt, but I was alive.

Which was more than could be said about the hellhounds and dragon. My eyes latched on to a familiar symbol etched into the nearest hellhound's shoulder—numerous thin black lines that morphed into thicker red ones, creating a makeshift circle. It was the same mark that had been on the gorgon and kraken, on the basilisk and fae.

If I had any doubt before about who'd been behind this attack, it dissipated at the sight of those markings.

Aaliyah.

"Z." Dair's familiar ocean scent engulfed me a second before his arms did. I squeezed my eyelids shut and leaned into his embrace as emotions bombarded me from all directions.

The first one was anger—anger at Aaliyah for trying to hurt me and my mates. Anger at the world in fucking general.

And then there was sadness, though I didn't know what it was directed at.

But underneath all of that, and growing larger and larger like a snowball moving down a hill, was hope and joy.

I spun in Dair's arms, tears of surprise and awe filling my eyes at seeing my mermaid mate standing before me.

Standing.

Near the edge of the tree line, I could see his discarded wheelchair and a jar of goo.

"How...?" I asked numbly, my fingers trailing over his muscular arms and gripping his biceps. My nails dug into his skin through his T-shirt, but if it hurt him, he didn't complain.

Instead of answering right away, Dair pressed his forehead to my own and breathed me in as deeply as I did him. His beautiful eyes fluttered shut, obscuring the clear ocean blue from view, before he reopened them and speared me with a look full of love and joy.

"Paco," he answered simply.

"Paco...?" Before I could further articulate my question, another body hugged me from behind, and though his natural scent was tinted copper from the blood on his body, Jax's arms around my waist were unmistakable.

"You're okay," he whispered repeatedly against my hair, his body shaking with each exhale. Dair released me, though reluctantly, and I turned to face my vampire lover. There seemed to be a war waging just beneath the surface—one second, his eyes were crazed, moving rapidly across my face but never sticking on one feature in particular, and the very next, coherency shown through. My heart ached for him, for the internal battle I couldn't help him fight. All I could do was be there for him, love him, until he was able to pull through on his own.

As he continued to murmur, "You're okay," over and over, I placed my head in the crook of his neck and wrapped my arms around his waist. My touch seemed to ground him, because a second later, his violent shivers stopped and the breath he released next was a deep exhale.

When he spoke again, his voice was soft. "You make me feel normal again," he whispered.

And then I was out of his arms and in Killian's before I could even think of a response.

"Yes. Yes. Everyone wants to see pretty mate. But Paco don't want to see no pretty mate. Paco wants to sleep," a growly, accented voice stated from the front of the shed. I froze, my muscles tensing like a bolt of electricity had been zapped through my veins, as I turned towards the mage.

The power he'd wielded...

It was incredible. I didn't even think the king was as powerful as him. With a single flick of his fingers, he was able to stop an army of resurrected supernaturals without breaking a sweat.

And how did I know he wasn't breaking a sweat?

Because the man was completely naked and was indolently tapping his cock against the railing of his front porch.

"Um...Paco, I presume?" I stage-whispered to Killian, who immediately placed his hand over my eyes.

"Don't look at the cock, Z. Do not look at the cock," he said an ominous tone, and I scoffed, biting down on his palm until he yelped and pulled it away with a narrow-eyed stare in my direction.

"Afraid I'll get horny?" I teased as Paco gestured for us to enter his home. The old giant immediately turned on his heel and stomped inside, giving me a view of his flabby ass.

"If you get horny, I'm afraid I'll have to rescind my offer of being your mate." Bash moved to stand in front of me, his eyes sweeping over my body from head to toe and cataloging any injuries. But besides a few cuts and bruises and the general feeling of shittiness, there wasn't anything majorly wrong with me.

"Awww, Bash-hole." I took a step closer until I could squeeze his cheeks. "You'd miss me too much."

He gave me a dry look and retorted, "I wouldn't miss—"

A cough rattled my body, blood erupting from my mouth, and I fell forward as my legs failed me. Bash cursed, the teasing atmosphere instantly diminishing as my mates looked at me with worry and fear. Before I could even get myself balanced, my body was scooped up into strong, muscular arms, and Bash strode towards the shed-like cottage.

"I can walk," I murmured...weakly, though. We all knew I was full of shit.

"And I can stop being an asshole for longer than a minute," Bash quipped angrily, though I knew the anger wasn't directed at me. "Now shut up and let me coddle you."

"You shut up." I stubbornly crossed my arms over my chest and scowled, even as his own lips twitched in amusement.

"You know, if you need something to occupy that dirty mouth of yours..."

"You offering me your cock, Bash-hole?" I blinked up at him innocently. "Are you sure I won't lose it in my mouth? After all, it's pretty small. I don't want to accidentally swallow—"

He growled sharply, his arms holding me even tighter against his chest as Killian opened the door to the cottage. "I can assure you, my naughty mate, that it's not small. You saw it once. Remember?"

I pretended to think about it as we entered a tiny, desolate room with very minimal furniture and a woodsy feel to it. "I didn't have my microscope, so I'm not sure—"

He placed his hand over my mouth and leveled me with a hard stare. "You're mean."

I pulled his hand away with a raised brow. "*You're* mean," I retorted immediately.

"I'll show you mean—"

"Enough! Paco wants to see the little female. Yes, Paco see," the crazed mage said, gesturing us forward and towards his bed.

I eyed a pancake resting in the center of his bed, and my eyebrows shot to my hairline, especially when Killian moved protectively in front of me and Bash and stuttered, "L-let's put her somewhere else."

I *so* did not want to know.

Bash eventually sat on the floor, keeping me in his arms until I was positioned comfortably in his lap. I didn't necessarily like this vulnerable position, especially knowing how powerful Paco truly was, but I didn't dare voice my discomforts. I felt so weak and tired, my body heavier than chunks of lead.

"Paco sees you used his potion." The mage turned towards Dair, who stood against the wall, his golden arms folded over his chest. When Dair nodded, his jaw clenched ever so slightly, the mage added, "Will wear off. Need to remember that. Paco only has one jar and will only have one jar. Too difficult for Paco to waste his time on making. And once you run out of special juice..." He trailed off with a sad shake of his head, and Dair's hands balled into fists.

I understood Paco's meaning well enough—the second Dair ran out of whatever substance was in that jar, he would be confined back to his wheelchair. He would have to use it sparingly until we could figure out how to get more. We could demand Paco give us his recipe and hope Bash could recreate it, but I had a feeling it was more difficult than that.

"What do you need Paco's help with? The female?" The mage leaned down in front of me, his cock brushing against my leg until Killian growled sharply. The sound was so primordial and possessive that my head snapped in his direction.

He blushed, ducking his head and shrugging his shoulders sheepishly. "Sorry. I don't like men who aren't your mates touching you."

"Join the fucking club," Bash muttered angrily, and though I couldn't see his expression, I had the distinct feeling that his gaze was fixed on how close Paco was to me, despite the fact his cock was no longer touching my leg.

Gah. I was going to need to burn my skin to rid myself of the feeling of his slimy snake cock.

"You sick, yeah? Paco sees you sick." He placed a sweaty hand to my forehead, and I resisted the urge to recoil. I could see my mates didn't like this anymore than I did, because Dair immediately straightened from where he was leaning against the wall, Killian growled sharply yet again, Ryland practically hissed like a feral cat, and Bash's arms tightened around me. Even Jax, who'd been staring absently out the window, whipped his head in my direction, his eyes flashing with an emotion I couldn't quite name.

But Paco didn't seem to mind the vitriol spewing at him from all directions. Instead, he shut his eyes and began to hum under his breath, his body swaying from side to side as he lost himself to the music.

"You trust this man?" Dair whispered urgently to Bash, and though my back was to him, I could feel his nod, his chin touching the top of my head for the briefest moment.

"Yes. I...I know him."

"You keep saying that," Killian pointed out. "But you haven't explained how."

"Well..." Bash sighed heavily, just as Paco's hand moved from my forehead to my nose, his fingers digging into my eyes and his thumb touching my lips. I gagged, attempting to pull my head away, but Paco grunted and held me tighter. "This is my grandpa."

Silence descended as we all processed this new revelation. My men stared at him with varying degrees of disbelief while I tried not to breathe too deeply, considering the fact I had a fucking smelly hand blocking my nostrils.

"Your grandpa?" Killian squeaked out. "Y-you mean the former mage king?"

"The one and only." Bash sighed tiredly, smoothing his hands up and down my arms. It appeared to be an almost absentminded gesture, as if he wanted to memorize the feel of my skin beneath his palms. As if he wanted to assure himself I was still here and alive.

"The former mage king..."

I tried to recall what I knew of him, but my mind came up blank. All I knew for certain was that he wasn't evil. At least not as evil as his son. The former kings had ruled the kingdoms with iron fists, but they hadn't had human work camps like they did now. The humans hadn't been enslaved and fed on.

That wasn't to say there hadn't been any bigotry or speciesism, but it hadn't been as prominent as it was today.

"Paco needs silence," the former king declared, his lips thinning beneath his scraggly white beard.

My men immediately stopped talking, their focus intense on Paco's hand on my face. When he finally reopened his eyes and released me, I breathed a sigh of relief, shifting as far away from him as my position in Bash's lap would allow.

"You poisoned," Paco declared with a wide grin, as if we would be so thrilled that he'd stated the obvious.

Bash's voice was curt when he responded, "Yes, we know that. How do we heal her?"

White eyebrows retreated into his hairline as he stared at us. "Heal her?"

"Yes," Bash gritted out. "I know that they have the cure in the palace, but I was hoping…"

"You want Paco to give the human an antidote," he said in understanding, nodding his head rapidly. "Paco understands. Yes, Paco understands." And then he just continued to nod and blink without saying a goddamn word.

"So?" Dair demanded, and Paco spun towards him, as if forgetting we weren't alone.

"So?" Paco quirked an eyebrow, and Dair scoffed, throwing his hands up in the air and pacing the room.

"This is ridiculous. He's not going to be able to help us, Bash. We're wasting our time when we should be heading to the Mage Kingdom and—"

"Mage Kingdom don't have antidote. No more antidote. Paco can help," the white-haired mage insisted. "But Paco needs ingredients."

Okay, now we were getting somewhere…

"Ingredients," I reiterated, shooting a concerned look at first Dair and then Killian. Bash's arms were practically iron bands around my waist, and I knew he had no intention of releasing me anytime soon.

Paco scratched absently at his chin before nodding once more. "Yes, Paco has all of the ingredients. Paco can make antidote."

"For fuck's sake…" Bash murmured in irritation.

"So you can save Z?" Killian's voice was hoarse with hope.

But that hope shattered with Paco's next words.

"No." He shook his head from side to side erratically as my heart crumbled into dust. "In order for antidote to work, Z needs to die."

Z

The spell was simple enough, at least according to Bash, who'd received a copy of it from his grandfather. All of the ingredients we needed were in the cottage.

The problem came from the end of the spell that specified that I had to be dead for exactly one minute before the antidote could be administered.

"Nope. Fuck this. Not happening." Bash tossed the book against the wall, his chest heaving and hands clenching into fists.

"Bash..." I began, but he whirled on me, fire sparking in his eyes.

"You're not fucking dying, Z!" he bellowed. "I'm not allowing that to happen."

"We don't have a choice," I said softly, venturing a step closer to him like one would a cornered animal. His eyes ate up the distance between us, darkness flooding his features, but he didn't move to grab me or pull me into his arms. He just stood there, glaring and panting and heaving. "Even if we went to the palace and found the antidote there—"

"Which Paco insists is no longer there," Dair added in a subdued voice.

"—I'd still have to die for it to work."

"He wants to inject you with more fucking poison!" Bash raged, stomping towards me until his hands landed on my shoulders. Despite the anger in his eyes, his grip was soft and comforting. Protective. "He wants to kill you even faster."

"He needs to do this, Bash." I gripped his wrists, removing his hands from my shoulders and placing them on my waist instead. "I need to die naturally from the poison and be administered the serum after exactly a minute. And we have less than two days to do it."

"I can't..." His voice broke as he pressed his forehead against my own. "I can't lose you. I can't...I can't watch you in agony, baby. I can't."

"I know." I lifted my hands to his cheek, loving the way his stubble brushed against my palms. "But we don't have a choice."

My words were the wrong ones to say. The tenderness I could see in his eyes vanished as quickly as it came, leaving me feeling oddly bereft, like my soul wasn't quite complete without that softness permeating it.

"No," he hissed out, shouldering past me. "I refuse to believe that."

"Bash!" I called out to his retreating back as he all but shoved Paco to the side and stomped out the door. If the giant was concerned at all, he didn't show it, simply turning back to one of the two potions he was brewing and humming happily beneath his breath.

"We'll check on him," Killian said, nodding towards Dair to join him. "Jax, stay with her. Ryland, stay with *him*." He glanced pointedly in Paco's direction.

When Dair looked like he was going to protest, Killian grabbed him by the ear and all but dragged him out. I couldn't help but snort. Apparently, Killian was becoming more dominant by the day as he grew into his incubus powers.

I couldn't help but find that insanely attractive.

But I was also grateful for him, because he knew what I needed even before I did—alone time with Jax. Since we saved him from Aaliyah, we hadn't had a chance to slow down and just talk. Everything had been so chaotic that we hadn't found time to catch out breaths.

Now, we had nothing to do but wait, and I was determined to break through the walls erected around my sweet mate.

"Walk with me?" I asked Jax, who was still staring out the window. He glanced in my direction, furrowed his brows, and then nodded once, accepting the hand I'd offered. Paco gazed at us curiously, scratching at his balls, but he didn't stop us as we stepped outside into the rapidly setting sun. It wouldn't be long until night fell... and until we found ourselves with one day left to return to the capital.

I couldn't see Bash, Dair, or Killian, so I guided Jax towards a pathway cutting through the forest of trees. I had no idea if it was a natural walkway or one Paco had made, but I found there were very minimal obstacles to hinder us.

I kept my eyes peeled for any threats heading our way, though I knew Aaliyah would take the chance to regroup. Attacking us back-to-back had never been her style, though that didn't stop my hand from tightening on the hilt of my blade tucked into the waistband of my pants.

We walked in silence, the only sounds coming from the rippling of wind against the boughs and a stream of water somewhere farther down. It was there we headed, Jax's hand warm in mine, until we stopped at a tiny river cutting through the forest in smooth, curved lines. A large rock sat directly adjacent to the shoreline, and I led Jax there, perching myself on the edge and patting the spot beside me.

Jax joined me without protest, pulling his knees up to his chest and wrapping one arm around them. His other hand remained tangled with mine.

Silence settled between us, but it wasn't uncomfortable. I didn't think a silence between me and my mates could ever be.

I watched him out of the corner of my eye, once again in awe of his perfect features and light brown hair.

His chest heaved as he took a heavy breath before he turned towards me, rendering me speechless with the force of his gaze.

"I'm not crazy," he whispered brokenly, a sob getting caught in his throat. "I'm not."

"I don't think you are." I shifted even closer to him on the rock until my thigh touched the curve of his ass.

He blinked rapidly, pulling his gaze off of me to stare into the distance. His grip on my hand tightened, though I didn't dare pull away. He could break every bone in my body, and I would still grip him just as fiercely as he held me. I imagined my touch might've been the only thing stopping him from metaphorically jumping head-first over the highest cliff he could find.

"Everyone thinks I'm insane, and maybe...maybe I am." He slowly released his legs and brought his closed fist to his forehead. "Sometimes, I can see things perfectly and know that I'm okay. That you're here. But other times..."

"Other times?" I whispered when it became apparent he wasn't going to finish.

"Other times, I see shadows and monsters and blood. They're everywhere, Z, and they terrify me."

"Oh, Jax." Without giving myself a second to think, I crawled into his lap and held him tightly. I wanted to hold all of his broken pieces together and make him whole with nothing but the strength of my love. But I knew that wasn't possible. Not yet.

"I don't know who I am anymore," he whispered against my hair as he rocked us back and forth.

I pulled away and gripped his chin, praying that he saw the sincerity in my gaze. "You're Jax. You're sweet and perfect and my mate and...I love you."

He blinked at me slowly, almost as if he hadn't quite understood my words, as wonderment crossed his face.

"You...love me?"

My throat clogged, turning impossibly tight, but I forced myself to nod. I'd almost lost him, and I vowed to myself I wouldn't let another day go without telling him how I felt. And what I felt...

Was love.

So much fucking love for this broken, scarred man before me. The older me would've been terrified by the strength of my emotions, but the new me, the one broken down by flames and reforged into something far greater, relished in these feelings. These feelings for *them*.

My men.

My mates.

My loves.

I would protect them with every fiber of my being, and if that somehow led to my death, then so be it. But I would die with a smile on my face and the knowledge that my mates knew and felt the strength of my love.

I didn't think it was possible for someone like me to love again, not after everything I'd endured. My parents' deaths. Lin's disappearance. S's death...

It was too much, and at the same time, not enough. Those events hadn't broken me, despite what I'd thought at the time. Instead, they'd made me stronger, a fighter, and I knew that my life purpose was to protect these men who'd weaseled their way into my heart. They were made to be powerful and righteous kings, and I would do everything in my power to see them on their rightful thrones.

"You. Love. Me?" he repeated slowly, pointing from me to himself as if he couldn't quite understand the meaning of my words.

I cupped his cheeks with my hand, swinging my legs to the side to straddle his waist, and placed my lips to his.

"Yes. How could I not?"

"I would die for you, Z." With every word he said, his lips moved against mine, sparks of electricity dancing in their wake. "I would die for you time and time again."

"I don't want you to die for me," I responded breathily, our lips continuing to move against each other's in a kiss that wasn't quite a kiss.

"Then what do you want?" Coherence flashed in his eyes as he held my stare, and I found myself dropping my hands from his cheeks to his strong, muscular shoulders. Goosebumps pebbled on his skin, but they had nothing on my nipples, which were suddenly hard enough to cut diamonds.

"What would you do if I answered 'you'?" I asked huskily, pulling back just enough to see his eyes.

A tiny grin pulled at his lips a single second before he pulled me back against him, claiming my lips with his.

But I didn't just want the taste of his lips on my tongue. I wanted all of him.

I moved off of his lap and settled between his knees, his legs automatically opening up to make room for me. His brows dipped lower, even as hunger filled his gaze.

"What are you doing, little mate?" he asked hoarsely as I slid my hands up his thighs. When I reached the waistband of his pants, I pulled them down just enough to stick my hand inside and caress his hardening cock.

"I'm so sorry for everything you've been through," I whispered, my heart flaying open and weeping for him. Weeping for this man who'd been left alone in the dark for longer than I wanted to admit. He needed me, needed this, almost as much as I did. "But you won't be alone anymore, Jax. I won't let you."

"The darkness in my mind..." His throat bobbed as he swallowed. "It's not as dark anymore when you're here. You're my light."

"And you're mine." I pulled his boxers down to his thighs and released his throbbing length from their confines, the tip already beaded with pre-cum.

Jax swore, his eyes turning hooded and half-mast, and I groaned with need, leaning down to run my tongue along the length of his shaft. I wrapped my hand around the base of his cock and leaned my head down, wrapping my lips around the tip. I worked my way down his hard dick, taking every inch of him I was capable of, while my hand fisted around the part I couldn't quite reach. I loved the way he tasted in my mouth, the saltiness of his pre-cum, as I worked him over with my tongue and teeth.

"Fuck," he hissed, his fingers tangling in my hair and guiding my movements.

I moaned my own desire over his length before popping him out of my mouth, my saliva dripping down my chin. Totally not sexy, but he still stared at me as if I were a goddess.

I moved my mouth down his length to reach his balls, sucking first one and then the other in my mouth before moving back to his throbbing member.

But before I could bring him to ruin, before I could destroy him the way I so desperately wanted to, he gripped my arms and pulled me to my feet, his lips colliding with my own. I knew he could taste himself on my lips, but that thought only spurred me on and I kissed him hungrily.

I moved away from him, only for a second, to pull my

shirt over my head, and that was quickly followed by my bra. He didn't give me a chance to take my pants off before his mouth fell on my nipple, and he bit down in a way that sent sparks of heat straight to my core.

He sucked and teased my breasts while I worked on unbuttoning his shirt, wanting to feel every inch of his taut, hot skin against my own.

"Z..." he murmured as he shakily moved his hands to my jeans and yanked them down, my panties following soon after. I stepped out of the material as he continued to lick and tease my breasts, his teeth grazing my sensitive nipple as his rough hand rolled the other one. "Everything is so, so clear," he whispered huskily.

"What's clear?" I gasped out, but instead of answering, he growled and yanked my hips, pulling me onto his lap. I could feel the heat of his cock between my legs, my wetness drenching his shaft, and I moaned low in my throat as he began to rub his length against me, not quite entering my channel yet. "Jax, dammit."

His eyes flickered from my face to my neck, where my vein pulsed in tandem with my racing heart.

"I love you more than fucking words, Z," he said, slamming me down onto his cock. I wound my fingers into his hair as I began to ride him, using the rock beneath my feet to propel myself up. His hips thrust to match my movements, his eyes never leaving my own. I closed my eyes and focused on his touch, the way he filled me so completely, and a growl of warning left his throat. "Eyes on me, little mate."

"Show me you're mine, Jax. Show me you own me

and love me," I begged, and a devilish light entered his eyes as he began to pound into me harder and harder.

He gripped my ass and bounced me on his cock, breaking eye contact only once to capture one of my breasts in his mouth.

Words escaped me as I gave up any semblance of control I thought I'd had and surrendered myself to my mate. I knew that if I were to fall, he would be on the other end, waiting to catch me. He would always catch me.

He slammed into me again and again as I brought one hand to my breast, kneading it, and the other to my clit. He moved his hand to my hair, gripping to the point of pain, as his eyes lowered once more to my neck.

"Bite me, Jax," I whispered. I was offering him more than just my love. I was offering him my trust as well. Before Aaliyah, he hadn't fed in years, afraid that he would do to an innocent human what he did to his childhood friend. But I knew my mate and I trusted him implicitly. He would never hurt me, he would never hurt anyone.

Indecision flared to life in his eyes—his want for me battling his own inner demons.

I tilted my head to the side in clear offering, baring my neck, and with a hiss that was all vampire, he lunged and bit down on my neck.

The pleasure was immediate and consuming, and I gasped out loud. There was pain at first, as his fangs pierced my skin, but then that pain transformed into something beautiful and new. Something I'd ever experienced before.

It was like I could sense Jax's essence inside of me, could feel his emotions intertwining with my own. For a brief, brief second, I could sense the love he felt for me and the hope that I would be able to dispel his madness once and for all.

But then I was lost to the sensation of his cock rutting inside of me and his lips on my neck drinking deeply. Euphoria was the only word I could think to use. It was almost as if his venom shot pleasure straight to my core, casting my vision in a bright, all-consuming light.

I came so hard that my breath caught in my lungs and I momentarily forgot how to breathe. My pussy muscles clamped down on his cock, squeezing him, and he came with a growl of his own, pulsing inside of me.

I sagged forward and rested my forehead against his sweaty shoulder. At some point, he'd stopped biting me, though I could still feel blood running down my naked body.

"Fuck, I love you so much, Z." He gently grabbed my chin until I was forced to stare into his eyes. My blood coated his chin and lips, dripping down the column of his throat, and my pulse hammered at the enticing sight. "You keep the shadows away."

"I love you too, Jax." I placed a single kiss to his lips, tasting my blood, before moving back and staring intently into his eyes. "Even with all of your shadows."

"Guys! You need to come...and holy crap. Those are some nice titties," Killian stuttered as he appeared on the pathway, his eyes dropping to my breasts. I laughed lightly, not bothering to cover myself up, before reluctantly moving off of Jax's lap. He released a sound of dismay as his cock slid out of me, and I glanced at the cum dripping down my thighs. Fuck, I needed to find something to clean this off before I got back into my clothes.

"What's up, Kill?" I questioned, though he seemed to be tit-notized—hypnotized by tits, if you were wondering.

"Err..." He absently rubbed himself through his pants, still not pulling his attention away from my breasts.

"I think we broke him," Jax mused with a wink in my direction, and that finally seemed to shake Killian out of whatever stupor he'd found himself in. He blinked rapidly, turning towards Jax with shock splayed across his face.

"You're... You...you fed!" he managed to say, disbelief evident in his tone.

"And you came running over here because...?" I pressed when it became apparent he'd lost his train of thought. At my words, his face drained of all color and he hurried towards me, removing his own shirt to help me clean the cum off my legs. Unfortunately, he wore a white tank top beneath it, so I wasn't able to see his impressive collection of tattoos. Though maybe I could convince him to—

"There's an army at Paco's house," Killian blurted out.

"What?" I stilled, only my eyes lifting to meet his gaze. Fuck. Fuck. Fuck! We still had time before I was required back at the capital. Why did they come? What did they want? Or was it Aaliyah planning another attack?

I searched the ground for my dagger, finding it beside my discarded pants, and I picked it up and began to march back towards the shed.

"Aren't you going to get dressed?" Killian called in alarm.

I spun to face him. "Dair, Bash, and Ryland are over there. They need my help."

Before I'd even finished speaking, Killian began to shake his head slowly. "The army won't hurt them."

"They won't...?" I trailed off, accepting the clothes Jax handed me. I got dressed as quickly as I could before facing Killian once more. "How do you know that?"

"Because it's not just any army, Z." Killian scrubbed absently at his cheek. "It's *your* army."

FOURTEEN

DAIR

If the kings didn't want the humans to rebel, they should never have given them a savior to rally behind. Of course, I doubted the kings realized that they'd created a living martyr out of Z, but the sentiment was the same.

She'd answered their unspoken plea to become the leader for the human race.

I stood shoulder to shoulder with Ryland, staring out into the sea of unfamiliar faces. All of them human. All of them whispering amongst themselves as they waited for Z to return. I heard whispers of the Liberator rippling throughout the crowd, though whenever I got near, they immediately shut down.

"I don't like this." Bash materialized on the other side of me, his eyes shrewd as he surveyed the assembled mass. I counted at least one hundred, if not more, humans. Tents had been erected around the perimeter of the property, almost as if they couldn't bear being separated from Z. The way they spoke of her...

It was almost reverent. Worshipful. They seemed to have placed her on a goddess level pedestal in their minds, and I was afraid of what that pressure would do to her.

To be quite frank, I was terrified in general.

Who assembled here today was a threat? Would word of this uprising reach the capital and the kings? What would we even fucking do with all of these men and women who'd left their homes to follow Z?

"None of us do," Ryland murmured from beside me. He'd left us when they first arrived to walk amongst their ranks, completely hidden by the shadows. He'd listened to their whispers, gauged their intentions, before declaring to us that they were relatively harmless.

'Relatively' being the important word.

Because like all fanatics, they could be swayed. And that was what they were—fanatics. I had no doubt they would sacrifice Z and all of us on stone altars if they believed it would help their cause.

"They're afraid of us," I whispered. As if agreeing with my words, a group of women turned in our direction, blanched, and then immediately whipped their heads away, shaking in fear. I was so used to women—and even some men—eyeing us with appreciative stares and hungry, wistful leers that this was unnerving, to say the least. I'd never had people fear me before, but all of these humans stared at us as if we planned to devour them whole.

"Can you blame them?" Ryland retorted bitterly. His shadows cinched tighter around him as he moved to perch on a tree branch. "We represent everything they fear and hate."

"Power. Royalty. Nightmares," Bash ticked off in a deadpan voice.

"Precisely. And what does our little mate represent?"

"Freedom. Humans. A return of power," I responded softly. "Hope."

And hope could be a very dangerous thing. It built people up, constructed armies out of men and women who didn't know how to shoot a gun, but when it faded, it made people bitter and jaded. They wouldn't hesitate to turn their rage on the person who obliterated their hope.

In this case, that person would be Z.

"Do you think Paco will—"

"Paco won't do shit," Bash said, interrupting Ryland. "He's never aligned himself with the new kings, but he's also never been an advocate for the humans. He'll watch and see how this all plays us. Besides, he's too fucking crazy to give a shit anyway."

Fuck my life. This day had been absolute shit. First, there was the knowledge that we had to kill our mate in order to save her life. Then there was the potion that had given me back my legs...but with the caveat that it would only last for a few hours at a time.

And of course, my insecurities couldn't help but rear their ugly heads, believing I was only good for Z when I was whole and on two feet. What use did she have for me in my wheelchair? The second I ran out of the slimy green potion Paco had given to me, I would be useless to her once more.

I shoved those ugly thoughts into the ground,

stomped on them with my shoe, and then spat on their grave.

"Oh my god." Z's voice was a breathy exhale, and I spun around just as she exited the forest, Jax's hand clasped in hers and Killian's palm on the small of her back. I noticed with some amusement that her hair was disheveled and her lips swollen. Good for them. I knew Jax needed her light to battle the monsters in his head, and if their coupling achieved that, then I was immensely grateful.

Though I couldn't ignore the sliver of jealousy embedding itself in my heart that I hadn't been able to participate.

"This can't be for me." Z began to shake her head adamantly, refusing to move a single step forward, despite Killian's urging.

"Is that my little sister I hear?" a booming voice inquired, garnering the attention of the entire crowd. The people parted as a familiar, dark-haired man stepped through, grinning cheekily and clutching the hand of a small girl.

"Axel?" Z's eyes widened in surprise as she stared at the former assassin.

"The one and only." Axel released the girl's hand to give an elaborate spin, shaking his ass for good measure and causing a growl to rip from Killian's throat before turning to face us once more. *Everyone* was fucking facing us—all eyes were trained firmly on Z, as if no one else mattered but her. It made me insanely protective, and I wanted nothing more than to step in front of her and shield her from their penetrating stares.

But I couldn't. She didn't need me to be her hero, not when she was perfectly capable of saving herself.

"How...?" Her gaze flickered to the little girl still standing beside Axel. Z's face morphed immediately, sadness blanketing her features, but before I could demand to know what was wrong, she spoke up. "Is this Miles's sister?"

Miles. My heart clenched when I thought of the kid killed at the Bloody Carnival. I'd never met him personally, but I knew his death haunted Z. He was the one she couldn't save, the innocent soul cast to damnation because of the wickedness of our world.

"Mary-Lynette," Axel introduced, smiling broadly. "I brought her here safe and sound, just like I promised. Did you know she's named after another Mary I know? Okay, not technically, but I'd like to think she is." He sighed dreamily, bringing a finger to his shoulder and brushing it down the blade of the machete resting there.

"Mary-Lynette," Z murmured, seemingly in a daze. She stared intently at the little girl, and Mary-Lynette stared back with the same intensity.

"Did you know my brother?" The girl's voice was soft but held an undercurrent of ferocity that I saw in Z every day. It made a tiny smile pull at my lips, even as my stomach muscles tightened in sadness for her loss.

"I did." Z nodded once, her expression grave. "He was a good kid."

"A good brother," Mary-Lynette agreed. For a moment, the two girls stared at each other, an entire conversation exchanged without a single word being spoken. It only lasted for a few seconds before Mary-Lynette turned to face Axel.

"She's a good kid, Z." For the first time since I'd met him, Axel's voice was serious. Grim, even. "But there's something we need to discuss about her." His eyes flickered to me and the other princes, distrust written across his features, before he clenched his jaw and added, "Later."

Z's brows furrowed, but she nodded. "Later," she agreed. "Now, how did you find me?"

The seriousness drained from Axel's face, replaced by amusement as his grin widened. He glanced towards the van sitting in front of Paco's shed.

"You should really check your vehicle for trackers, little sister." He gave her a sheepish, *what can you do about it* smile, and her lips hardened into a straight line.

"So you stalked me. And brought me an...army." Her voice was devoid of any inflection.

"They're your followers," Axel responded without any shame whatsoever. "I just picked them up along the way. Word of your sexual prowess has spread throughout the kingdoms."

"Do not say sexual prowess," Killian hissed, causing Axel's eyes to shoot to his face in surprise. His eyebrows raised.

"Damn, son. When did you turn so possessive?"

Killian's cheeks turned bright red, and he immediately released Z's arm. I hadn't even realized he'd gripped it in his haste to assert his ownership.

"Oh...um...I..." he stuttered, taking another step away, and Z threw him an amused, slightly curious smile.

Apparently, his display of possessiveness didn't bother her as much as she usually let on.

"And you brought them here because?" Z pressed, getting our conversation back on track. The same distrust Axel had directed at my brothers and me was emanating from Z's eyes now. I knew she didn't trust him any more than she trusted the kings. Axel had spent too long being their yes-man that it was surreal to think he'd ever turn against them.

Instead of answering, Axel simply winked. "I can't give all of my secrets away, now can I? I have to maintain some air of mystery."

Z released a heavy breath, running her fingers through her tangled blonde hair.

"I honestly don't know what to say to all of this." She stared pointedly out at the crowd of people who were eerily silent, staring at her as if the world ended and began in her name. I could understand that expression only too well—it was the same one my brothers and I wore daily when we were with her.

But why the fuck were these random strangers staring at her with hearts in their eyes, as if they were seconds away from falling to their knees and worshipping her?

Before I could voice my discomfort to Ryland, a twinge of discomfort had me shuffling from foot to foot. It was a familiar sensation, and I mentally cursed the sin I was descended from.

Mermaids came from Envy, and as such, we were forced to spend twelve hours a day on land and twelve in water, never truly a part of any world and always wishing for what we couldn't possess. I couldn't remember the last time I'd been in water, which meant it'd been too fucking long and my body was failing me.

I cursed again as pain rippled down my spine, the touch colder than ice, and turned helplessly in Bash's direction. Instead of meeting his eyes, though, I found myself face-to-face with Z.

Her face was creased with concern as she stared into my pained eyes before understanding dawned.

"You need water," she stated, and I watched as guilt splayed itself across her face. Instantly, I moved to take her hands in mine, ignoring the whispers that began in the crowd at my initiation of contact. I didn't give a fuck what they thought about our relationship. She was our mate, and I would never hide it, regardless of my status as the prince.

"It's not your fault, sweetheart. You didn't know."

"I should've paid attention—" I cut her off with a kiss to her mouth. It was the briefest graze of lips, but it had heat entering her cheeks immediately.

"It's not your fault," I repeatedly sternly, and though she didn't protest, guilt still swam in her expressive eyes. After a moment, she took my hand in hers and began dragging me towards the pathway.

"Come on. I found water with Jax a little bit earlier."

I hesitated, digging my feet into the dirt. As much as I wanted to be alone with her...

"Shouldn't you remain with them?" I whispered, jerking my chin in her followers' direction. They continued to stare after her with wide, awestruck eyes, and her lips twisted with disdain.

"No. Right now, I need to be with my mate. Axel can handle all of...that." She waved her hand in their direction with a disgruntled growl, and I smirked.

"Not a fan of being a general of an army?" I teased.

She pursed her lips. "That's the thing, Dair. They're not looking at me like I'm their general...they're looking at me like I'm their queen."

WE FOUND THE RIVER EASILY ENOUGH AND continued walking until the stream transformed into a brilliant lake. The waning sunlight glistened on the top of the water, casting streaks of orange, red, and gold across the dark blue surface. It wouldn't be long until the sun fell completely and darkness took over.

As I swam in my mermaid form, Z settled on the edge of the bank, her knees pulled up to her chest and her arms wrapped around them. Her gaze was distant, staring at something I couldn't see on the horizon.

I swam towards her, treading water and staring at her beautiful, angelic face in the rapidly dimming sunlight. Sometimes, I found myself struck stupid by her beauty and perfection. Take now, for example. There were a thousand things I should've said to her, but instead of doing any of that, I simply stared like an imbecile.

Her dark lashes fluttered against her cheekbones, and she heaved out a breath, stirring a few strands of hair that had gotten caught on her lips.

"I don't know what to do, Dair," she whispered, resting her cheek on her arms and meeting my bright blue gaze. "About the kings and those humans and...everything." The despondent note in her voice had my heart clenching with the need to go to her, pull her in my arms, and promise her everything would be okay.

But that was a lie, and we both knew it.

We were pawns on a game board with no rulebook. Our movements were dictated by fate itself, and no amount of running away would allow us to escape it. Z was trapped by the spell the kings had placed on her, and we were trapped by our love for her.

"Don't think about that," I told her, diving beneath the surface and swimming even closer to her. I paused when I was level to where she was sitting and rested my arms on the rocky dirt, my tail swishing in the water behind me. "Tell me something about yourself."

She blinked in shock, obviously not expecting that change of subject from me.

"What?"

I offered her a dimpled smile, one I knew short-circuited her brain waves, if that dazed look in her eyes was anything to go by. "You're my mate, Z. I want to know everything there is to know about you."

"Oh...um..." She released another breath, though this time, it took the tension out of her shoulders. "What do you want to know?"

"Tell me about your parents," I suggested. When her expression fell, I bit down on my lip hard enough to taste blood and mentally chastised myself. "You don't have to—"

"Mom used to sing when she cooked." She picked at a thread on her sleeve, not meeting my gaze. My heart juddered wildly in my chest as she opened up to me. For so long, she'd kept impenetrable barriers around herself, refusing to allow any of us entry. Only now, they were beginning to crumble into dust. "I don't remember the song, but I would dance with my dad in the living room while she laughed and clapped." A tiny smile graced her perfect features.

I didn't dare breathe, as if that one sound would have her retreating into herself yet again.

"My favorite dish was…" Her nose scrunched up as she struggled to remember. "Lasagna!" she declared after a moment. "My mom made the best fucking lasagna. Dad used to joke that it was what made him fall in love with her."

"They sound wonderful," I said sincerely, and sadness flitted across her face once more.

"They were," she agreed softly, her attention still on that damn thread. She tugged sharply, almost as if she wanted to rip it from her shirt, before sighing and dropping her arms to her sides. "Sometimes I wonder why I'm still alive and they're not. I wonder why I was spared when they weren't. And then I wonder what I could've possibly done in this life to deserve you guys." Her legs dropped next, and she shifted until they were underneath her. She nervously licked her upper lip while I waited for her to gather her emotions. "I just don't understand."

"Fate is a mystery to us all," I responded simply. "We never know what the universe is going to throw at us next. Sometimes, the greatest joy can only be achieved by experiencing unspeakable pain. We were meant for you, Z, just like you were meant for us." I swam closer and placed a hand on her knee, rubbing my thumb back and forth gently. "We each offer you something different, something that makes you feel whole. Killian's your innocence. He reminds you every day what you're fighting for —*who* you're fighting for. You also know you can fall with him. He might not catch you, but he sure as hell would throw himself over the edge to be with you.

"Devlin's your best friend, your confidant. He takes the lead when you feel too weak to do it yourself. He's a reminder that you're not alone, that you'll never be alone again. Lupe is your protector. If you have to charge into battle, you can bet your perfect ass that he'll be right by your side. He might prefer to fight with words rather than fists, but he'll do anything for you. We all would.

"Jax brings out a softness in you that I don't see with anyone else. Every day that you're with him, you're reminded it's okay to feel. It's okay to lose yourself to your emotions.

"Ryland is your wit and your rock simultaneously. He was the first one to recognize what you were to all of us, and he constantly pushed you towards that conclusion yourself. He's the person you can rely on when it feels as if the world is falling down around you. He'll fight with you, yes, but he'll also sit in absolute silence for days if that's what you want.

"Bash is your anger, but he's also your motivator. He pushes you to be a better person. You may not realize he's doing it, but that anger you experience fuels you. It changed you into the woman sitting before me today."

A single tear slipped down her cheek. I imagined before she would be too terrified to show such an emotion in front of me. Now, it came unbidden, and she didn't lift a hand to brush it away.

"And you?" she whispered, her voice a low murmur.

"Hopefully, I'm the person you can lean on. A reminder that you'll always have someone in your corner. I don't know what will happen next, but I'll be with you every damn step of the way. *We'll* be with you. I don't care what the consequences are."

More and more tears cascaded down her cheeks, but when she didn't say anything about it, I didn't bring it up either. Instead, I moved my hand from her knee to clasp hers, giving it a reassuring squeeze.

I didn't know how long we stayed like that, my hand intertwined in hers while we remained in two separate worlds, one of land and one of water, but by the time we finally pulled away, night had fallen.

And the monsters always came out to play in the dark.

FIFTEEN

Z

I left Dair a few hours later, when the sun had finally disappeared completely and a silvery streak of moonlight bathed the forest in white.

I kept one hand on my dagger as I ventured down the familiar pathway, back towards Paco's shed-cottage-deathtrap.

What the fuck was even happening with my life? These people had come...for *me*? Why? Was it because of what I did at the Bloody Carnival? What would the kings think of this?

Those thoughts plagued me as I picked up my pace, suddenly desperate to find my men and lose myself in their embraces. The memory of my coupling with Jax had heat rising to my cheeks, though I bit down on my lip to stop the girly smile that wanted to emerge. That urge to smile faded when I thought about what was waiting for me.

What did we do about these humans? Would Paco allow them to remain on his land? Would he tell the kings? Bash seemed adamant that he didn't give a shit enough about the world to do anything, but I wasn't so certain. That mage... He'd once held absolute power. It ran through his veins and permeated his very soul. He couldn't just switch it off, despite his eccentricity. Still, we needed him, needed his power and potions, and until we received what we wanted, we had to remain on his good side.

I was so lost in my thoughts that my brain almost failed to register the pounding of footsteps breaking branches. I ducked behind a tree, my dagger extended, and waited until the figure passed my hiding space, heading in the direction I knew Dair still to be.

Before the stranger could take another step, I leapt forward and placed the blade against his neck.

"Who the fuck are you?" I demanded.

"Let go of me," a decidedly feminine voice squealed, struggling in my arms. I stared at the back of her thrashing head before releasing her. She stumbled, curses spilling from her lips, before spinning around to face me. One glance in her young, elfin face confirmed she was human, though I'd already suspected as much. Unlike the nightmares, she didn't emit any power.

Rocking back on the balls of my heels, I nonchalantly dropped the blade back into the waistband of my pants. Despite lowering my weapon, I wasn't relaxed.

Not at all.

But I didn't need a dagger to kill her if the need arose. My hands were plenty capable.

With her face shrouded in darkness, it took me a few tries to make out her features. The moonlight illuminated a pasty, freckled face surrounded by stringy red hair. She was probably a few years older than myself, though her face had a sickly tint to it that made her appear younger. Her bones stood out prominently beneath her translucent skin, almost as if she hadn't eaten a full meal in days.

A pang took up residence in my chest, and I instinctively brought my fist to my heart and began to rub at it. I remembered far too well how it felt to go hungry. To be weak. To feel nearly out of your mind with hunger pangs.

"Liberator, I need your help." Her voice shook, and she began to fidget with the long sleeves of her dirty sweatshirt.

Curiosity filled me, alongside a heavy sense of trepidation. "I don't know—"

"It's my sister," she blurted, her eyes widening in her gaunt face. I couldn't quite tell what color they were in the darkness, but just then, they resembled pools of oil. "I need your help to free her."

"Free her?" I cocked an eyebrow as she tugged, tugged, tugged at her sleeves. The sweatshirt practically engulfed her tiny frame, only the tips of her fingers poking out.

"She was taken to Lazy Evenings a few weeks ago, and I haven't been able to get a hold of her since. I'm freaking the fuck out, but I don't know what to do. And I know you freed those humans at the Bloody Carnival. So you need to help me free her, because I don't know what to do and I don't—"

"Hold on." I raised a hand to cut off her ramblings. "What's Lazy Evenings?"

"It's a..." She twisted her head in both directions, as if ensuring we were truly alone. "A brothel. Mages use it."

Chunks of coal entered my stomach. "And I'm assuming the humans there aren't...willing participants?"

She began to shake her head rapidly, fear flaring to life in her eyes. "No. Please, Z. I need your help."

My conversation with Dair had already left me feeling flayed open and bleeding. I wanted to give in to her, I truly did, but...

As if my body was in agreement with me, white-hot pain twisted up my insides. I gave the girl my back so she couldn't see the agony that splayed across my face.

Fuck, how could I help her when I could barely help myself? When my body was failing me and leading me to an early grave?

But what else could I do? Say no?

"It's a few miles into the Mage Kingdom," she continued, obviously taking my silence as assent. "We can leave now and get there in less than an hour. I'll—"

"All right," I cut in, turning back around. I watched her shoulders slump in noticeable relief. "Let me get my mates and—"

"No!" She appeared horrified, her feet taking her backwards a few steps. "No! We can't trust them. They're nightmares." She spat the last word as if it were something unholy, her pretty face twisting in disgust.

"Axel's a nightmare," I pointed out. "And you guys seem to trust him."

Almost...scarily so. I didn't know how I felt about the shadow assassin, but the ease with which the humans followed his lead wasn't sitting right with me.

"That's different," she protested indignantly.

"Look, you can trust the guys—"

"No!" she hissed venomously. Even in the darkness, the anger emanating from her eyes was evident to see. "I'll just do it myself."

Without another word, she shouldered past me and stalked in the direction of Paco's shed. I was left staring after her in dumbfounded disbelief, my mind racing a mile a minute and my heart struggling to keep up.

What the fuck was that about?

I could sense the animosity between the humans and my mates, but I'd never seen it firsthand before. Not that I could blame them.

Before I met the guys, I'd considered them a scary story human mothers told their children to stop them from misbehaving. They were the men prophesied to either end the world...or save it. But I knew my mates, and I knew that they would do everything in their power to right the wrongs their fathers had made. They weren't the great evil society portrayed them to be.

But that didn't stop the fear. The hurt and anger. The wariness.

Humans had the right to fear them.

By the time I arrived back at Paco's house, the girl was nowhere to be seen and the lawn had been completely transformed.

Dozens of tents were located along the length of the property, humans walking in and out of them. I counted at least ten fires, the red and gold flames casting the entire camp in shadows. I didn't spot Axel or Mary-Lynette, but I did see Killian perched on the back bumper of our van.

I weaved my way through the crowd, trying to ignore how fucking creepy it was when people brushed their hands against me or bowed their heads subserviently and whispered, "Liberator," until I was standing in front of my incubus mate.

He seemed relieved to see me, his smile widening before placing his hands on my hips. A delicate blush stained his cheeks when he realized what he'd done, but before he could drop them, I brought my own hands over his to keep them in place.

"Where are the others?" I queried as he grinned up at me, that perpetual blush still firmly on his cheeks.

"Ryland is...canvasing," he admitted softly, and I knew "canvasing" was just another word for spying.

"And Bash and Jax?" I questioned.

"Helping Paco with the potions." Darkness fell over his expression, but before he could get too lost in his thoughts of what was to come, I placed my thumb between his eyes, smoothing out the wrinkles.

"I thought incubi weren't supposed to have wrinkles," I mused, dropping my fingers to his cheeks and squishing them together.

His eyes crossed as he stared at his protruding lips. "I've never been a normal incubus, Z."

"What even is normal?" I finally released his cheeks and smoothed my fingers through his hair. The garnet streaks were highlighted by gold and burgundy, the color somehow resembling the fire burning a few feet away.

"Not a stuttering incubus who's afraid of sexual intimacy," he blurted.

"Or maybe all of the other incubi are not normal." I

removed myself from between his legs and plopped down on the bumper beside him, reveling in his body heat.

"You're hurting my head, Z." He flashed me a sheepish smile, that customary blush returning with a vengeance. "How do you even do it? How do you make me feel better about myself?"

"Because I don't understand why the fuck you would ever feel bad," I retorted immediately.

I thought back to what Dair had told me earlier. Killian *was* my innocence. He was too pure for this world, too pure for me, and I would never understand how or why he fell in love with me. I was abrasive to his gentleness, cunning to his openness, cruel to his kindness.

But he loved me. I could see it in his eyes whenever he smiled in my direction, whenever he blushed or ducked his head. I could feel it in the way his body molded to mine, even now, as if he didn't want even a sliver of space to separate us.

My cheeks caught on fire, no doubt resembling his own, when I thought of the way he dominated me unintentionally the last time we were in bed together. I knew it was his incubus powers coming out to play, but I couldn't deny it was sexy as fuck to see quiet, timid Killian playing my body like an instrument. He didn't just command my pleasure; he demanded it.

"Wanna play a game?" Killian hit his shoulder against my own, and I lowered my head into the crook of his neck to hide my smile. The movement felt so...instinctive. It was as easy as breathing to fall into his embrace.

Why had I always been scared of this?

Why had I been scared of loving them?

"The sexy kind?" I teased, pulling away to face him. "Because we might want to go somewhere a little more private." I glanced at the humans trying their hardest not to stare at us, but more than a few gazes shifted our way. "I'm pretty possessive, Killian. I don't want any female seeing what doesn't belong to them." To emphasize my point, I dropped my hand onto his thigh and gave it a squeeze.

He squealed like a piggy, and a snort of laughter escaped unbidden. "I wasn't...I wasn't propositioning... unless you want..." When another bark of laughter escaped me, he glared down at me with narrowed eyes. "You were teasing me, weren't you?"

I placed my forefinger and thumb together. "Just an itty-bitty bit."

"An itty-bitty bit?" His eyes flickered from my face to my fingers before he leaned down and nipped the tip of my thumb. This time, *I* was the one who squealed, the noise garnering the attention of a few of the human men standing nearby. They looked seconds away from marching over to us and forcibly removing Killian from the equation.

Fuck.

To show them that he hadn't harmed me, I leaned forward and pressed my lips to his.

He took over immediately, his hand fisting in my hair as his tongue tangled with my own.

"This wasn't the game I had in mind," he whispered, pulling away but keeping his forehead to mine.

"I like this one though," I protested lazily, my eyes

drifting to those men once more. This time, they didn't look murderous, but they *did* look angry and disgusted.

I really, really had to figure out what to do with these damn humans, but that was a problem for future me. Besides, what were they going to do tomorrow when I returned to the capital? Follow me? The mere thought was laughable.

But that didn't change the fact that they stared at my mates like they were the enemies. It made my hackles raise, indignation, fear, and anger warring within me.

Peeling my gaze away from theirs, I focused back on my sexy mate.

"So the game...?" I pressed, determined to forget about the humans for the rest of the night.

"Oh, um." He pulled away from me, flushing with embarrassment, before gripping my hand and playing with my fingers. "Some of the kids were playing it earlier, and I thought it would be fun—"

"You want to play a kids' game?" I teased, loving the way his blush deepened. I didn't think I'd ever get tired of seeing him flustered.

"You don't have to if you don't—"

"Killian, what's the game?" I bumped his shoulder with my own, and he smiled at me. It was a smile that stole the breath from my lungs and made me lightheaded. He should probably register that smile with the defense department in the capital, because it was totally a lady killer.

"Would You Rather," he stated, ducking his head. "We don't have to play if *you* don't—"

"Would you rather," I tapped on my chin in consideration, "know exactly when you were going to die or how you were going to die?"

He gaped at me in horror. "You're...you're a sadist!"

"You wanted to play!" I insisted, hitting his shoulder once more.

Killian brought a finger to his lips as he pushed his bottom one between his teeth, nibbling on the poor flesh. He didn't immediately rush to answer, and I appreciated the fact that he was taking his time to answer instead of just blurting something out. "How. I think it would be awful to know the exact time you were going to die. You could never truly live with that guillotine hanging over your head."

"But what if you knew you were going to die when you're ninety," I pointed out. "Then you could take all of these risks, knowing that it wouldn't kill you."

"That doesn't mean you'll be living during all of those years," Killian countered. "What if you jumped off a bridge and became paralyzed from the neck down? Or what if you became a slave or forced into prostitution or—"

"But if you knew how you were going to die, then it might prohibit you from doing things you love," I insisted. "Like, what if you knew you were going to die during sex? Would you just never have it?"

He blushed. "I-I wouldn't know. I mean, I don't know what it feels like. And, um...I mean, I'm sure it's...um..." He shook his head from side to side before asking, "Z, would you rather have love or have power?"

I gave him a droll look. "That's an easy one."

"Is it?" He quirked an eyebrow.

"Love, of course." I felt like such a fucking sap for saying that out loud, but when his eyes gleamed even brighter, I knew I'd gotten it right. "What's the point of all that power if you don't have someone to share it with? How can you truly be happy if you're all alone?"

"And that begs the question...is it possible to be happy and alone?" Killian mused, scratching at his jaw.

"I think so..." I trailed off as I considered it. "I mean, I don't think it's for everyone, and I truly believe that every person on this planet struggles with loneliness, but that doesn't mean it's not possible."

"But if you're alone, you can't create genuine human connections. And if you don't have those connections..."

"Then you don't realize what you're even missing," I finished for him, though I wasn't sure if that was what he was even going to say. "So to them, that's their absolute happiness. Saying that, I imagine it's true on the opposite spectrum as well—people who are constantly around other people don't understand the joy you get from being alone and focusing on yourself."

"Ah. I see my little mate and brother are having an... intriguing debate." Ryland's quiet voice came from directly above me, on the roof of the van, but I didn't startle at his sudden appearance. A part of me knew he had been there, watching and observing us. His presence was a soothing balm to my heart and soul, alleviating the tension that had been sitting on my shoulders.

I tilted my head back to smile at him and felt a feathery soft kiss on my lips.

"We're playing Would You Rather," I told him, and

even with the shadows concealing him, I knew his eyebrows rose in surprise.

"Oh, really?"

"Yes." Grinning wickedly, I asked, "Ryland, would you rather never receive pleasure during sexual encounters or never allow your partners to receive pleasure from your sexual encounters?"

Killian winced. "Oh. That's a good one."

"An easy one too," Ryland declared dismissively. "But you need to rephrase your question. Partner, not partners. There's only ever going to be one woman I'm pleasing." He caressed my cheek from above me, leaving a trail of goosebumps in his wake.

Unable to help myself, I asked, "So you'll be open to pleasing other men...?"

"No, you silly, naughty girl." He pecked my lips again. "Only women. And only you. Though I wouldn't be opposed to a threesome, foursome, or moresome...as long as I don't have to put my lips anywhere near a dick."

Liquid pleasure exploded in my insides, and I began to squirm on the bumper of the car. It was suddenly way too hot out here, and at the same time, it wasn't hot enough.

"Killian, what about you?" I lazily brought my finger to his palm, tracing upwards to his forearm and then his bulging bicep. His breath stuttered as he stared at me with dilated pupils.

"W-what about me?" he murmured, his lips parting.

"Would you be down for a threesome, foursome, or moresome?" I questioned in a low voice.

"Um...I would prefer not to have a dick up my butt,

but I wouldn't be opposed to...um...sharing you...and oh my god." He closed his eyes as I brought my hand down his chest and over his rapidly hardening cock. "Your hand feels fucking amazing."

"Imagine what my lips could do," I teased.

Warm breath wafted over my neck a second before Ryland began trailing kisses to the shell of my ear. I arched my neck to give him better access, trying to ignore the penetrating stare from the nearby humans. If we were going to continue this, which I really, really hoped we would, then we needed to move to a new location.

Preferably one that Jax, Bash, and Dair could join us at.

Could I handle five at once?

Seven at once?

My vagina sure as fuck wanted to try. She enthusiastically started a parade and declared today a national holiday.

"And if I didn't answer your question from before..." Ryland began in a low, seductive tone. A shadow curled around my chest, pinching my nipple until I gasped. Another one rubbed against my clit, while a third caressed my ass. Ryland's own hands remained on my shoulders, kneading the skin gently. "I would much rather pleasure my little dove."

"How about we move this tantalizing party elsewhere?" I suggested, jumping off the bumper and extending my hands towards both of my mates. They eyed each other for a moment, surprise twisting their features, before greedily accepting my proffered hands.

We moved down the pathway from before, but

instead of heading towards the lake, we veered to the right until we were in a clearing far enough away that no one would hear us.

Hopefully.

"I think—" My words were cut off as Killian claimed my lips in a desperate, toe-curling kiss. Ryland's hands moved to my shirt, pulling the material over my head so he could paw at my breasts. He bit down on my nipple hard enough to sting before taking my chin and forcing my lips to his.

Killian, now dislodged from my lips, moved to my breast and began to trace tender kisses around my aching nipple, never quite touching me where I so desperately needed him to. I couldn't help but note that his eyes flickered to Ryland's face, almost as if he wanted confirmation he was doing this right.

Ryland's hand moved to my free breast, plucking and twisting my nub, as his lips traveled to my neck.

For a long moment, this pattern continued. One would kiss my lips while the other would worship my tits before switching out.

My hands moved from the smooth skin of Killian's face to the rough, jagged lines of Ryland's. My shadow mate once hid from me, using the shadows as his own personal shield, but he no longer felt the need. All of his beautiful scars were on display for me to see, his indigo blue eyes ensnaring my very soul and holding it hostage.

We didn't hide from each other.

Not anymore.

"Kill." I buried my fingers in the incubus's red hair as he continued to kiss around my nipple, still not touching the pointed peak. His green eyes flickered up to my face, and I groaned low in my throat, bringing one hand up around Ryland's neck to hold him to me. I could feel my shadow's smirk against my skin, content to let me take the lead. "Use your tongue to tease me."

A flare of defiance entered Killian's eyes, almost as if he remembered the last time we were together and he dominated me, before he obliged. It seemed as if his need to pleasure me, *worship* me, outweighed his desire to control me. But maybe...

Maybe he was *still* controlling me. I may have been calling the shots right then, but I had no doubt that my pleasure was currently in Killian's hands. Or tongue, as the case may be.

His tongue lightly pushed against my nipple as a gasp lodged itself in my throat.

"Like that?" he whispered as he moved his lips between the valley of my breasts to give my other tit attention. I had no idea if he was teasing or if he legitimately wanted to know, but either way, my core gave a painful throb and I whimpered.

"Roll your tongue around my nipple," I begged as Ryland bit down on the shell of my ear.

Killian did as instructed, his tongue tracing around my beaded nub before sucking it fully into his mouth.

"Don't be afraid to use your teeth," Ryland interjected, and I swore I nearly came from that alone.

Ryland was naturally dominant in the bedroom as well, and a twisted part of me had always wondered how a threesome between the three of us would work out. It had fueled more than one late night masturbation session, if I was being completely honest.

Killian bit down on my nipple, and my entire body jerked as Ryland forced my lips back to his, claiming me with a bruising, possessive intensity. There was no doubt in my mind that I was his. Theirs.

Killian brought his hand to my pussy and began to rub me through my pants, and pleasure collided with a rippling wave of ecstasy.

"Fuck, yes," I moaned as I reached blindly for their cocks. Ryland had already freed his from his jeans, and I wasted no time wrapping my hand around the mushroom tip and giving it a squeeze. Killian was slightly slower, his movements shaky as he fumbled with his zipper, but he eventually freed his impressive length as well, not bothering to remove his pants completely.

I lowered myself to my knees between them, not giving a damn about the dirt and grit that got stuck to my knees.

Turning towards Killian, I wrapped one hand around his base before leading the tip of his cock to my eagerly awaiting mouth, hollowing my cheeks so I could swallow him deep. My other hand began to stroke Ryland in tandem.

"Oh my...butterballs!" Killian gasped, his face flushed with pleasure. "That feels really fucking good."

I tugged on my shadow prince slightly, forcing him to take a step closer, as I moved my mouth from one man to the next, using my saliva as lubrication. Their cocks were so close to each other that the tips touched, though neither seemed to mind as they gazed down at me with hungry, lustful eyes. I felt like I was the center of their world, and it was a heady sensation.

I couldn't remember the last time someone had cared about me that much. *Loved* me that much. It made me fiercely possessive of them, and I never wanted to see that spark in their eyes dissolve. I could die a happy woman with their gazes fixed on me, worshiping my skin through look alone.

Ryland began to remove his shirt, and Killian, after a brief moment of hesitation, did as well.

The differences between my two lovers were stark. Both were muscular, though Killian was more defined, with a prominent, chiseled eight-pack. While my incubus had smooth, pale skin covered in colorful tattoos, my shadow was an image of dark, masculine perfection. It was like the moon and the night sky standing side by side, and my pussy walls tightened around air.

These men...these ethereal, perfect men...were mine. My loves. My mates. And hopefully, my future.

"Are you feeling needy, my love?" Killian murmured huskily, and a dark thrill ran through me, knowing he was once more turning into dominant Kill. He pulled at my hair until I was forced to release his cock from my mouth, and my hand automatically dropped from Ryland's as well.

"Get naked," Ryland instructed darkly.

I moved faster than I ever had before, kicking my shoes and socks off before tugging down my pants and panties. While I undressed, they did the same, until all three of us stood naked in the moonlight. The moon had completely risen now, painting the world in streaks of silvery gold. Warmth rushed through the breeze, chasing away the chill from the last few days.

"Hands and knees, little dove." Ryland moved until he was on his knees in the dirt, and I quickly did as instructed, giving him my ass.

His hand smoothed over the curve of it before slapping each cheek hard.

"Fuck!" I hissed.

"Naughty language, love," Killian purred, his incubus allure coming out full force. He moved to his knees in front of me and gripped my chin between his hands.

"Maybe she needs something to occupy that naughty mouth of hers?" Ryland suggested.

Without needing to be told twice, Killian guided my lips once more to his cock. His hand fisted my hair at the nape of my neck as he began to fuck my mouth, words of worship and praise leaving him on a breathy exhale.

Behind me, Ryland tapped his cock against my ass, not yet entering me.

"Are you ready for me, little dove?" he whispered silkily.

"I..." A groan was torn from my mouth when Killian's cock reached the back of my throat.

"Why don't you warm her up first?" my incubus suggested.

"With my tongue or fingers?" Ryland asked with a chuckle, the noise low and devilish, and Killian laughed.

"Tongue, of course. Though I'm sure our girl is already soaking."

But instead of entering my slick channel like I

expected, Ryland's tongue circled the tight ring of muscles of my ass.

I gasped, releasing Killian's cock, but one slap from Ryland had me deep throating Kill once more.

What were these men doing to me? Destroying me, that was what. And not just physically either—this connection between us went far beyond something simply visceral. It was a merging of souls as well as bodies, eight hearts joining together until we became one being.

One tangle of limbs currently in the throes of intense, mind-blowing pleasure.

Ryland removed his lips from my ass, and a second later, the tip of his cock spread through the juices of my sopping pussy.

He entered me slowly, inch by inch, and I gasped around Killian's cock at the intrusion. Ryland was big —*really* big.

"You feel so tight, little dove," he rumbled, pressing down on my back with his hand and forcing Killian's cock deeper down my throat. "So fucking tight."

I murmured something around Killian's cock—maybe a plea to move, maybe a confession of love. It was sorta hard to think clearly with dick in your mouth and pussy.

Ryland began to thrust into my tight channel, spanking my ass until I was forced to release Killian's cock or risk choking.

"Yes! Yes! Yes!" I cried as I felt my orgasm approach. I didn't care that I was being loud enough to wake the entire camp. I didn't care that I was basically getting spit-roasted by two sexy as sin nightmares. Nothing mattered but the sensations they evoked, the fire that lit up my veins whenever I was with them.

My breasts bounced from the force of Ryland's thrusts, and Killian took my lapse in concentration to pull at my nipples. The jolt of pain had pleasure coursing through my pussy.

I could feel my orgasm approaching, I could feel my body falling apart, but before I could reach my climax, Ryland pulled out of me. I didn't have a second to be alarmed before he moved to his back and pulled me on top of him, once more lining up his cock with my core.

Killian scrambled to his feet and stood slightly to the side of us, his erect cock bobbing against his stomach.

I twisted my head so I could once more take him into my mouth as Ryland pistoned his cock inside of me.

"Take my cock all the way inside of your mouth like a good girl," Killian whispered as his hand tangled in my blonde hair, guiding my mouth.

With Ryland's hands on my waist helping me keep my balance, I gripped Killian's left thigh tightly. My other hand wrapped around his base.

It wasn't long before he was so far inside of my mouth, I was practically gagging.

"Just like that. Yeah. Just like that," Killian praised as Ryland positioned my hips so he could hit that sweet spot inside of me.

His hands moved to my breasts, squeezing tightly, and soon, the three of us became nothing more than a flurry of limbs and pleasure. I couldn't tell where I ended and they began.

When I finally exploded, it was with Ryland's hand

wrapped around my throat, squeezing gently, and Killian's hands tugging at my hair, the sting of pain amplifying my pleasure.

My pussy squeezed Ryland's cock, milking him for all he was worth, as he grunted, spilling his seed inside of me.

Killian pulled out of my mouth just before he came, aiming his cock so his cum covered my tits and landed on Ryland's chest.

Not one of us said anything, suspended in time and space. At that moment, there was no poison coursing through my veins, killing me slowly. No humans camped outside Paco's shed whispering my name with a reverence it didn't deserve. No kings hellbent on destroying us. No evil, bitchy sisters who wanted to destroy the world. It was just...us.

And it was fucking perfect. What would've made it even better was all of my mates being present.

Killian didn't remove his cock from where it lightly brushed against my tit, and Ryland didn't pull out of me. We just sat there as the stars twinkled in the sky above us, seemingly pleased with our mating.

Utterly sated and unable to hold myself upright a second longer, I placed my hand on Ryland's chest and practically fell forward. He caught me instantly and placed a tender kiss to my forehead. It didn't even matter to me that we were camped out on the uncomfortable floor of the forest. Nothing mattered but my mates and the love I felt for them.

"Fuck," Killian murmured dazedly as he dropped

down on the other side of me. He kissed my shoulder as his hand sneaked around me, cupping my breast.

"Fuck is right." I laughed breathlessly as I remained cuddled between the two of them.

The silence was broken when Killian blurted, "I've never had a threesome before."

"You've never had sex before," Ryland retorted, and I didn't need to see my incubus to know that he was blushing.

My heart swelled with emotion, and desire swirled through my veins. What would it be like when I completely claimed Killian as my own? I heard being with an incubus was absolutely insane, inspiring pleasure that no human could possibly imagine.

And a sick part of me felt an insane amount of glee that I would be the first, and only, girl ever to experience this with Killian. It wasn't as if I had expected all of my mates to remain virgins before we met when I sure as fuck wasn't one, but it was nice to know that I would be Killian's first.

"Soon." I pressed my lips to Killian's hand, a promise and a vow. In response, he nestled closer to my body, his cock digging into my ass.

A cough jerked my body forward, and I spasmed in my mates' arms.

"Z?" Killian asked in concern, but I couldn't stop coughing. It felt as if my lungs were being shredded and forced out of my throat. Blood dripped down my chin and stained the dirt beneath us.

"I'm. Okay," I panted, though my voice was weak and shaky.

Killian's face turned grim. "No." He swallowed. "You're not."

"Come on." Ryland grabbed my clothes off the ground and tenderly began to dress me. I let him, too weak and tired to do the simple task myself. "Let's get back to the others." His eyebrows furrowed together in concern as he stared intently into my eyes. Whatever he saw had sadness rippling across his face. "Now."

SIXTEEN

DEVLIN

The fire in my veins burned white-hot as I stormed down the staircase and into the foreboding darkness of the dungeons. Only one candle sat on the opposite end of the hall, its orange light barely able to penetrate the shadows surrounding us.

Everything here was dank and depressing, with stone walls, dirty floors, and the scent of piss permeating the air.

Lupe stood beside me, his expression grave and hands balled into fists. Both of us were on pins and needles as we neared the cell located at the very end of the hall that we knew housed the shadow king.

He stared despondently at the far wall of his cell, his shadows contained by the cuffs wrapped around both of his wrists. This was powerful magic—magic I had only seen once before, when Zack was able to stop Diego from accessing his powers during the Damning.

Which meant that bitch Aaliyah was involved.

"I'm not surprised they sent the two of you." His gaze

didn't move in our direction, though his hands did tighten into fists. Without his shadows obscuring him from view, I could make out every scratch marring his face from the kings' torture. Every bruise on his bare torso. Every wince of pain he quickly tried to hide.

"Your Highness," I began stiffly, but the shadow king simply laughed, the noise low and raspy, and waved his hand back and forth as if he could dismiss my words.

"Please. I'm no more a king than you. Call me Seth." He finally twisted his head to stare at me, and I was struck by the blue of his eyes. Not because the color was unique or anything like that, but because they were *Ryland's* eyes. The same cerulean shade I saw daily in my brother's face was now staring back at me from this beaten, disheveled shell.

"Seth." I tested the name out on my tongue, not quite sure how much I liked it. For as long as I could remember, the kings had held a god-like power in my mind. They were invincible, indestructible, and powerful beyond measure. Even the shadow king, who we'd all decided was the nicest of the bunch, was both revered and feared.

To see him reduced to this...

Horror engulfed me, squeezing my throat in an impenetrable iron vise.

What would the kings do if they discovered the truth about Z? Would they continue using her as their pet assassin, forcing her to do their bidding and work against her closest friends and confidants? Or would they decide she was more trouble than she was worth and kill her? Knowing my father and his malevolent friends, the former option was more their style. They saw all of us as only pieces on a game board, and they wouldn't hesitate to move Z like a marionette into enemy territory.

"If you're going to torture me, get it over with," the shadow king—Seth—said in an indolent manner. He nestled himself further against the wall and squeezed his eyelids shut, adopting a pose of nonchalance and innocence. "I'm not telling you shit."

"But it's true you worked with the Alphabet Resistance?" Lupe hedged, but Seth simply pantomimed zipping his lips shut and throwing away the key.

I stared intently at the shadow king, almost as if I could will him to reveal all of his secrets, before sighing heavily and grabbing Lupe's arm. The large man didn't struggle as I dragged him away from the cell, with its pungent smell and steel bars, towards the opposite end of the hall, near the candle.

"We can't torture him," Lupe hissed in revulsion. "I won't. Not again."

I knew he was no doubt thinking of T—Z's friend and a member of the resistance, whom he'd been forced to get information out of. We'd left T back at the inn with the other human servants, but I knew it haunted Lupe whenever he saw his mottled, bruised face and the scar on his cheek that would never quite heal properly.

"He won't tell us anything," I warned, glancing over my shoulder in the direction of Seth's cell. Fuck, it felt weird to call him that. His title, the King of the Shadows, evoked images of wealth and power. Seth made me think of the pathetic, beaten man rotting away in a cell miles beneath the capital. "I don't know what to do here, Lupe. The kings own Z, and if we don't do what they say, I have no doubt they'll hurt her to hurt us. But she'll never forgive us if we give over information about the Alphabet Resistance to the kings. And that's assuming the shadow king tells us in the first place. Plus, how the fuck do we explain all of this to Ryland?"

As I was speaking, articulating the numerous thoughts running rampant through my head, Lupe's expression changed and tightened, shock giving way to resolve, and then that resolve transforming into unread-ability. Before I could question his behavior, he placed a large hand on my shoulder and gave it a squeeze.

"I'll handle this for us," he vowed, his tone solemn.

"Lupe..." I eyed my best friend warily. "What are you going to do?"

Lupe ducked his head until his blue eyes met my violet ones. There were lines around his eyes and mouth, lines that I'd never noticed before. It gave him a haggard look, almost as if he'd aged years in seconds, and I couldn't help but note the similarities between him and his father.

They really did look similar.

But I couldn't argue with him and whatever decision he'd apparently made, not when Z's life was on the line. Not when I would make the same decision as well.

I hated that Lupe was embracing his wrath, embracing the beast he'd struggled for years to contain, but we didn't have a fucking choice.

We never had a choice.

We were born in sin, and we'd die in sin. It was the way the world worked.

So instead of mounting a protest, I nodded stiffly,

straightened out my cuffs, and then climbed the long staircase out of the basement, leaving my brother alone to face his demons.

What was happening to us?

In our quest to stop our fathers...were we becoming even bigger monsters than them?

I DIDN'T MAKE IT TOO FAR BEFORE I WAS BOMBARDED by a sickly sweet perfume. My nose wrinkled in distaste a second before a tiny body practically plowed me over, her arms wrapping around my waist and constricting like a boa.

"Devlin! I haven't seen you in forever. I've been worried." I detangled myself from the brown-haired genie with a grunt of disgust.

"Laurel," I said curtly, staring into her violet eyes a few shades darker than my own. She smiled widely, revealing a single dimple in her right cheek, and brought a hand to my wrist. I automatically stepped away with a grimace, hating her touch on my skin, but that only seemed to broaden her smile.

Some might have considered her pretty, with her curly brown hair, an hourglass figure, and long lashes that curled slightly. But she didn't hold a candle to Z, a fact that would infuriate her if it came to light.

"You're a tough man to get a hold of, Devlin Genie," she purred as something ugly and slimy lodged itself in my throat.

Weeks ago, I made a deal with Laurel to find my

stolen lamp and have it returned to me. At the time, I'd believed it housed the soul of Z's ex-boyfriend, S, but someone had stolen the soul before I could retrieve it. It all proved to be a complete fucking waste of time, but because I'd wished on Laurel's lamp, I owed her a favor.

Or my soul.

And it seemed she had come to collect.

"What do you want, Laurel?" I bit out. I was desperate to get away from her, to get away from it all. I wanted to scrub at my skin in my shower, eliminating days of filth that clung to every bare inch of me. And then I wanted to find my favorite black suit, put it on, and fall back into a role of familiarity, one where my life wasn't rapidly steering itself towards a brick wall. One where I could take control of my surroundings once more, instead of relying on chance and circumstance—two words I abhorred.

"You owe me, Devlin." Her hand moved to my chest, her fingers splayed just above my heart, before she lowered it to my stomach. The path she took was slow and torturous, and every muscle in my body locked together. I held myself perfectly still as her fingers touched the waistband of my pants, but before she could dip them inside, I grabbed her wrist and gave it a punishing squeeze.

"Don't touch me," I hissed out, horror and disgust percolating in my stomach like days old milk. If she forced me to touch her...

I would rather die.

Laurel pouted, fluttering her long lashes up at me as if she thought she had even the smallest chance in hell of seducing me. "You don't want me touching you, Dev? You don't want me to wrap my lips around your cock?" She wrenched her hand free and placed it on my cock before I could stop her, rubbing me through the material of my pants. I was about as hard as a limp noodle, and she knew it.

The only touch my body ever responded to was that of my mate.

"Don't." I grabbed her wrist once more. "Touch." I squeezed until her face scrunched together in pain. "Me." Releasing her, I gave her a tiny shove that had her stumbling back a few steps.

But instead of appearing indignant or even upset, she simply threw her head back and began to laugh.

"Oh, Devlin. I missed our verbal sparring. Haven't you?"

"I'll kill you before I'll ever allow you to lay a hand on me," I warned her vehemently. I didn't care what my father would do to me. This bitch wasn't going to get a single piece of me, no matter the deal.

"Relax, firecracker." She quirked her lips up and sashayed back towards me, standing until we were chest to chest. She bit her bottom lip as she peered up at me, one of her hands moving to her cleavage and tracing the skin there.

"Not. Happening," I hissed, and she released another breathy laugh, finally stepping away.

"All right. Fortunately for you and your flaccid dick, I don't want that from you." She began to circle me like a vulture studying its prey. Her eyes were just as predatorial as that damn bird.

"Then what do you want?" I growled out.

She paused when she was in front of me once more, but this time, she kept a respectable distance between us. She placed her hands on her hips and tilted her head back, her lips twisting into a scowl.

"I need you to break someone out of the palace's dungeons for me."

"What?" I balked, staggering back a step in disbelief. "You want me to free the shadow king?" That was a death sentence if I ever heard one. If the kings discovered we helped him escape...

It would be very, very bad.

"No." She shook her head. "Not him. The other prisoner."

"The other...prisoner?" I cocked an eyebrow, trying to remember who else had been down there with Seth, Lupe, and me. I couldn't recall any of the other cells being occupied, but that wasn't to say they weren't. It was a big fucking prison, and there were still two more hallways with more cells than I could count.

"A shifter," she clarified. "Cell G." Something soft touched her features as she gazed at something over my shoulder.

What the...?

Understand washed over me. "You love him," I stated in wonderment.

The softness faded, replaced by something hard and dangerous. "Your job isn't to ask questions," she hissed out. "Your job is to do what I say. Once you complete this, your debt to me will be fulfilled."

She turned on her heel, preparing to walk away, but I

called after her. "What did he do?" A perplexed expression knitted her eyebrows together, so I rushed to elaborate. "What did he do to end up in the dungeon?"

"Oh." A cunning smirk pulled up her ruby-red lips as her gaze turned faraway and distant yet again. When she finally came back to the present, her eyes were hyper focused, but her smile remained just as cruel. "Nothing you need to worry about. Just get him out, and we'll be even. Got it?"

Nothing you need to worry about.

This was a horrible fucking idea, yet I knew I had no choice. I had to free this mysterious prisoner from the capital's prison or my soul would belong to Laurel.

Now, how to do that...

I couldn't very well walk in and use my cunning to break him out. And I couldn't have Lupe wish for his escape either, not when my father would be able to see our contract if he so desired.

Which meant...

Which meant I had to ask my father for his help. Which meant I had to play the dutiful son he'd always wanted me to be. Which meant I had to move myself on the game board away from Z and towards the kings.

My nails dug into my palms hard enough to break skin as I moved farther down the hall, bypassing the throne room and ballroom until I reached my bedroom. Once inside, I locked the door, turned on my shower, stripped down, and then scrubbed my body raw. My skin was a bright red by the time I finally pulled myself out from beneath the spray and dressed in a pitch-black suit with white cufflinks. I combed my brown curls back and completed the look with a plum-colored tie.

Control.

You need control.

I thought of Z the last time I saw her, unconscious and in pain, and my heart gave a damning squeeze, even as my expression turned stoic.

For her, I would become the thing I hated.

For her, I would embrace the monster inside of me.

For her, I would be the Crowned Prince of the Genies.

I straightened my violet tie, checked my reflection once more in the mirror, and then stalked out of my room with an imperious set to my chin. Servants and nightmares alike got out of my way as I walked, their eyes widening in fear and awe. It was the same look they wore around my father and the rest of the kings.

The only way to free a prisoner and not be deemed a traitor was to have an official pardon from one of the kings. Which meant I needed a favor from my father. Which meant...

Which meant I was selling my soul to a different genie.

Pushing open the heavy oak doors to the throne room, I found the kings exactly where I'd left them, whispering amongst themselves. Their silence was instant when they caught sight of me, and I noticed my father straighten imperceptibly in his throne, as meticulously groomed as always.

"Devlin?" he demanded. "What's the meaning of all of this?"

I clasped my hands behind my back and pushed my chest out, meeting each of their gazes unflinchingly.

"Why, I thought it was obvious?" Bile burned in my mouth, but I shoved it back down. "I'm here to embrace my duties as the crowned prince." I paused, allowing that revelation to sink in. Unlike my brothers, I hadn't ever openly defied my father, but I knew he saw the rebellious streak in me. Taking a deep breath, I braced myself for what I needed to do. "How can I serve you, Father?"

Z

My peaceful sleep was interrupted by the barely audible sound of the van door opening. My eyes shot open, and I tensed where I lay between Killian and Ryland in the backseat of the vehicle, all of the seats pushed down to make room for the blankets and pillows we borrowed from the humans. Jax and Bash had chosen to stay inside Paco's shed and help him finish the potions. Hopefully, I'd be able to take the elixirs tomorrow and finish it once and for all. Either I'd die...or I'd live to fight another day. I was hoping for the latter, thank you very much. Since Dair was still in the lake, and I knew he had no intentions of coming back tonight...that meant the figure peering in at us was not one of my mates.

I wrapped my hand around the hilt of my blade, barely breathing as the figure inched closer and closer and then rested their hand on my ankle.

I jerked upright, Ryland's arm falling from my waist and Killian's hand leaving my own as he murmured something sleepily. I didn't pay them a glance, though, as I leapt forward and tackled the intruder, the momentum forcing me out of the car and onto his body on the pavement.

"Motherfucker!" the man rasped, and I peered down at him intently, my blade pressed to his throat. He appeared to be a human a few years older than me, with sandy-blond hair, deeply tan skin, and blue eyes that were as dark as pitch in the firelight. His face was creased in horror and pain as I jabbed my knee into his stomach. "Don't hurt me."

"Why were you spying on me?" I demanded, pressing both my knee and knife further into his skin simultaneously. He wheezed but didn't even try to fight me off. He was either the stupidest man I'd ever met...or the smartest. The verdict was still out on that one.

"I wasn't..." He blinked rapidly up at me. "I just wanted your help!" The last words were almost a shout, though he quickly clamped his mouth shut and flushed bright when I gaped at him.

"Help?" I quirked an eyebrow, removing my blade from his skin slightly so he could nod.

"Yes. I know my girlfriend, Natalia, talked to you earlier. About her sister?" he pressed, and it took me a moment to remember who he was talking about. Natalia must've been the girl I'd met in the woods, the one whose sister was a prostitute at... What was the name of that place again? Lazy Evenings?

"And you want me to free Natalia's sister," I finished for him, my lips pursed ever so slightly. I wanted to help them more than anything, but I was weak and so very,

very tired. If they wouldn't accept help from my mates, then I didn't know what we could do. We were at a stalemate, plain and simple, and one of us would have to bend.

But the stranger's next words send a jolt of pure ice zigzagging through my veins. "No." He once again shook his head, not seeming to care that his shaggy blond hair collected debris and dirt from the ground. "I want you to help me save my girlfriend."

"Your—?'

"Natalia went after her sister, Ali," he admitted. "I told her she shouldn't, I told her not to be stupid, I told her that we needed backup, but she was fucking insane. She left a few hours ago and promised to message me every thirty minutes." He moved his hand down his body, towards his pocket, and I tensed automatically. But he seemed unconcerned with how close he came to death as he removed a cracked tablet from his pocket and held it out to me.

It wasn't password protected—stupid—and I was easily able to see the messages between this stranger and the woman named Natalia. When she first left about six hours ago, she would message him every thirty minutes on the dot.

But there hadn't been a new message in over two hours.

Fuck.

Guilt bombarded me, slashing at my chest, and the grip I had on the knife faltered. I dropped the hand holding it back to my side completely before it could nick his skin, and relief washed over his face.

Why did I let her leave, knowing her mental state? Why didn't I stop her? Why didn't I force the issue with bringing my mates along? Why didn't I suggest she bring other humans with her?

Why? Why? Why?

"Fuck." I thrust the tablet back into his chest and climbed off of him. He hurried to get to his own feet, his cheeks crimson and his eyes dancing with worry.

And hope.

It was nearly impossible for me to miss the tiny sliver of hope that materialized in his eyes, as if I were the answer to every prayer he'd ever had.

I was sure he wouldn't be looking at me with such reverence if he knew I sent his girlfriend away when she needed help.

Fuck. The guilt felt like sticky tar that clung to my skin, hardening by the second, until no amount of scrubbing could remove it completely.

"You'll help me?" he asked softly, giving me doe eyes. He placed his hands together in the universal pleading pose, and fuck, I didn't really have a choice, did I?

"All right," I agreed, albeit reluctantly. I still felt weak, though I knew that wouldn't change until I had the cure. At the same time, I doubted I would get worse anytime soon either. There was a reason Paco was adamant I needed to get more of the poison in my bloodstream to die from it.

So that meant I could go with this man to free his girlfriend and I probably wouldn't die from the poison. Probably. Hopefully. Maybe. I was seventy percent positive that I wouldn't kick the can early. Okay, make that sixty percent.

"But if we're doing this…?" I cocked an eyebrow, realizing I hadn't gotten his name.

"Toby," he supplied, bouncing on the balls of his feet.

I pursed my lips. "If we're doing this, Toby, then we're doing it my way. You'll listen to me at all times, understood? I don't want you playing hero and ending up dead." I'd seen enough death in the last month to last a lifetime. I didn't want another one on my conscience.

"I promise," he agreed quickly.

"And we need to get my mates involved," I finished firmly. He opened his mouth as if to protest, but whatever he saw in my eyes had him nodding, though begrudgingly.

"All right," he said simply. "If you think you can trust them."

"I do." That wasn't even a question.

I could sneak off, free Natalia and her sister, and then face the consequences of my actions when I returned home. The old me might've done that, but the new me knew I needed to rely on and trust my mates if this unconventional relationship between us was ever going to work. I loved them, but more than that, I trusted them. They would stand by my side through any battle, any war, and all I needed to do was extend the invitation.

That wasn't to say I wasn't scared shitless about what could potentially happen to them while on the battlefield, but I knew that it wasn't my choice to keep them hidden away. They were grown men who could make that decision for themselves. We were a team, and I was determined more than ever to fight as one. Survive as one.

And wasn't that the whole point of...everything? Survival?

As Toby went to gather supplies, I turned back to the van, unsurprised to see Ryland and Killian still fast asleep. The past few days had been a long and grueling, and I knew my mates were exhausted. They needed that sleep more than I did.

What was a surprise, however, was the fact they'd reached for each other in their sleep and were now tangled together, Killian's head on Ryland's chest and my shadow's arm wrapped around his middle. I bit my lip to stop the laughter that threatened to escape.

"Kill. Ry," I said, and Ryland sleepily began to kiss Killian's forehead.

"Hey, little dove," he murmured, his voice drowsy with sleep.

Killian mumbled something unintelligible, craning his neck back to seek out Ryland's lips. His eyes were still shut as he murmured my name, their lips mere centimeters from touching...

My laughter bubbled out, and their eyes snapped open immediately.

For a moment, they simply stared at each other in horror, their faces so close, they could probably feel each other's breath on their lips.

And then Killian squealed like a girl, practically doing a backwards somersault to escape my shadow mate, and Ryland moved to a crouching position, his shadows tightening around his form.

"Awww. You guys were cute cuddling together," I teased, and Ryland's ice-blue eyes flashed in my direction amidst the darkness of his shadows.

"That was naughty, little dove. You deserve a spanking."

Heat flared in my stomach at his suggestive words, but I shoved the fire aside, dousing it with water.

Not now, Z, I mentally chastised myself. *You have people to save, nightmares to kill, butts to kick.*

"Spankings will have to wait," I said lightly, ignoring the way both of their gazes flashed with banked fire at my words. I already knew Ryland had a kinky streak a mile long, but Killian's had honestly surprised me. I didn't even think he realized what he was doing the last time we engaged in sexy foreplay, but his incubus allure came out tenfold whenever we were together.

"And why do these spankings have to wait?" Ryland questioned lazily, and a second later, I felt something slap my ass cheek. I gasped, my stomach muscles clenching as the shadows moved from my butt to my core, plucking at my clit. Arousal sparked inside of me, but I forced it away yet again to focus on the matter at hand.

"Mission. Super—" The shadows pinched down on my clit, eliciting another gasp from my mouth. "—secret mission."

"A supersecret mission?" Killian quirked a red brow as excitement danced in his eyes. "Oh! Are we going after bad nightmares? Maybe I can finally use one of the catch-phrases I came up with when I kill someone."

"You came up with a...?" I stared at him in amusement.

"Pow! Wow! Stab!" Killian pantomimed stabbing someone in the stomach and then lowered his voice to a low, seductive murmur. "*Would you like fries with that shake?*"

A burst of laughter escaped me before I could contain it, and Ryland didn't even bother to hide his.

"That's your murder catchphrase?" I wheezed out.

Killian crossed his arms over his chest, appearing indignant, though his eyes flashed with amusement. Fuck, I loved that man. "What's wrong with it? Would you prefer, *Would you like butter with your toast?* How about, *This salad doesn't come with any croutons, but I can grab you ranch dressing?*"

"Okay, fine!" I threw my hands up in the air in defeat. "You can use weird-ass food sayings whenever you stab someone. Happy?"

But I had no fucking intention of ever letting Killian take a life. Yeah, not happening. I had enough blood on my hands for the both of us. He was my innocence, the one bright spot in a world full of darkness and pain. No one would take that from him as long as I drew air in my lungs.

The jovial atmosphere in the van diminished when I began telling them about Toby, Natalia, and Natalia's sister. Both of their faces turned grave, chiseled from stone, and they didn't speak right away when I finished.

"This isn't safe, Z," Ryland warned me tersely. "Especially with the pois—"

"I know," I said, cutting him off. "But we need to do this, Ry. That woman came to me for help, and I turned her away." That familiar, white-hot stab of guilt twisted up my insides. "And now she's captured. Maybe even already dead. I need to do this."

"And we need to be with you," Killian stated simply, already crawling out of the car. "I'll grab Dair if you guys grab Jax and Bash." He paused when he was halfway out the door, twisting his head over his shoulder to stare at me. A blush stained his cheeks as he ducked his head. "Th-th-th-thank you for trusting us. Thank you for letting us help you."

My heart swelled with love for this man, for *all* of my men. I wouldn't have even been able to tell you when my feelings for them grew, when my mates went from infatuations to crushes to men vital to my very well-being. They were embedded in my soul now, a part of my genetic makeup, and I needed to tell them that. Soon.

"We're a team now," I told Kill, shifting my gaze to include Ryland as well. "No more secrets."

"No more secrets," the two of them agreed immediately.

Nodding once, I crawled to the trunk in the back of the van that held our weapons. I began sifting through the collection present, grabbing a sword, two daggers, and an axe.

We were really doing this—driving to an unfamiliar location, saving humans we didn't know, and killing an unknown number of nightmares. All while I fought off the poison coursing through my bloodstream, weakening my body.

And now for the famous last words...

What could possibly go wrong?

EIGHTEEN

JAX

A lot could go wrong with this mission.

Even with my mind steadily sinking in and out of sanity, I knew that this trip to the brothel could end horribly for all of us.

I moved towards where Z was loading up a limo Axel stole with Bash, trying to ignore the landscape constantly changing and morphing around me. Right now, the trees had been replaced by metal contraptions that rose from the ground. Hideous, distorted faces were shaped into the very top, where the boughs were supposed to be. The "tree" nearest to me displayed a young woman with her face twisted into perpetual agony, her lips opened in a silent scream and anguish visible in her metal eyes. The grass beneath my feet was red with blood, so red that I couldn't see a sliver of green anywhere in the vicinity. When I looked up, the night sky was a mirage of disembodied limbs—a nose where the moon should be, hands and feet in place of stars, and carved up torsos everywhere else.

I shook my head from side to side rapidly, struggling to orient myself to the here and now.

I'm safe.

I'm with my mate and my brothers. My mate...who loves me. Whom I love.

I'm not dead.

Memories of that pitch-black abyss bombarded me, but I shoved them away. I refused to even think about that brief, brief moment when death had claimed me. When death had taken me away from my brothers and my very reason for living. When the world had been nothing but a barren expanse of nothingness...

The scenery changed around me in a bright flash of color. Now, instead of metal trees, hundreds of Sashas stood in the forest in lieu of them. Her hair fell around her face, and her eyes sparked with malice. Blood dripped, dripped, dripped down her cheeks, staining her white dress.

"You did this to me." Her voice reverberated all around me. I couldn't escape it, couldn't run away fast enough.

"I'm sorry," I whispered.

Harsh, feminine laughter grated on my nerves, and I lifted my head back to see Aaliyah's smirking face staring back at me.

"Feed, Jaxon," she purred, and I quickened my pace in Z's direction. "Don't you want to feed?"

Now, hands were erupting from the ground, their fingers gnarled and bloody. I could see tendons and muscles as the zombie-like creatures attempted to pull themselves out of the dirt.

"Doesn't Z's neck look so...delicious? Do you hear her pulse pounding? See the blood rushing?" I wanted to place my hands over my ears to tune her out, but I knew if I did that, Z would become suspicious. My sweet mate was always so perceptive.

As if my thoughts had summoned her attention, Z glanced up from where she bent over a duffel bag with Bash and smiled sweetly. That smile lit me up from the inside, shooting through my bloodstream like erratic fireworks.

And when I finally touched her arm, running my fingers across her silky smooth skin, the nightmares vanished and I was once more back in the front of Paco's house with the humans.

"Everything okay?" Z asked softly as the last of the fog cleared from my mind. I remembered where I was—at Paco's house—and why I was there—to save Z from the poison. All of the other pieces steadily clicked into place, until I felt like I was taking control of my life for the first time ever.

"Yes," I replied, shocking myself with the sincerity of that.

No more blood.

No more darkness.

Only light.

A vampire could go insane if he didn't drink any blood. On the opposite end of the spectrum, he could go crazy if he consumed too much of it. It was a fine line we had to balance, made even more precarious by our sin of gluttony.

And then there was me—insane for no other reason

than the fact that my brain had cracked. First because I didn't consume blood, and then because I did.

When would I ever feel whole again?

"Who's ready to kick some ass?" Axel materialized behind me and clapped a hand down on my shoulder. I flinched instinctively at the contact but forced myself to clear my expression when Z's shrewd gaze whipped in my direction. Her eyes narrowed slightly, but I kept my face perfectly blank.

"What's the plan?" Bash loaded up a gun full of specialized mage bullets. Each one was able to do a completely different thing when they hit their target—the blue electrocuted them, the red lit them on fire, the green stopped their hearts, and the purple fried their brains. All effective tools for killing any nightmare. We were fortunate Paco had a surplus lying around in his shed, though Axel had to be wiener slapped to receive them.

Strangely enough, I thought the ex-assassin actually *enjoyed* it.

"I give Mary some sweet loving and allow her to kill people," Axel answered sincerely, reaching behind his shoulder to caress the blade that sat there.

Z gave him a long, long look, one that might've made me jealous if there hadn't been a hint of annoyance in her eyes, before sighing and addressing us all.

"We head in, kill the mages, head out. Simple." She exchanged a wary look with Axel, one that had my hackles rising, and shoved a knife into her sheath. "Let's go."

We arrived at a large mansion framed by birches on either side. The paved pathway curled around a marble fountain, flashing lights illuminating the water in the darkness in shades of pink, red, purple, and green. One glance at the fountain confirmed it was spelled to do so, the familiar green glow most mages possessed surrounding it. We paused at the gate so Axel could speak to a guard, declaring he wanted to enter through the back so his wife wouldn't get word of his infidelity, before we were led around the building towards the staff entrance, where there were no guards and only one rickety doorway.

Nobody questioned the crazed shadow and the dark power he exuded.

In the limo Axel had stolen for us, Toby stripped out of his shirt and waited obediently for Axel to secure a collar and leash around his neck. Fear flashed in the young human's gaze, but he didn't protest once, even when Axel tugged experimentally on the leash.

It was decided that Axel would go in posing as a client looking for prostitutes. Toby would be his human slave. The rest of us were too recognizable, despite us being nightmares. We couldn't afford to have our fathers discovering what we had been up to.

"What the fuck are you doing?" Bash barked, his eyes widening in horror. My jaw went slack when I saw Z stripped down to her bra, the swells of her breasts visible over the fabric. When she began to tug down her pants, one of Ryland's shadows wrapped around her wrist, stopping her.

"What?" She whipped her head up to glare at us all.

"W-wh-why are you stripping down?" Killian stuttered, a myriad of expressions flashing across his face. First, surprise, then lust when he took in her creamy smooth skin, and finally, anger and possessiveness.

My own jealousy, an emotion I wasn't entirely familiar with, sparked to life in my bloodstream. I couldn't remember a time I had ever felt jealousy before, but just then, it was impossible to deny. I didn't want others seeing what didn't belong to them.

"For fuck's sake, Z!" Bash hissed through gritted teeth as she finally wiggled her way out of her pants, despite Ryland's shadows attempting to hold them in place. The thin lace panties she wore left very little to the imagination. I whipped my gaze in Toby and Axel's direction, ready to murder them if they so much as glanced her way. Toby was staring purposely out the far window, a blush staining his cheeks, but Axel...

Axel was staring at Z's chest intently.

My fangs lowered, seconds from embedding themselves in his neck and drawing out his blood until he fell at my feet dead, when the assassin's nose wrinkled in disgust.

"Don't see it." He shook his head vehemently.

"Don't see what?" Z questioned, not at all ashamed by her near nudity. I wondered how many times she'd gone out in public like this, how many men had set their eyes upon her perfect flesh.

But then I decided I didn't want to know the answers to any of those questions.

"Don't see the allure," Axel answered simply.

Z snorted. "In me?"

"In women." He crinkled his nose, and then, before any of us could stop him, leaned forward and squeezed her tits. Surprisingly, Z let him, her eyes dancing with amusement, even as Killian, of all people, lunged forward and tried to grab at the former assassin.

Axel glanced from Z's tempting tits to his cock and then back to her tits once more.

"Nope." He released her before Ryland's shadows could strangle him or Bash could cast a nasty ass spell. "Not even a twitch." He rubbed at his flaccid dick with a manic glint in his eyes. "Axel junior is still fast asleep."

Bash practically hissed at him, moving forward to wrap his arm around Z's waist possessively before pulling her onto his lap. All he needed to do next was piss on her, and then he would've firmly asserted his authority.

I could tell he'd realized his error when Z began to wiggle in his lap. Her expression was at first annoyed, but then it turned mischievous when he grunted, his eyes fluttering shut with arousal.

"Stop trying to distract me," Bash gritted out, grabbing her hips to hold her still.

Z simply turned to stare at him over her shoulder, and his eyes lowered from her lips to her chest and then went back to her lips. "I'm not distracting you. It's not my fault your cock has a bigger brain than you, Bash-hole." She finally pulled herself off his lap, and Bash released a noise of distress, his hands reaching in her direction as if he wanted to drag her back towards him. But then his eyes glued themselves to her ass as she lowered at the waist, moving towards the door of the limo, and all was right in the world.

"I need to pretend to be one of the working girls," Z explained once she was far enough away we couldn't grab her. Toby exited the vehicle, followed immediately by Axel, but Z lingered, still crouched over.

"Fuck no," Ryland seethed.

"Not happening, baby," Bash retorted.

"I'm not asking your permission," she sniped. "I told you guys about this rescue mission because we're a team and I trust you." Her words filled me with warmth and bubbles and all of the other light and airy things in this world. But then coldness replaced the heat and the bubbles popped one by one. "I don't need to be protected. I've done a damn good job of protecting myself for years."

"What if we want to protect you?" Killian asked softly, and when all of us turned to stare at him, he blushed, running a hand through his red hair. "I-I me-mean..."

"I know what you mean." Z threw him a gentle look.

"Z." So far, Dair had remained silent throughout this entire exchange, but I could tell he had something important he wanted to say. "We understand you're perfectly capable of looking after yourself, but sometimes, it's okay to lean on us. It's okay to rely on other people, because I promise you, we won't let you down. We won't abandon you." He paused, allowing his words to sink in, before continuing. "Saying that," he threw pointed looks in all of our directions, "we understand that you need to do this mission by yourself."

"Fuck that," Bash said with a snort. Ryland seemed to be in agreement as his shadows writhed and danced like angry, hissing snakes.

Dair cast them frosty glares. "We're too recognizable. Not only that, but we're not trained for combat." Killian ducked his head sheepishly, Bash glowered, and I kept my face perfectly blank. Only Ryland sat up straighter in his seat, jutting his chin up.

"I am," he insisted, and I recalled somewhat dazedly that his father, the shadow king, had trained him in sword fighting throughout his childhood.

"And that's why you should go with," Dair continued, and this time, Z was the one who opened her mouth to protest. Dair waved her arguments away with a simple flick of his golden hand. "It makes the most sense, Z, and it's a win-win for all of us. We want to look after you, but we understand that this isn't a fight we can help with at the moment. But at the same time, Ryland is able to have your back in secret." He nodded towards Ryland, who immediately pulled the shadows close around his body like an obsidian cloak. Even though I knew he was there, I couldn't see him. "This is a fair compromise."

"Compromise." A distant look glazed over Z's eyes. Her jaw set, and a hardness marred her features. Her pouty lips pursed slightly before immediately straightening out. She released a heavy sigh, the muscles in her shoulders loosening, and relented, albeit reluctantly. "All right. I suppose I should get used to compromising more."

"We're a team," Dair told her gently.

"A team," she agreed immediately. She turned to address all of us then, the movement drawing attention to her impressive chest and the clear view we had of her tits. I wasn't the only one who had to fight off a hard-on. "All right. Ryland, come with me but stay hidden. The rest of you, wait here. I'll call you if I need backup." She leaned towards one of the limo benches and grabbed a walkie-talkie, tossing it in my direction. I caught it easily and held it out to Bash. Not because I didn't want to have a direct line of communication with Z, but because I knew Bash would freak the fuck out every second she wasn't in his line of sight.

He didn't love easily, but when he did, he loved harder than any man I'd ever met.

She looked as if she wanted to say something to us, her mouth opening and a softness thawing the frost in her eyes, but she immediately pressed her lips together, her cheeks filling with flames.

"I...I'll see you later," she stuttered out, all but running out of the vehicle.

"Fucking hell," Bash murmured, staring intently at the walkie-talkie, as if he could see Z through it.

But I couldn't focus on him.

Or anyone else, for that matter.

The second she left, the walls of the limo began to drip red with blood. Darkness permeated the small space, and the faces of my brothers twisted and distorted until I couldn't recognize them. Killian's eyes drooped down his face like ice cream melting on a hot summer day, and his skin blistered and cracked like hell itself lived beneath his skin. Bash's head was no longer connected to his body, but instead, sat next to him, his eyes lifeless and vacant.

Dair had three heads, but each one displayed a different face—one had his mouth opened in a silent scream, another was grinning maniacally, and the third was a picture of anguish.

The darkness in my mind once more consumed me.

NINETEEN

Z

When that woman, Natalia, mentioned a brothel, I'd expected the building to be a rundown, desolate shed teeming with scantily-clad prostitutes. I was right about the scantily-clad part, but instead of venturing into a shed, I found myself at the back door of a sprawling mansion.

It was gorgeous, with stone pillars, a wide balcony, and a fountain, but the beauty of the building only added to my unease and trepidation

Something that held such horror shouldn't be beautiful.

That made me hate these nightmares even more. Their malevolence was like a black storm cloud hovering over us all, promising torrents of rain, white-hot lightning, and booming thunder.

I turned towards Axel and Toby. The old assassin was cackling evilly and staring up at the mansion as if he were imagining eating all of them for dinner. Toby, on the other hand, kept flicking his gaze in all directions as if he couldn't decide where to focus his attention. His face was screwed up in fear.

I had to give him credit though—despite the terror twisting up his features, there was a determined glint in his gaze that increased my respect for him.

Though I couldn't see him, I sensed Ryland hovering in the shadows nearby, his presence settling my fears and soothing my nerves. Anxiety gnawed at my insides, cutting a hole in my heart like moths chewing through clothing. I half wanted to dance on the balls of my feet in preparation of the fight to come, while the rest of me worked to regulate my breathing to conquer the growing panic.

"Be safe." I paused to stare intently at both Axel and Toby. To Axel, I added, "And don't stab people just to fucking stab people."

He placed his hand over his chest and staggered back a few steps in mock-horror. "You wound me, little sister. I thought you liked my stabby ways."

"No stabbing," I told him firmly. I glanced once more at Toby, hoping my face conveyed everything I couldn't say out loud.

I'm sorry.

I should've stopped her.

I'll fix this.

But instead of wording any of that, I gestured for them to head towards the main entrance.

"Go."

Soon, it was just me...and Ryland.

"Let's do this," I told my shadow mate with a bravado I didn't completely feel. To be honest, I was a mess. My internal organs were tangled into hundreds of knots, each one tightening by the second, until I feared I would topple over.

How could I fight when my body was failing me the way it was? How could I keep my promise and save these humans?

I wasn't sure I could, but I sure as fuck would try.

With the skimpy clothing I wore, I wasn't able to hide any weapons on my body. That was okay, though. If you were a real assassin, a real killer, you knew how to use the environment to your own advantage.

I didn't need weapons to make these bastards pay. Especially with...

My thoughts trailed off as I fingered the necklace a disgruntled Paco had created for me. It hung just between my breasts, appearing like a part of my costume. A nice accessory to go with the bra and panty combo I was rocking.

Taking a deep, shuddering breath, I moved towards the back door.

According to Toby, there were only a few guards posted at the front entrance. I thought that was moronic on the mages' part, but Toby explained it was arrogance. The mages who ran the brothel didn't believe anyone would be stupid enough to fight back against them. And why would they think differently? Humans had been the nightmares' punching bag for hundreds of years. For so long, we accepted this mistreatment in relative silence.

But maybe we were another extinct supernatural creature coming back to life. Maybe we were phoenixes rising from the ashes of our ancestors.

Once I entered the mansion, the smell of stale air, sweat, and cigar smoke immediately bombarded me. There were very few lights in this section of the mansion, giving the entire area an eerie, desolate feel. Smoke entered my nostrils as I moved on silent feet down the hideous floral carpet of the hallway.

Human woman with dead eyes and haunted expressions stopped to stare at me as I walked. All of them wore outfits similar to mine or nothing at all. Bruises covered the majority of their flesh, and that sick feeling inside of me intensified with every step I took.

I moved towards the end of the hall, where the smoke seemed to be coming from. This was the only part of the mansion that wasn't silent. Music blared from the speakers, a soundtrack to the horrible, depraved sight I was forced to witness.

It appeared to be a sitting room with a fireplace against the far wall, intricate woodworking, and a chandelier hanging from the ceiling. Couches were positioned in a semicircle around the room, every cushion currently occupied.

Human men and women were in a variety of lewd positions as mages laughed haughtily, smoking on their cigars and chatting amongst themselves.

Directly in front of me, a young human female was bouncing on the cock of a man significantly older than her with a pudgy belly and a bald, sweaty head. Another human woman was pawing at her breasts, pinching her nipples with a vacant look in her eyes. A young man was completely naked and on his hands and knees while a mage rammed his cock into his ass. A female mage in a green gown stood over them, sipping on her whisky and eyeing the human with hungry eyes.

The humans all varied in age and gender, ethnicity and body type, but one thing remained the same—the dead, empty look in their eyes. It felt like I was staring into dozens of abysses, falling head over heels like Alice down the rabbit hole.

My heart cracked in two when I saw a young woman's body lying naked and discarded near the roaring fireplace. Even in death, I could see the resemblance between her and her sister clearly.

This must be Ali, Natalia's sister.

We couldn't save her in time.

Was Natalia dead too? Or was she here somewhere, facing unspeakable horrors, just as her sister had before death claimed her?

Fuck. Fuck. Fuck!

Ryland released a distressed noise from behind me as he witnessed the horrific sight. I swore my stomach bottomed out, the contents spewing across the floor as my heart raced a thousand miles a minute.

This world...it was evil. Absolutely, undoubtedly evil. Nothing we said or did could change the fact that the world we lived in was steeped in shadows and darkness. In bones and thorns. In monsters and beasts.

The more I looked, my stomach a tumultuous mixture of dread and fear, the more I saw, and the more I realized that we, as a civilization, really were fucked.

Embodying their sin of sloth, most of the mages weren't actually doing any of the work themselves. The woman riding the mage's cock was being propelled up and down by wispy strands of green magic. Two women being fondled had similar green streaks wrapped around their wrists, forcing them to palm each other's breasts.

Bile filled me.

As did determination and a rage so white-hot, I feared it would set this entire room ablaze. Although... maybe that was what needed to happen. Maybe this room—and the rest of the world—should deteriorate into nothing but soot and ash, and a new civilization should be reborn.

Before I could take a step into that room of horrors and raise hell, rough hands clamped down on my arms, pulling me back against a chubby body. Those same hands moved from my arms to my breasts, squeezing tightly before clumsily reaching for my nipples.

If this fucker couldn't even find my nipples, I wondered if he'd ever been able to find a female's clit. That was probably why he was here, raping unwilling females, because nobody would be stupid enough to fuck his disgusting, disease-ridden cock.

"What's a pretty thing like you doing hiding away?"

Experience had taught me I had seconds to escape, to fight back. I'd just made my body go limp, forcing him to hold all one hundred pounds of me, and lifted my foot to jam it backwards into his knee when the man fell away from me with a pained grunt that was quickly muffled.

I spun around quickly, making sure to keep a few feet between us. I knew my limitations, and taking on larger opponents was definitely one of them. It was why I preferred to use my bow and arrow over short-range weapons. Humans weren't allowed to possess guns, so I'd had to get creative with ways to kill people with my petite body type.

The mage was an average man, albeit weathered with age. His hair was speckled with white and seemed to be styled into a bowl cut. Either he'd done a shit job of cutting it himself, or the barber was a woman he couldn't find the clit of.

As I watched, amused, two shadowy tendrils wrapped around both his wrists and forced his hands behind his back. Panic flared to life in his gaze, but he couldn't speak with the third shadow over his mouth. His eyes sparked with his mage power, but before he could call on his gifts, a knife materialized in Ryland's hand and my shadow mate slashed it across his throat in a demented, bloody smile.

Ryland's ice-blue eyes shone in the darkness of the hall as he held the blood-covered blade tightly in his grasp. Shadows converged on the two of them, obscuring the disgusting mage completely from view.

I gave my love a brief nod of solidarity, one he returned, before he diminished from sight once more, taking with him the man's body and the blood spilled on the floor.

No wonder shadows made the best fucking assassins and spies. Damn. I was a little jealous I didn't have those powers.

"I'm here!" a flamboyant voice called enthusiastically, forcing my attention back to the crack in the door leading to the main parlor. A headache formed behind my eyes as I watched Axel swagger into the room, Toby trailing behind him on a leash. The human's eyes flicked from face to face, searching desperately for his girlfriend. When his gaze landed on Ali's crumpled, naked form, horror etched itself onto his features, followed immediately by sadness and grief.

I'm sorry, Toby. I'm so, so sorry.

The mages present turned from one another to stare at Axel, who simply flicked his hair away from his face and then plopped down onto one of the couches. His shadows curled around his hands, and when they dissipated, he had a lit cigar between his fingers. He brought it to his lips to take a drag...and then began to cough dramatically, his face twisting into a scowl. He tossed the still lit cigar to Toby, who struggled to catch it, before flashing a blindingly white smile at the party goers. I trusted that smile just as much as I trusted a shark circling the water in search of fresh blood. "Now the party can truly begin."

The mages appeared confused but quickly dismissed Axel as irrelevant. Why would they worry, after all, when Axel was a nightmare just like them?

I only prayed that Axel's confusing loyalty to me outweighed the one he felt towards his fellow nightmares.

Somewhat satisfied that Axel could keep an eye on the humans, I moved back down the hallway, towards where I noticed the kitchen to be.

Naked men and women hurried in and out of the room, carrying trays of alcohol and other snacks. Their lifeless eyes barely spared me a glance as they hurried to do the mages' bidding. My eyes snagged on one woman standing a little bit apart from the others, almost as if she wasn't sure what to do.

A familiar woman.

Like the others, Natalia was naked and covered in hideous bruises. Ropes were wrapped around her body in a style I might've found artful if it hadn't been for the circumstances behind them. They were tied around her breasts, causing the skin around her nipples to turn purple, and crisscrossed her stomach.

When her eyes fell on me, they widened imperceptibly, a myriad of emotions flitting across her face. At first, I saw hope, but then that hope quickly transformed into fear and anger.

I hurried towards her, searching the kitchen for anything I could use to free her from the bindings. As if he'd heard my thoughts, Ryland materialized beside me, handed me his blade, and then disappeared from view once more. Ignoring Natalia's whine of fear, I hurried towards her and sliced through the rope. She released a grunt of pain and immediately rubbed at her bare breasts, still that ungodly purple color.

"What are you doing here?" she asked anxiously, crossing her arms over her chest. I wanted to give her something to cover herself up, but I didn't dare. Not yet. If a mage were to see her in normal clothes before I could implement my plan, everything would be ruined.

"I...I..." I opened and shut my mouth repeatedly before deciding to tell her the truth. "I screwed up when I turned you away before. And I'm sorry. I should've helped when I had the chance."

Natalia released a pained laugh, still rubbing at her boobs, though she kept sneaking furtive glances to where Ryland had disappeared to, as if she thought he was looking at her nude, beaten body. I wanted to promise her that my shadow mate would never violate her like that, and even if she *wanted* him to look, he was loyal to me and our mate bond, but I knew my words would fall on deaf ears. And after what she'd been through, I didn't even *want* to reassure her.

She deserved to be fucking furious.

"It's not like you being here would've made a difference." Natalia wrapped one arm around her chest while she pushed a strand of orange hair behind her ear with the other hand. "Ali was already dead when I arrived." Pure agony distorted her features, and she blinked rapidly to hold back the tears.

"I'm sorry," I whispered sincerely. Her grief was almost palpable. It made my heart ache for her. I knew what it felt like to lose the people you loved, and I wouldn't wish that on anyone.

"I want them to pay. To suffer." She finally dropped both hands to her sides and clenched them into fists.

"They will," I promised, holding up my necklace. Her brows furrowed together as she stared at the potion visible in the translucent vial clasped to the end of the stylish string.

"What's that?"

"It's a poison," I explained, moving towards a tray full of glasses. The human standing there stared at me impassively, not a flicker of emotion in his gaze, before stepping aside. He didn't speak, didn't blink, just watched with a deadened look that had my heart racing.

"A poison?" For the first time since I saw her in this hellhole, intrigue entered Natalia's eyes as she watched me pour a generous amount into each glass. I then poured scotch into all of the glasses until the poison was no longer visible.

"It's one I'm...familiar with."

Understatement of the century.

This was the same poison Zack had given me, the same one coursing through my system, killing me slowly.

But according to Paco, if I gave these mages exactly three teaspoons...

It wouldn't kill them slowly.

"You ready to get your revenge?" I quirked an eyebrow at Natalia, who grinned sharply. She grabbed the tray from me and sashayed out the door.

Surprisingly, the human male followed us out too, a wicked glint appearing in his eyes that had fear strangling my airways. I was just grateful that malevolence didn't seem to be directed at me.

Pasting a fake grin on my face, I entered the main living room and moved through the crowd, dancing to the beat and ignoring the hands that grabbed at me. I watched out of my periphery as Natalia whispered to one of the girls and then handed her a glass of poisoned scotch from her tray. That girl immediately turned to a mage sitting on the couch, perched on his lap, and then offered him a sultry grin. He cupped her bare breasts, twisting her nipples, as she giggled and placed the cup to his lips. He opened his mouth eagerly, allowing her to pour the liquid in.

The second his eyes flickered away from her to speak to his companion, her eyes turned dead. Empty. Emotionless.

Ruined.

All of these humans were ruined beyond repair because of the depraved things these mages made them do. I wasn't sure they'd ever recover.

It seemed as if word had spread amongst the humans. Almost the entire tray was empty as they handed out scotch to all of the men and women present.

The man who had been in the kitchen with us was kissing a mage woman while an older man reached around him from behind to jerk him off. The human handed the glass to the woman first, and while she drank, he turned around in the man's arms to kiss him. When he finally pulled away, it was only to grab the glass from the mage woman and hand it to the older man.

A devilish smile pulled up my lips.

Axel, reclining on the couch where I last saw him, smirked and winked at me. Toby was staring intently at Natalia, who didn't seem to realize he was there as she flitted from mage to mage with a sultry grin, passing out drinks.

When she passed me, I grabbed the two remaining drinks from the tray and moved onto the dance floor. Immediately, my body was sandwiched between two sweaty, ancient men who rolled their lengths against my body. I giggled like I actually enjoyed the feel of their micropenises digging into my hips.

The shadows in the far corner of the room twisted and writhed in agitation, but fortunately, the men and women present were either too drunk or too high to care. I gave Ryland a warning look over the bald man's head, and the shadows immediately calmed down.

"Drink?" I inquired, raising my voice to be heard over the music.

The men agreed and accepted the drinks eagerly.

And then the fun part began.

One of the mages began to scream in agony, blood gushing out of his nose, ears, mouth, and eyes. As panic splayed itself across his face, the other mages began to scream as well. The mage woman I noted earlier grabbed at her throat as she doubled over, convulsing. Blood poured from every pore of her body as her eyes rolled into the back of her head. The two men I was with released me as if my touch was toxic, green balls of power materializing in their palms. Before they could wield their magic, however, the poison took effect and forced them to their knees, where roaches like them fucking belonged.

Their screams were music to my ears.

"We have company." Axel rose gracefully and removed his machete from his back, swinging it around in his hands like a baton.

Toby immediately removed the collar from his neck and screamed, "Natalia!" at the top of his lungs. The girl turned from where she was hovering over a dead mage's body, her mouth flying open as tears filled her eyes.

"Toby!"

The main door was pushed open, and a dozen guards rushed inside, their weapons raised. But Ryland was prepared for that as he fired his magical gun at every man who entered, the bullets exploding in their chests. Some of the bullets caused them to instantly burst into flames, while others had them falling to the ground and seizing as white-blue electricity crackled over their skin.

We did it. A semi-hysterical laugh threatened to break free as I stared at the fallen bodies surrounding me. *We did it.*

Something wet touched my upper lip, and I rubbed it away impatiently. When I glanced at my fingers, I was surprised to find them stained red with blood.

What the...?

Dizziness coursed through me, like a wrecking ball destroying my mind in one fatal swoop, and I swayed precariously to the side.

The sounds of gunfire and shouts reverberated through the mansion as the humans attacked the mages and guards with a vengeance. Punching, clawing, screaming...all of their rage, anger, and hopelessness had led to this one final showdown.

I could see Bash, Dair, Killian, and Jax at the front entrance, shooting at the remaining guards. And there was Ryland, fighting back-to-back with Axel. And Toby and Natalia. And the haunting young man with the dead eyes. And—

Darkness shrouded my vision, and I fell.

TWENTY

It'd been an hour, and she still hadn't woken up.

I stared intently at Z where she lay on the floor in Paco's shed, her head in Killian's lap.

Fortunately, I had been paying enough attention to my sweet mate back at the brothel to catch her before she fell, though no words were capable of describing the terror I felt as her eyes rolled into the back of her head. The fight had already been won by that time, since the mages didn't have a chance with the poison destroying their bodies, and Axel and Natalia had been working together to go room to room and free the rest of the humans.

Me? I ran like hell with my mate in my arms. I knew I should've stayed and finished the mission, but I couldn't concentrate knowing how close Z was to death's door. Her face had been so pale, so sickly, that panic had eroded what remained of my mind. Killian, Jax, Bash, and Dair had hurried after me, all of us climbing into a car parked in front of the building. The idiot mage who'd been driving it had left the keys in the ignition. From there, all we'd had to do was drive the hour ride to Paco's house.

And now, we waited.

Waited and twiddled our damn thumbs as the archaic mage surveyed Z with a clinical intensity that had my heart pounding out of rhythm as my gut lurched with fear.

"Paco..." Bash growled out, pacing in the tiny shed. He scrubbed at his ash-blond hair, the strands sticking out in all directions like he'd stuck his finger in an electrical outlet.

"Shh!" The old man began to wave his hand erratically in Bash's direction, though what he was trying to articulate through that gesture, I had no idea.

My shadows coiled around my stomach like a constricting snake as I glared at Z's forehead, despite my anger not being directed at her.

Losing her...

It was unfathomable. I imagined it would be similar to wading through an endless ocean of black tar, my hands roaming blindly in the dark. There was no light without Z.

Why hadn't she told me she was feeling that sick? I never would've allowed her to go on this mission to begin with if I knew... Though telling Z not to do something would've only resulted in an acerbic tongue-lashing.

What if she'd been fighting against a mage when she passed out? What if she'd been injured? What if...what if...what if...

My heart felt like a wave shredded to pieces on the jagged stones of the shore.

Whispers of what Z did for Natalia had spread throughout the camp. I knew my little dove would snort and laugh at the ridiculousness of it all, claiming she wasn't a hero, but the rest of the humans begged to differ. The ones who'd been hesitant to follow Z now whispered her name with reverence. They'd inquired about Z's condition no less than twenty-six times since we'd returned from the brothel, though we always kept our answers vague.

She's fine.

She's recovering.

She's doing great.

Fucking bullshit.

"I want to learn to fight." Killian's voice dragged me out of my thoughts and had my head snapping in his direction. When he realized we were all staring at him intently, his cheeks turned crimson and he lowered his lips to Z's forehead.

"You want to *what*?" Bash stared at his best friend in disbelief, his blond brows crawling up into his hairline. "Kill, you don't fight. You hug."

Killian threw him a withering glare. "Maybe, but the world is changing, and I want to change with it. I don't want to be a pampered prince anymore. I want to learn to fight. I want to be by Z's side when she charges into battle, not waiting in the car." His lips compressed into a thin, stubborn line. The pain in his eyes was like a blazing beacon that called to the broken part of my own soul.

"You caught a fly once and set it free," Bash pointed

out. "You can't kill anyone, Kill." He actually looked distressed by the prospect, and I couldn't say I blamed him. For as long as I could remember, my brothers and I had protected Killian from the worst this world had to offer. He had a light inside of him, a flame that shone brilliantly and burned through the darkest of nights. We didn't want his hands to be stained with blood, and I knew Z felt the same.

He was the one person we refused to let this war tarnish.

"You can't protect me from the world," Killian pointed out. He turned his gaze to me, and I swore the fucker was giving me puppy dog eyes. That might work on Z, but it wouldn't work on me. Nope. Nada. Not me. I had a will of motherfucking steel. "Please, Ryland. Can you train me to fight?"

"Fine." My traitorous mouth said the word before my brain could catch up.

Where did my balls go? And how did I find them again?

"Z's going to want to train you herself when she wakes up," Dair said, absolute certainty that our girl would open her eyes again ringing in his voice. I wanted to have that same conviction, but every time I stared at her, I saw the way those mages in the brothel died right before my eyes. The blood that had poured from their mouths, ears, eyes, and noses. The pain twisting up their features, their haughtiness transforming into agony. The way they screamed just before death claimed them in a cruel, unrelenting vise.

And the fear that had flashed in their eyes just before

they fell to the ground.

They'd known they were going to die, could feel it in their bones, and I wondered if that was how Z felt every damn day since Zack poisoned her.

If my mate died, I'd follow her into death, consequences be damned. All of the kingdoms could fall into ruin for the number of shits I had to give.

"Z's going to want to train all of us," Bash retorted with a self-deprecating twist of his lips. "Can you picture that? Us as fighters?"

"Well, now I'm picturing it." I smiled too, envisioning my mage brother in badass leathers and sunglasses as he twirled a blade around his fingers. It was almost too comical to picture. Bash was a lazy son of a bitch and had never found the motivation to train like I did when we were younger. He preferred to spend his days in his room having orgies than in the training yard.

Bash narrowed his green eyes at me. "Why do you look so amused?"

I worked to keep my expression placid. "No reason."

"You don't think I can fight, do you?" He cocked an eyebrow at me, though I swore I saw amusement in his dark green gaze.

"I think..." I gave him a wry smirk. "I think that if you and Killian got into a fight, Killian would kick your ass."

The incubus's head snapped up from where he was staring down at Z. "W-wh-what?" he stuttered, surprise lacing his tone.

Dair smirked and folded his arms over his chest. "I agree. Bash is too..." He trailed off as he contemplated what word he wanted to use.

"Wimpy," Jax finished absently, though he didn't peel his attention away from the window.

Bash's eyes flared with indignation. "I am not." His power cackled and fizzled, green currents erupting on his skin and congregating in his palms.

"Just a teeny bit wimpy." I placed my forefinger and thumb together as rage distorted his face. My shadows moved me out of the way just in time to stop his assault, and he ended up running face-first into the wall. Cursing, Bash swiveled in my direction, his hair standing on end with the force of his power.

"If I'm so wimpy, why don't you stop hiding and face me like a man?" he questioned dangerously, and I stealthily used the shadows to materialize directly behind him.

"Like this?" I breathed in his ear, and he spun towards me with another curse.

"You're such an—"

"It's time." Paco removed his hands from where they rested on Z's shoulders and turned to face us, his expression uncharacteristically grave.

"T-time?" Killian asked, brushing Z's sweat soaked hair behind her ears.

Paco nodded and stood from his crouch, moving towards his collection of freshly brewed potions beside his bed. He grabbed two bottles—one of them a verdant green and the other a sparkly purple.

"What the fuck do you mean?" I demanded, pulling the shadows tighter around my body and using them to propel me protectively in front of Z.

Paco didn't even spare my silhouette a glance as he

kneeled beside my mate once more with the two potions in his hands.

"Time to administer more poison," he answered simply, unscrewing the green bottle.

"What? No!" I knew this was the plan, I knew we'd talked about it, but all I could see were those mages falling to the ground, a perpetual state of grief and agony twisting up their features. They deserved it for the sick and vile things they did, but Z didn't. Not my sweet mate. Not my little dove. Turning desperately towards Bash, hoping he would back me, I held his gaze and pleaded, "Bash, no! You can't allow him to do this."

Bash gritted his teeth together so tightly, I was surprised he didn't crack a tooth. "We don't have a choice, Ry. You know Z has to die from the poison in order for the cure to work."

"You saw what happened to those mages at the brothel." I was practically pleading at this point, more than willing to fall to my knees if that was what it took to save my little dove from this fate. If I could've experienced her pain for her, I would in a heartbeat. But what I couldn't endure was watching her suffer.

"She needs to return to the capital by..." Bash turned towards the clock on the wall, surprise darkening his features when he discovered it was already one in the morning. "She needs to return to the capital by tonight. We don't have time to wait."

My shadows twisted and writhed, hissed and snapped. They felt like live wires about to whip around and electrocute anyone who came too close. They were sentient and dangerous, their sole purpose to protect our oblivious, sleeping mate in the center of the shed.

I lost control of my rage, the full brunt of it pouring out of me in a wave.

"No! I can't allow you to do this." Darkness closed in on us from all sides, pushing off the walls like a slow-moving, sticky tar. It crawled across the floor, devouring everything it came into contact with, as panic invaded my lungs.

I couldn't breathe, couldn't see, couldn't think.

The anger and fear... They ran through my blood like magma. I was the reaper of death, and anyone who touched me would fall dead at my feet.

"Ryland, calm the fuck down!" Dair demanded as my shadows crawled forward like pitch-black molten lava.

"Ryland!" Killian sounded terrified, but I couldn't stop. Wouldn't stop.

My shadows had a mind of their own.

The muscles in my shoulders were so tense, they physically spasmed, the full reality of what I was doing wreaking havoc on my insides.

Protect Z.

Worry about the consequences later.

Something sharp stabbed into my neck, and my shadows instantly retreated inside of me. I turned my eyes to Bash, who stared back at me without a flicker of remorse. Betrayal reverberated through me.

"I'm sorry, brother," he whispered as my body tilted to the side.

I was unconscious before I even hit the ground.

Z

I was back inside the strange stone palace, once more in an ostentatious green gown that cascaded around my ankles. I brushed impatiently at one of the blonde curls cascading down my shoulder, forcing the unruly strand behind my ear.

Everything was exactly as I remembered it, down to the shattered window that I'd fallen out of. The only difference was the notable absence of Aaliyah.

Where was that bitch hiding?

I spun in a circle, nearly tripping over the trim of my dress, and glared daggers at the fucked-up paintings on the wall. One displayed a woman in a brown dress, her face obscured by a burlap sack. Her hands were tied behind her back, and in the distance, I swore I could see malevolent shadows standing on a hill, watching the woman. I had no idea what the painting was trying to depict, except for a general sense of fuckery, but unease still skirted down my spine. It almost reminded me of a person shuffling their sock-clad feet across carpeting and then reaching out a finger to zap me.

The painting beside it showed a second woman, this one in a drab gray dress, leaning beneath a guillotine. Directly beside her was a bucket full of decaying heads, their eyes vacant and their mouths open in a scream I couldn't hear. Unlike the first painting, this one displayed the woman's face clearly—the horror and fear emanating from her eyes, the twist of her features as she awaited death, and the spark of defiance in her cunning smirk. The same number of men that stood on the hill in the first painting surrounded the woman now, though their faces were devoid of any features, as if someone had taken sandpaper and scrubbed off their eyes, nose, lips, and ears.

"Z," a soft, breathy voice whispered from behind me. I spun, heart racing, to see Mali standing before me.

My entire body froze as if I'd been jolted by electricity. I could barely breathe through the tightening in my throat.

Mali.

My best friend who...

Who betrayed me.

She looked well. Better than she had when I last saw her, fleeing from the scene of Diego's murder with tears in her eyes. Over the course of the Damning, she'd discovered she was mates to one of the competitors, a sociopath who hadn't hesitated to kill everyone in his pathway, including innocents. Mali had inadvertently led me to a trap, believing that Zack would make a deal with me.

A bunch of horse shit.

Because of her naïveté, Diego had died, stabbed by the

man she claimed to love. I sent her away without a second thought and hadn't heard or seen from her since.

Until now.

Her brown hair was perfectly coiffed, framing a face that appeared fuller than I remembered it being. Her dewy eyes were glossy with unshed tears, and her hands trembled where they plucked at the skirt of her vibrant red dress. I noticed blood on the corner of her mouth, almost as if she'd just recently partaken in a feeding.

What the fuck was she doing here? With Aaliyah?

The familiar sense of betrayal rushed over me like a swooping, ice-cold tidal wave. It seeped through my skin and embedded itself in my bones and bloodstream.

I knew I had no right to feel this way. I'd sent her away, after all. I couldn't stand to be around her, knowing that Diego's blood rested on her hands.

But to know she went crawling to my enemy?

I wanted her to suffer.

"Z." Mali's lower lip began to tremble as she took a hesitant step towards me. I automatically countered it with a backwards one of my own, wishing desperately I had some sort of weapon to defend myself if she chose to attack. Hurt flashed in her eyes at my retreat, but instead of commenting on it, she asked, "What are you doing here?"

"Obviously your bitch of a master brought me here," I snapped, trying to remember what had happened just before that. My memories were hazy, shifting constantly like someone was repeatedly running their hand through a pool of water, causing them to distort. The last thing I remembered was the brothel...

True fear flashed in Mali's gaze as she took a few more steps closer. I found that I couldn't back up any more. My body was already flush against the far wall, and there were no windows in this particular area. I would prefer jumping into the sea below than facing my traitorous best friend.

"Z, there's so much I need to tell you while you're here, and I don't have a lot of time," Mali began urgently, her eyes flicking in all directions.

"Leave me alone, Mali," I hissed, but she ignored my acerbic tone and gripped my wrists, her vampire strength rendering me immobile. I could pull away and risk breaking a few bones, or I could hear what she had to say.

The former option sounded pretty appealing right about now…

"The kings have been here to visit Aaliyah," Mali told me, and I froze, finally giving her my complete attention. "They want her to help them live forever."

"So it's true," I breathed, stunned. "They're trying to become immortal."

"Aaliyah made a deal with them," Mali confirmed, once more glancing in all directions, as if she expected the redhead to be hiding behind the couch. "I don't know the details of it yet, but I know that the second the kings complete their part, Aaliyah will make them immortal. They won't die of natural causes, and no man-made weapon will be capable of killing them."

"Fuck." We had known about this, of course, but hearing it confirmed had goosebumps rippling across my skin. "What else can you tell me?"

"A lot." Mali's eyes turned sharper, shrewd almost, as

a wicked grin pulled up her lips. "The bitch trusts me." She finally released my wrists, seemingly satisfied that I wasn't going to run away, and continued with her report. I didn't know if I could trust her, but at this point, I didn't have a lot of fucking options. Mali, Atta, Axel... I had the distinct impression that one of them was going to betray us, but I had no idea which one. "Aaliyah talks a lot about the prophecy."

"The one about the princes becoming more powerful than their fathers? And either ending or saving the world?" I questioned, and she nodded.

"She also mentioned..." She hesitated, biting on her lower lip, and I nodded to encourage her to continue. Swallowing, she tried again. "Aaliyah also mentioned that the princes weren't born. I have no idea what she meant by that, but..."

Icy fear infiltrated my heart as if someone had injected frost into it directly. My mind replayed Tavvy's final words before Dair killed him.

"If the rumors are true, you and those men you call your brothers magically appeared. Out of thin air."

From what I'd gathered, Dair hadn't told any of the others what Tavvy said. And I knew I hadn't either. I dismissed Tavvy's words as the ramblings of a crazed, dying man, but if what Mali said was true...

I needed to tell my mates.

"What else?" I asked urgently.

"The basement." Mali pointed towards a long hallway decorated in metal knights standing at attention. They held swords, javelins, and daggers directly over their hearts.

"What about the basement?"

"It's where Aaliyah raises her monsters." She lowered her voice to a whisper. "It's where she has her portal to Hell."

"What—" Before I could continue my line of inquiry, Mali's face twisted in surprise and shock a second before she was thrown across the room. I screamed her name, rushing towards her, but she continued to fly backwards down a long hallway until a door slammed shut, hiding her from sight. "Mali!"

"What a traitorous little swine." Aaliyah's face twisted into a look of utter disgust as she stomped towards me, her red, revealing dress trailing behind her. The skirt was long, almost resembling a wedding train, but it had two slits up either side, revealing more leg than I ever wanted to see on that she-bitch. Her neckline dipped almost completely to her bellybutton, and her shiny red hair was perfectly straight, giving her a severe, harsh look.

"What the fuck did you do to her?" I hissed out, and I swore something akin to jealousy flashed in her brilliant green gaze.

"You care about that vampire, don't you? After everything she's done?" She trailed her fingers over the top of the couch as my gaze followed her with the intensity of a hawk. She didn't wait for me to answer, not that I would've given her one, before continuing, "Why do you hate me, sister of mine?"

"I'm not your sister," I scoffed, and once more, that white-hot jealousy I noted earlier entered her gaze.

"You don't have to love me now, Z, but just know that everything I'm doing, everything I have done, has been for *you." Her voice crawled over my skin like an invasion of skittering insects.*

"I never asked you to do anything for me," I snapped, balling my hands into fists. "I don't want your help."

"But big sisters don't always listen," she retorted, finally removing her hand from the back of the couch to study her red painted nails, the exact same shade of her dress and lips. "They do what's best for their family."

"I don't understand what you mean," I growled out. "I have memories of my mom and dad, and I never saw you in any of them. I think I would remember your ugly mug."

Rage flashed in her eyes for a brief moment before it immediately simmered away, replaced by amusement. She threw her head back and laughed haughtily, the noise grating on my sensitive nerves.

"Is this what sisters do? Banter?" She cocked her head to the side curiously. "But no matter. To answer your question, of course you wouldn't remember me. Those...humans were not your real parents." She pulled her upper lip away from her teeth in disgust.

"Don't fucking talk about them like that," I raged, stepping closer and preparing to deck her across the face.

"Why? It's only the truth, sister." Sadness darkened her perfect features as she sighed heavily, dropping her gaze to the ground. She hadn't moved from where she stood beside the couch, though I could see it was taking every ounce of her willpower. I had no idea why she was giving me my space. Because she feared me? Or because she feared my reaction to her? Either option gave me a splitting headache.

"Why are you doing all of this?" I demanded, figuring

if she was in a talkative mood, the least she could do was answer my burning questions.

"I just want to get the world back to the way it was before the Sins arrived," she whispered, and I spotted a single tear cascade down her cheek. When she lifted her head, however, the tear was gone, and I wondered if I'd imagined its presence.

"Before the Sins created nightmares," I elaborated slowly, terror inflating me like helium in a balloon.

Her lips twisted into a scowl. "You hate nightmares, Z. I know you do."

"Not all nightmares are bad," I insisted, thinking of my mates and Diego. Of Axel and even Mali. Of Paco in his shed, with his flabby ass cheeks and pancake covered bed.

"You didn't always believe that," she pointed out, sounding slightly irritated.

I resisted the urge to growl. "People change. They take in new information and form new connections."

"Can you honestly tell me that if your precious mates weren't nightmares, you would still be so against my idea?" Aaliyah glared at me. "A world without nightmares sounds like...like a paradise."

"It's genocide," I protested. I hated nightmares and what the majority of them represented, but there had never been a time in my life where I wanted all of them to fucking perish. There had been hundreds of good ones I'd met over the years, not even including my mates. And what about the children? What about the millions of inno-cent nightmares?

"We have power, Z," Aaliyah told me. "Lots of power.

Take me, for example." She once more brought her gaze to her nails, surveying them in the sunlight streaming through the open window. I took note of that sunlight—when I passed out, it had been night. And if this was a true location and not just a product of my imagination, it meant Aaliyah's headquarters were in a completely different kingdom. Probably the Shifter Kingdom. Aaliyah's next words stopped my internal musings. "I can exacerbate the sins of all nightmares, but I can also eliminate them completely."

"What...?" I gaped at her wordlessly. "What does that even mean?"

And why are you telling me this?

"I can amplify the sins in nightmares," she reiterated. "Just like I did with your vampire mate... I made him out of control with bloodlust until he couldn't concentrate on anything except getting his next fix of blood."

"You destroyed his mind!" I bellowed, rage filling me.

She waved away my words dismissively. "His mind was never fully there to begin with. You can't break what's already broken, am I right?" She winked at me as if we were best friends and conspirators, but I simply glared back at her. Her smile wilted. "But I can also use my powers on the opposite spectrum as well." She paused for dramatic effect before saying, "I can take away a nightmare's power. I can make nightmares human."

My god.

My legs wobbled, threatening to give out underneath me, and I slid down against the wall until my butt touched the cold tiling of the floor. I couldn't see through the red fog that clouded my vision.

If what she was saying was true...

It could change everything.

"You're capable of it too," Aaliyah continued, her lips quirking upwards at my near meltdown. "You just need to learn how to harness your powers."

"Why are you telling me all of this?" I demanded, finally finding my way to my feet. My legs shook underneath me, but I placed one hand on the stone wall to hold myself up. My eyes spewed vitriol at the grinning psychopath before me. "Why are you working with the kings if you hate nightmares so damn much?"

"Because..." One second, she was by the couch, and the next, she was directly in front of me. She placed a hand on my chest, and to my horror, a window materialized behind me. "You're not the only one I plan to stab in the back."

And just like before, she shoved me.

My arms pinwheeled in the air as I struggled to regain my balance, but before I could fall to the turbulent sea below, the castle crumbled into dust. I crouched down, raising my hands above my head to protect myself from fallen rocks and cement, but the scenery changed.

I was no longer in the stone palace but a dungeon.

What in the...?

I appeared to be in a cell where an unfamiliar man hung suspended on the wall, a manic grin pulling up his pink lips. His face was covered in bruises, but his ice-blue eyes were eerily familiar.

Ryland's eyes.

On closer inspection, I saw that this was an older version of my shadow mate. The same dark skin. Same blue eyes. Same cropped black hair. The only difference was the permanent scars marring Ryland's face, scars I still didn't know the origins of.

Behind the shadow king stood my shifter mate.

Lupe's hands were bloody as he plunged a knife into the king's shoulder. The shadow king didn't scream, didn't make a single noise of distress, but his entire face twisted with pain.

And Lupe...

His eyes were empty, devoid of the softness I'd come to associate with my studious, passive mate. He didn't spare a glance at the blood speckling his face and hands as he roughly yanked the knife out of the shadow king's shoulder and tossed it onto a table...a table full of other bloody weapons of torture.

A noise of distress escaped me, and both the shadow king and Lupe whipped their heads in my direction. Lupe's eyes widened almost imperceptibly as shock, shame, and fear danced in his eyes.

"Z!" he begged, running towards me.

Before he could reach me, the vision changed, and I found myself in a different section of the same dungeon. Instead of my shifter mate, however, I found myself standing behind my genie one.

Devlin looked horrible, his familiar suit rumpled and his brown curls disheveled. His olive skin appeared almost ashen as he pulled open the cage to a second cell.

Was I going to witness him torture someone too?

And why was Lupe even torturing the shadow king to begin with?

What the fuck was going on?

Before I could articulate any of the questions out loud,

Devlin stepped inside the cell, and after a moment, I followed him.

It took my eyes a moment to adjust to the dark, but when they did, I saw a lanky man sitting on the ground, shackles around his wrists and ankles. He looked extremely familiar, but I couldn't figure out why. Not with the long beard and gashes on his face.

I opened my mouth to call out to Devlin, to make him aware of my presence like I had with Lupe, but before I could get a word out, the world shattered like a rock being thrown at a mirror.

And I fell once more.

But this time, I fell straight into a pool of burning lava.

TWENTY-TWO

BASH

Z's head snapped upwards as a scream ripped from her throat.

If I ever thought my heart was nothing but a dead lump of coal, that noise proved me wrong. I swore what remained of the black organ shattered into thousands of pieces.

My mate was in *agony*, and there was nothing I could fucking do.

When Paco injected Z with more of the poison, she had fallen completely still. I'd worried she'd stopped breathing, but Paco had assured me she was still alive.

And then the screaming started. I could live a million years, and those anguished cries for help would haunt me every fucking night. I wanted to punch something, anything, but more than that, I wanted to cry.

She was nearly hysterical, words escaping her lips that I couldn't make out. I heard our names, though, while her tears wet her cheeks as she sobbed.

Another scream laced the night air, and Ryland, who

had awakened from his sedative a few minutes earlier, roared, punching at the wall the way I desperately desired to.

"Please! Make it stop! Please!" she begged, thrashing in Killian's arms. The incubus's face was perfectly blank, silent tears dripping down his cheeks. He had a deadened look in his eyes that would've made me worried in any other circumstance. But right then, I could only focus on my mate.

My screaming, terrified mate.

"How much longer is this going to take?" I barked at Paco, who'd pulled up a chair and clasped his hands together on his knobby knees.

"Soon," Paco answered, not peeling his gaze away from Z.

"We can't fucking do this!" Ryland bellowed, moving to stand directly in front of me and jabbing a finger into my chest. I'd never seen him so volatile or emotional before. His black hair stood in all directions as pure panic swirled in his blue eyes. "We can't kill her!"

"We don't have a choice!"

"You keep saying that—"

"Enough!" Dair didn't pull his gaze away from Z's hand intertwined with his. Tears flowed freely down his face as another scream wrenched itself free of Z's mouth. "Just..." He choked on his words. "Just stop fucking fighting."

I glared at Ryland, wanting to see if he'd back down or if I'd have to sedate of him again, but with one disgruntled curse, Ryland stalked away from me and used his shadows to hover in the air above Z.

The only other person in the room with us was Jax, though the vampire didn't spare Z a glance. He just... stared out the window. Just stared, his face utterly devoid of any emotion whatsoever. I wondered if this had finally broken him, finally shattered what little remained of his mind completely. Hearing Z's agonized screams was a lot for all of us to handle, but for him? I wasn't sure he'd ever come back from this.

I knew I couldn't.

When Z first started thrashing and crying, tiny whimpers escaping her, I'd tried to use my magic to take away the pain.

But the poison was made by sadistic fuckers, and nothing I did stopped the tortured moans. I could handle the crying, the whimpers, the thrashing. What I couldn't handle were the screams.

I was about to lose my goddamn mind and kill everyone in this room. Already, I could feel my powers sizzling through my body, sparking like green lightning.

"Z..." I crawled back towards her, ignoring Ryland's warning growl. Killian gently placed her head down, allowing me to take his place, and I didn't hesitate to cradle my mate's head in my lap. I stroked her golden hair away from her sweaty face, cataloguing every tightening of her features, every whimper, every flash of blue eyes before her lashes fluttered shut. I would make Aaliyah pay for this, even if it was the last thing I did.

I placed my forehead against hers and squeezed my eyes shut to hold my tears at bay. It didn't work, and more than a few landed on her skin.

"I'm so sorry, baby. I know it hurts. I know. I'm so

sorry." It felt as if someone had doused me in gasoline, lit a match, and then ran away while I burned. Everything was on fire, and I knew the burning sensation would only be rectified by my sweet mate's survival. If she died, I would turn to ash. "Did you know I had dreams about us?" I whispered, aware that my brothers were listening in and not giving a damn. "Visions of the future? I didn't understand them at first, but we were so happy in them, baby. So happy. I think that was why I pushed you away when we first met. I didn't want to love you the way I did in my vision because I felt like I didn't deserve it. I've done...a lot of horrible things. I hurt people. I used women for my pleasure and then discarded them like trash. I lied and stole and cheated. And I coveted...I coveted you, because I wanted you even when I knew I shouldn't. I love you, Z. I love you so damn much that I don't know what to do with all of these feelings."

I took a shuddering breath and lifted my forehead from Z's, my eyes fluttering open.

Z's blue gaze speared me in place as she shakily lifted a hand and brought it to my cheek. I desperately kissed her palm as my tears cascaded with wild abandon. I didn't even make a move to brush them away as I fell apart in her arms.

Her chest heaved a second before her hand fell from my face, whacking against the ground. Her eyes fluttered shut, and her pursed lips straightened out.

And then my sweet mate, the love of my existence, went still in death.

TWENTY-THREE

LUPE

What have I done?

I stared at my bloody hands as rage coiled inside of me like a ravenous beast thirsting for blood. My eyes drifted from my hands to the doorway, where I swore I could still see Z's shocked eyes staring back at me, piercing my soul.

I never wanted her to see me this way. Like I was a monster, a beast, a creature forged from pain and suffering.

But maybe that was what I was now. My father had made me a monster, but only Z held the reins to my beast.

As if in agreement, my bear roared inside of me, rocking backwards onto his legs and pawing at the air.

Was the figure I'd seen truly Z, watching me with confusion and a tiny bit of horror in her eyes? Or was it merely a hallucination? Was my subconscious telling me that I was traveling down a dark and dangerous path, one that would change everything? She needed to know that this wasn't me. I wasn't my father, and I wasn't prone to violence. I would never, *ever* hurt her.

There may have been blood on my hands, but it was only to save her life.

Still hanging suspended from the ceiling, the shadow king released a raspy laugh, the sound quickly turning into a cough.

"She sees the true you, Lupe," he hissed. "A monster, just like your father."

"Shut up," I told him, my entire body shaking like a dandelion. I was two hundred and fifty pounds of pure muscle, yet one look from Z was able to rip away all of my defenses and leave me broken and shaking like a scared little boy. I hadn't felt this out of sorts since I discovered my mother had died, murdered by humans from the same resistance I now wanted to help. The same resistance that the shadow king, Seth, was a part of.

"I'm not your enemy." I tried to convey to him with my eyes that he could trust me, that I was only playing a part, the same as him, but his expression simply darkened. The pure, venomous rage he harbored towards me was impossible to ignore.

"You say that...but I don't see anyone else stabbing knives into my skin," he seethed, and I visibly blanched.

Without responding, I dropped the knife I'd been holding and stormed out of the cell, taking deep, desperate lungfuls of air as soon as I was in the hallway. The candle at the far end of the wall danced, creating strange shadows on the gray cement.

I lowered my hands onto my knees and worked to regulate my breathing.

In and out.

In and out.

In and—

Pain took root in my gut, curling through my veins like flames. The sensation sent a dagger of fear into me as I gasped, blinking rapidly as I tried to understand the source of such pain. I placed a hand over my chest, rubbing at my skin, as agony bombarded me, shooting errant fireworks through my bloodstream.

What in the...?

A cord materialized in front of me, glimmering like it was crafted from the stars themselves, and I knew innately that on the other end of the cord would be my sweet mate. I watched with awe and a little trepidation as the cord began to vibrate erratically, jerking from side to side as if someone were tugging at it.

I gasped, clutching at my chest, as fear snared me.

No. No!

The cord snapped in two, the silver transforming into a hideous shade of brown. It continued to writhe on the floor, twitching in all directions, before it crumbled into a million pieces of dust.

No! No! No!

My bear roared inside of me in denial as I fell to my knees. Emotion coiled through my chest like barbed wire —agony, fear, anger... I couldn't decide on one.

Fur sprouted on my arms as I surrendered myself to the wrath always hovering just at the edges of my mind.

No! No! No!

I was aware of nothing else except the pain and agony. I screamed, the noise deafening in the silence of the prison, as I fell to my knees, my keen claws digging into the stone floors.

"Z!" I screamed until my voice was hoarse, until the candle toppled over and the walls began to shake. I screamed until my throat hurt fiercely and the tenuous control I had on my rage snapped as effortlessly as the mating bond had.

Then Lupe was no more, and only the wrath remained.

TWENTY-FOUR

DAIR

There was an empty hole where my heart should be.

I felt...numb. So, so numb. Every breath felt like being cut by thousands of minuscule daggers. They dragged at my skin, slashing until I was choking on my own blood.

Z...

I was dimly aware of screaming, but I couldn't focus on that. I couldn't focus on anything besides my mate's cold hand in my own. Her face was pale, too pale, and I yearned to see a flash of color in her cheeks.

The screaming grew louder, and this time, I could make out words.

"SAVE HER! FUCKING SAVE HER!"

The voice was familiar, but in my numb state of mind, I couldn't focus on who was shouting. Nothing mattered anymore.

My mate was dead, and there was nothing I could do about it.

I felt as if my soul had shriveled into dust the second the bond connecting us severed. The sensation was unlike anything I'd ever experienced, and I felt almost disembodied, as if I were watching the entire scene play out from above. Lurking, but not necessarily participating.

"SAVE HER! FUCKING DAMMIT!"

It was only then that I realized the screams were coming from me.

I ripped my gaze from Z to Paco, who was staring intently at the clock on the fireplace mantle, his lips pursed.

"FIX HER!" I raged, spit forming on the corner of my lips. "FIX HER!"

Bash was screaming at his grandfather as well, while Killian cried softly. For once, Jax's gaze wasn't fixed out the window but instead, was focused on the love of our lives. The reason we all got out of bed in the morning. I didn't see Ryland, but I heard him just outside the shed, his screams of anguish and rage permeating the still, night air.

"Paco needs patience!" the old mage retorted, still not moving his gaze away from the clock.

He had mentioned something about a time limit, right? Like he had to administer the cure within a certain time? Or was it the opposite? Did he have to administer the cure *after* a certain time?

My brain was utterly fried, and I struggled to fit together the pieces of this puzzle.

All I could think was...

This is the end.

I didn't want to live in a world without Z. The mere thought sent bile rushing up my throat. Maybe I'd drown myself in the sea in the most ironic way of death a mermaid could have.

Or maybe I'd—

"It's time," Paco told us, placing one hand on Z's jaw and forcing her head back. With his other hand, he pulled her lips apart so Bash could pour the second purple liquid into her mouth. Immediately, Paco placed his hand over her mouth, forcing her corpse to swallow the liquid, and I swore, not even the crickets outside were chirping. A deathly silence fell over the shed as we waited, waited, waited.

A shadow appeared above my shoulder, but I didn't peel my attention away from Z to greet Ryland. How could I, when my entire world could be ripped away from me in a matter of seconds?

"Why isn't she waking?" Bash demanded, the words a sharp growl that had the fine hairs on my arms standing on end.

Paco held up a hand. "Wait."

We waited.

And waited.

And waited.

The hope I'd felt before dissolved into smoke when Z remained still and lifeless. If anything, she appeared even paler than before, a stark contrast to the vibrant woman who'd fallen into my pool of water during the Damning weeks ago.

"Come on, baby. Get up. Get up. Get up," Bash whispered repeatedly.

We waited with bated breath. I could feel my heart physically spasming, clenching with fear and horror. All of our hopes depended on that one damn potion. What if Paco made it wrong? What if it did nothing to save her? What if she remained dead, a pasty corpse of the woman we all loved? What would we do?

Before my thoughts could send me into a downwards spiral, Z's fingers began to twitch in my hand. I held my breath, scarcely believing what I was seeing.

"Z..." I whispered.

And then the most beautiful thing occurred—her bright eyes snapped open, and she gasped, panting for breath.

TWENTY-FIVE

Z

My world was shrouded in nothing but fire. I couldn't even begin to describe the pain I experienced as death washed over me like an ice-cold tidal wave. I tried to fight it, tried to resist the current, but it was impossible. One second, I was staring up into Bash's dark green eyes, hooded with emotion, and the next...

I was nowhere.

I wouldn't have been able to tell you what, exactly, I experienced in that one minute I was dead, but I could've sworn I saw a familiar man and woman standing side by side, his arm wrapped around her waist.

My parents.

They beckoned me forward, identical grins on their faces, and I wanted nothing more than to run towards them and allow them to pull me into their arms. I missed them fiercely, and I knew the only cure for that would be holding them as tight as I could and never letting them go.

But then their images rippled and dispersed until I was once more floating in that abyss of darkness.

So much darkness.

But now...

I gasped, jerking upright and glancing from side to side desperately.

"What in the...?"

Five of my mates huddled around me, their eyes bright with tears and disbelief. I spotted Paco just above their shoulders, silently moving his naked ass away to give us some privacy.

"Z." Dair was the one who spoke first, and before I could even catch my breath, his lips were on mine. I froze, muscles tensing, before immediately wrapping my fingers in his golden-blond hair and deepening the kiss. His familiar sea scent barraged me, and I wanted nothing more than to lose myself in it. In him. Everything was always so easy with Dair. He was like a tranquil spring current that I didn't hesitate to swim in, secure in the knowledge that no harm would ever come to me.

I was pulled away from Dair before the kiss could get too heated and met Killian's greedy, searching lips. I teased him with my tongue, and he opened for me immediately, wrapping his arms around my waist and holding me to him.

"I thought I lost you," he whispered between pants of breath.

"I thought you did too," I admitted, unable to shake off the unease of being in that strange darkness. It'd been so tempting to stay there, to surrender to the inevitable.

There would've been no wars or armies, no malicious kings or sadistic bitches. And...

And I would've been reunited with my parents. S. Even A, my adoptive father.

Thoughts of my mates kept me from succumbing completely. I knew if the situations were reversed, if one of them had died, I would've lost my damn mind.

So I fought, kicking and screaming, until my soul snapped back into my body like a rubber band that had been pulled too tautly. At least, that was what it had felt like. One second, there was complete and utter darkness, a bottle of spilt ink I was wading through, and the next, there was light.

Ryland and Jax both took their turns kissing me passionately, the latter shaking in my arms as he murmured my name repeatedly, peppering kisses across my face.

"I love you, Jaxon," I whispered in his ear, too soft for anyone but him to hear. He shuddered in my arms, a delicate ripple I felt in my own body, as his arms constricted tighter around me.

"I love you too. More than anything."

It was only then that I realized we were missing one person.

My eyes narrowed as I searched the small hut for Bash, unable to see his ash-blond hair anywhere.

I turned towards Ryland, who was on the other side of me, and cocked an eyebrow. "Where is he?"

Ryland's lips pursed as he smoothed his hands through my sweaty hair. "Outside," he confessed, and pain rushed through me, though my rage quickly tempered it. Why would he leave me after everything that just happened? After I just fucking *died*? After what he told me? Did he regret those three words? "But you should get some rest—"

"I want to see if he's okay," I interjected, stumbling to my feet. Ryland immediately caught my elbow to keep me from toppling over, his face scrunched together in rage.

"My god, woman, you nearly died!" he bellowed, his tongue caustic and acidic. Despite his cruel tone, there was near panic in his icy blue eyes. This entire situation had shaken him, shaken *all* of them, and I didn't know if they'd ever recover from it completely. I knew I wouldn't if I'd been forced to watch one of them die.

The mere thought had bile rushing up my throat.

"Ry..." I gently took his hand in my own. My whole body felt sluggish and heavy, as if the entire force of Earth's gravity was pushing down on me. Despite that, there was a skip to my heart that hadn't been there prior. I may have been tired, but I no longer ached fiercely like I'd been run over by a truck. "I'm okay." I turned towards Paco and repeated, "I'm okay, right?"

"Paco does not sense any more poison in little girl," Paco exclaimed with a toothy grin. I bit down on my lip to stop myself from arguing about the "little girl" comment. The man had saved my life, and he deserved my complete and utter respect.

Or at the very least, a day free of retorts.

"She's cured?" Killian breathed, almost as if he scarcely dared to believe it.

"Cured, yes." Paco nodded his head, and the relief that spread through the room was almost palpable.

His words set off another round of kisses and declarations of love as each of my men sought to hold me, touch me, love me. I allowed them to, relishing in their embrace, before remembering my sulking mage. I needed to know what his problem was, even though an insidious sort of fear slithered through my mind and grasped my heart. I didn't know if I could handle it if he rejected me.

But what other reason would he have to leave?

"Go to him." The order, unsurprisingly, came from Dair. My sweet mermaid always seemed to know when my other men needed me. The blond prince pulled my attention away from Jax and gave my hand a reassuring squeeze. Warmth migrated from where our hands touched, settling in my chest. "He needs you right now."

"We all need her," Ryland murmured, but he didn't protest as I moved on wobbly legs to the backdoor of the hut, pushing it open and stretching my taut muscles. I still felt sore, uncomfortable, but nowhere near the level I'd been at when I was dying from the poison.

Because I was...cured.

Cured.

A giddy laugh wanted to escape me at that one word. I always thought I'd die before my time. As an assassin, you came to learn that death was inevitable. But honestly? It didn't scare me. At least not at first. It was only after I met my mates that I came to the realization that I *wanted* to live. Now, instead of fighting to die, I fought to survive. When I discovered Zack had poisoned me, I kept it quiet, believing it was my burden to bear alone, my torture to endure. I'd assumed I would die from it, but here I was, alive and well and loved by seven incredible men.

Heat radiated through my body accompanied by a kaleidoscope of emotions. They created a beautiful tapestry of color in my mind's eye, and I leaned into it like a flower twisting towards the sun.

Movement to the left startled me, and I shoved the plethora of emotions aside to focus on my mage mate.

Bash was pacing, tugging repeatedly at his blond hair, and seemed unaware of my presence. In the moonlight streaking through the boughs of trees, his eyes appeared lighter, almost like emeralds, and glimmered.

"Thank you," I whispered, and his head snapped in my direction.

"Z." My name was a prayer on his lips, though his tone held a healthy amount of trepidation. His entire body shook as his arms raised, reaching for me...before immediately dropping back to his sides. "I'm so fucking relieved to see you're okay."

"Because of you." I ventured a tentative step closer, watching his face carefully. Everything about Bash was chiseled, masculine perfection, from the sweep of his eyebrows to the curve of his jaw. While he was usually clean-shaven, the last few days had seen blond stubble on his chin, giving him a rugged look.

I found it sexy as hell.

When Bash turned his gaze away from me, focusing on a branch sprouting off the nearest tree, I took the final steps forward until I was directly in front of him. "I know you helped Paco with the cure."

"You died, Z." His voice shook. "I held you while you fucking died."

"I know. I was there." I tried for a joke, but it fell flat. There was nothing but despair and heartbreak in his green gaze. Agony reverberated from him in waves that almost felt tangible, as if I could reach out and grasp his pain in my fist.

"I can't...I can't lose you." He finally turned to face me completely, his features shadowed, and I carefully clasped his hands in my own.

"You won't. I promise you, Sebastian. I will fight to remain with you and the others until I'm incapable of fighting anymore." His eyebrows furrowed at my use of his full name, but he didn't comment. Instead, he simply stared at me, a myriad of emotion glimmering to life behind eyes I always thought were impassive and incapable of love, but now I realized they were teeming with life and passion. "You can't get rid of me. I suppose you can say that you're stuck with me."

"Like mold," he deadpanned, a tiny twinkle appearing in his eyes. My own lips twitched into the beginnings of a smile. I much preferred this verbal sparring version of Bash over the somber one.

"You're an ass," I quipped.

"And you're the pain in it," he responded without pause.

We stared at each other for a long moment, the only light in the forest the golden glow from the moon high above. The tension between us crackled and hissed like a live wire, adding to the foray of fireworks and lighting already coursing through my body.

"I…" Swallowing, I began again. "I heard what you said."

His expression didn't change, not even a twitch, as he blinked at me. "Oh."

"You said that…you loved me." I kept my voice low and soft, staring up at his handsome face with hearts in my eyes. For what felt like the first time in my life, I didn't hide my emotions. I wore them for everyone to see, for him to see, and he could either tenderly cup my heart or crush it. Either way, the choice was his. Vulnerability shot through me as I shuffled from foot to foot, finally forcing my gaze away and lowering it to the ground. The intensity in his mossy green eyes was too much for me to handle. "Do you… I mean…did you mean that?"

"Did I mean it when I said that I loved you?" Bash asked for clarification. There was no teasing in his tone. His voice was uncharacteristically serene. Solemn, even. One glance beneath my lashes showed a grave expression on his face as he regarded me.

My heart stuttered.

"You don't have to…um…"

"I hate that you even have to ask me that," he gritted out, shoving a hand through his hair almost distractedly. "I know I don't do a good job of showing you—or anyone else for that matter—how I feel, but I thought it was obvi-ous." He reached for my arms and pulled me against his strong chest, so close, I could feel his heart beneath my palm. The *thump-thump-thump* was slightly erratic, as if he was as worried about this conversation as I was. "Of course I love you. How could I not? You're everything I always wanted and everything I never thought I deserved. I may not have a lot to offer you, I'm lazy and cruel and sarcastic as fuck, but everything I am is yours... if you'll have me."

Now, he was the one staring at me with stark vulnerability in his gaze. Color darkened his cheekbones as he held my stare, his thumbs smoothing circles over the skin of my waist where my shirt had risen up.

"Of course I love you, Bash-hole." I brought my hands around his neck and fingered the soft hair at the nape of his neck. "Now shut up and kiss me."

He obliged.

His kiss was different than all of the others. I didn't want to say gentler, because in no way did that word ever describe Sebastian Mage, but there was a tenderness and reverence in each press of his lips that I hadn't experienced in a long time.

He *worshipped* my mouth, and it was like our hearts merged, twin balls of light becoming one being. All of the angst and yearning and anger...they all translated to this one moment, where I felt as if I could touch his very soul through the force of my kiss.

One of his hands moved to my right breast, kneading the tender flesh, while the other cupped my ass, pulling me flush against him. His hard cock dug into my belly, and when I finally broke the kiss, he was breathing just as hard as me.

I moved my hands from his neck to his chest, unbuttoning his shirt as I went. His green orbs locked on me, he slid it over his shoulders, unveiling his muscular chest to my greedy eyes.

"You don't know how long I've wanted this," he whispered as I took a step away from him. My eyes lapped up all of the smooth, pale skin on display before dipping down to that delectable trail of blond hair. I wanted to take even more of his clothes off, unwrapping him like a present at Christmas.

"Then show me," I breathed. And then, because I couldn't help myself, I added, "Unless you're scared. Are you scared, Bash-hole?"

Wicked heat entered his eyes as he claimed my lips once more, his tongue prodding at the seam of my lips until I opened for him. Each slash of his mouth against my own sent fire through my veins.

I tried to reach out to him, tried to touch the smooth skin of his chest and shoulders, but discovered that I wasn't able to.

I pulled my mouth away from his. "What the...?" Lowering my gaze, I found my hands clasped in front of me, a single tendril of green magic keeping them immobile.

That fucker had placed a spell on me!

"Are you scared, baby?" Bash taunted as his hands moved to my breasts, twisting my nipples through the fabric of my shirt and bra.

I moaned in answer, and with another naughty grin, he flicked his fingers, and suddenly, my clothes were on the ground beside him, leaving me completely bare to his viewing pleasure.

"This doesn't seem fair," I rasped, my naked chest heaving.

His eyes darkened, turning molten in the copious

moonlight. "You nearly died, Z. I need to...I need to feel you. I need to know that you're here, that you're okay."

If my hands weren't bound together, I would've placed my palm on his cheek. Instead, I stared at him, hoping he could read the earnestness in my gaze.

"I'm here, Bash. I'm okay."

The magic holding me hostage faded, and I used the opportunity to run my hand down Bash's smooth chest before he could change his mind. His shoulders weren't as broad as Dair's, nor were his abs as pronounced as Killian's, but Bash was a work of art all on his own. I desperately wanted to memorize every dip of his impressive six-pack and the cock I'd only seen once before.

Back then, it'd been limp and flaccid. He'd been unable to get it up after coming into contact with me. But now...

Now it dug into my bare stomach, straining against the confines of his jeans.

He rested his hand just below my breast, his thumb brushing the underside, as he kissed me once more, our bodies molding together.

"You're so beautiful, Z," he whispered against my lips as he plucked my nipple. When he began to trail kisses down my neck, I stopped him.

Confusion, and a tiny bit of hurt, appeared in his eyes, though he quickly tried to mask it.

"If I'm moving too fast..."

I dropped to my knees without preamble and unbuttoned his pants, gripping his hard cock and stroking him from base to tip.

"You want to know I'm okay, right? You want to know I'm still alive?" I breathed on his cock, causing it to jerk.

"Z, you don't have to—Oh fuck!" His hands moved to the back of my head, not yet pulling at my hair, as I licked the underside of his cock like a lollipop. Grinning up at him through my fringe of lashes, I took him deep in my mouth, maintaining eye contact the entire time.

When I released him, I didn't give him a moment of reprieve, instead circling my tongue along the tip and then licking the length of his dick once more.

"Fuck, Z." He tried to hold himself still, tried to remain calm, but I could see him falling apart in my arms. His abs tensed beneath my hand as I brought my lips around his throbbing member once more.

It occurred to me that we were only a few yards away from hundreds of humans who could listen in.

But I didn't care.

Let them hear. Let them see. The world needed to know that these men were mine and I was theirs.

"Baby," he growled as I trailed my hand up his chest, resting it just above his heart. He placed his hand over mine, holding it hostage, as I removed his cock from my mouth and began to kiss along the side. I realized quickly that Bash loved it when I traced the vein along the length of his cock with the pad of my tongue, his eyes dilating before turning half-mast with pleasure.

"You like that?" I teased, doing it again.

"You're playing a dangerous fucking game."

Before I could retort, his magic coiled around my body, forcing me to my feet. He wrapped his hands around my neck and smashed his lips to mine. I reached between our bodies to stroke his cock, determined more than ever to keep the upper hand.

Something soft brushed against my clit, and I gasped.

"What the fuck?" I wheezed.

Both of Bash's hands were around my throat, so where did that—

The mysterious presence dipped between my slick folds and began to make a circular rotation that had my knees buckling.

Bash simply smirked at me—that cocky as fuck smirk I wanted to both punch off his face and kiss senseless.

"Your magic," I breathed as something plucked my clit.

"We're lazy sons of bitches, baby." He paused, dropping his gaze to where my hand was wrapped around his cock. A second later, sensations flooded me as both of my nipples were twisted, my clit was played with, a finger speared my tight channel, and someone brushed the curve of my ass.

"Motherfucker."

"But we're almost as good at sex as incubi," he finished, nipping at my ear.

He released me, twisting me so I was gripping the trunk of the nearest tree, my ass sticking out.

He kissed first one shoulder and then the next before sliding kisses down my back. When he reached my ass, he nipped at the skin there before soothing it away with the pad of his tongue.

I groaned, removing one hand from the tree to squeeze my own breasts, as one of his fingers breached the tight ring of muscles of my ass.

"Do you like this, baby?" he purred, and I mumbled something inarticulate, lost in the heady haze of pleasure. "Then why don't you spread yourself for me."

My hands moved of their own accord, captured by his magic, to spread my ass cheeks apart.

"Bash..." I whimpered, my body shaking with need and lust.

"Is this okay, baby?" I couldn't see him, but his voice sounded lower, as if he'd dropped to his knees behind me.

"Yes. God, yes. Please, Bash."

I didn't even know what I was pleading for, but my mage mate obliged, licking the tight hole while I went mindless with pleasure. His other hand crept inside of my pussy, circling my clit, and it wasn't long before my orgasm hit me like a freight train.

"Fuck, yes! Bash! Oh my god!" I praised as I shook and shuddered. I would've fallen if Bash's magic hadn't banded around my chest, keeping me upright. "I need you."

"What do you need, baby?" I could hear the amusement in his voice as he kissed up my spine, stopping at the shell of my ear. "Say it."

"I need your cock!" I all but begged.

"It's yours, baby. It's always been yours. Just like I am." I could feel the head of his large dick lining up with my pussy, but before he could enter me, I shook my head.

"Other hole," I whispered.

He froze, and I desperately wished I could see his expression.

The growl he released was low and primitive, causing goosebumps to ripple up my arms.

He lined up his cock up with my back entrance but didn't immediately enter me. His hand tenderly traveled up and down my spine as he kissed my neck repeatedly.

"Are you sure?"

"Yes, Bash," I whispered, arching into him.

"I'm gonna go nice and...slow." He grunted out the final word as he entered me. My mouth dropped open, eyes widening at the uncomfortable intrusion.

"Fucking hell," I groaned as he gripped my waist to steady me. With his other hand, he pressed down on the small of my back until I was at a ninety-degree angle. This new position pushed his cock even deeper inside of me, and I gasped at the unfamiliar, but not unwanted, sensation.

He began to slide in and out of me, his hands touching everywhere they could reach. My ass, my back, my bouncing breasts. His lips moved from my neck to my cheek, before eventually finding my lips and claiming them in a searing kiss. I twisted my head to deepen the kiss as he fucked me relentlessly.

Something began to rub at my clit, creating circular patterns, and I glanced down to see a finger of green magic spearing my channel.

"Yes! Yes! Yes!" I praised as his hand reached around our bodies to cup my dangling tit. His magic pressed down on my clit at the same time he jerked inside my ass, his balls slapping against my skin, and my orgasm hit me like a freight train, stealing my breath away.

All of my muscles clenched and tightened, and I knew the second they did so around Bash's cock. He pulled out of me just before he exploded with a roar, his cum squirting against my back and painting me in a way that asserted ownership. Possession.

I fucking loved it.

We both took a long moment to catch our breaths. My head was still lowered, one hand resting against the bark of the tree, and Bash was practically draped over my back, his sweat soaked chest brushing deliciously against my skin.

"I love you," he whispered, kissing my ear. He paused before adding, "Even when you annoy the shit out of me."

"I love you too," I responded breathily. Pausing as well, I jokingly retorted with, "Even when you *think* I'm annoying the shit out of you."

"Naughty girl. Do you really think that—"

Someone cleared his throat, and Bash was immediately in front of me, shielding my nudity from any wayward eyes. He relaxed, though, when he noticed Dair standing in front of us.

The tent in my mermaid's pants was impossible to miss, and his eyes smoldered with lust. I was just about to ask him if he wanted to join us—I got a second chance at life after all. Why not make the most of it?—when he shook his head vehemently, seemingly in response to one of his own thoughts, and nodded towards our discarded clothes.

"Get dressed," he instructed. Bash and I exchanged a wary look but worked to do as he said.

"Why?" I questioned, and when Bash gave me a *you're an idiot* look, I whacked him in the arm and elaborated. "I mean, I obviously know not to walk around all of these humans naked, but why do we have to end our fun times right now?"

"Awww you're pouting, baby," Bash said with a cocky as fuck grin. "Do you want more of my big cock?"

"It means you didn't satisfy her enough the first time," Dair quipped. And the look Bash threw him? Acid. Complete acid.

"Ha. Ha. Ha. Very funny." I rolled my eyes at their immature banter and finished pulling on my clothes. "But seriously, what's up?"

"We need to discuss what's going to happen next," Dair confessed, glancing in the direction of the shed. "Come on."

Z

We followed Dair back inside the hut, where Paco, Ryland, Jax, and Killian had been joined by Axel, Toby, and Natalia.

"Looking good, little sister!" Axel called as soon as he caught sight of me. His mischievous eyes flicked to my sex tousled hair before drifting to Bash, his shirt haphazardly buttoned and half tucked into his pants. "Got some good deep dicking?"

"For fuck's sake..." I murmured, moving to stand beside my men.

Jax immediately wrapped his arms around my waist and burrowed his nose in my hair, inhaling deeply. Axel, Natalia, and Toby all gave him strange looks, but I didn't pull away from my vampire mate. Instead, I stroked his silky brown hair, offering him the comfort I knew he so desperately needed.

Only a few minutes ago, it was Bash who needed the reaffirmation that I was alive and well. Now, it was Jax. I was determined to give it to him, regardless of the curious looks from the others.

I noted, somewhat sadly, that Natalia looked absolutely wrecked. Her face was a vision of grief and barely suppressed anger, her lower lip wobbling despite her eyes being dry. Toby wasn't much better, though he put on a brave face as he hugged his girlfriend closer to his side.

"We're glad to see that you're better," Toby told me with a respectful nod. "Is it true that Paco cured you from the...poison?" He glanced at Axel for confirmation, almost as if he didn't truly believe that mere hours ago, I'd been inches from death. Hell, I'd faced death, fought it off, and emerged victorious.

"I'm better now," I assured them all, turning my sympathetic eyes in Natalia's direction. "And the brothel?"

"Destroyed." Her voice was weak and raspy, but the defiant glint in her eyes made my respect for her grow. "Burned to ash."

"And the mages inside of the building?" Ryland inquired, and Natalia blanched, her face draining of all color. She shifted even closer to Toby, and he gave her a reassuring squeeze.

Not meeting the shadow's questioning gaze, Natalia muttered, "Dead."

"We have all the liberated humans with us now," Toby explained, and I couldn't help but glance in Paco's direction, wondering how the eccentric mage felt about his home being turned into a camp for rebellious humans.

But if he was concerned or even remotely upset, he didn't show it as he hummed beneath his breath, grabbing a bristled broom from where it was perched against the wall and sweeping at the floors.

"I'm glad we were able to save them." I took a hesitant step towards Natalia but then thought better of it. Maintaining my distance, I held her gaze and bowed my head slightly. "I'm sorry for your loss."

"We're all going to lose people in this war, Liberator," Natalia told me, her face still ashen beneath her mane of orange hair. "But if we can't bounce back from the amount of death and carnage we're destined to experience, there's no chance in hell that we'll win. That's the difference between us and *them*." Her pretty face twisted in disgust, and she spat on the ground. "They don't care about anyone. They don't grieve people the same way we do."

"That's not true." Dair's voice was soft but acerbic. I almost wanted to describe it as bitter. His sea-blue eyes, the exact color of a sunlit ocean, peered back at her before turning to me and softening. "Not all nightmares are the same. We grieve, just like you do. We fear death."

Why did his gaze burn a hole inside of my chest? It reminded me of a candle being lit up and infiltrating all of the shadows that crowded my heart and soul. There was something so calming and serene about his piercing gaze, something that made warmth explode inside of me.

Natalia opened her mouth as if to protest, but Toby quickly clamped his hand down on her shoulder to stop her. She pursed her lips but chose not to comment again.

"We need to get to the capital," I interjected, glancing at all of my mates. "Now that I'm healed, I need to return to the kings."

"Why would you go back to them?" Natalia demanded, seemingly unable to hold her tongue. A perplexed expression knitted her brows together over eyes that dripped with disdain.

I cast her a level gaze. "Because I don't have a choice."

Either I traveled back to the capital to receive my next task...or I died. Those were the only choices I had with that damn spell placed on me.

"What do we do about...all of that?" Killian gesticulated towards the front door of the shed, where we all knew there were hundreds of humans gathered in tents just outside.

"Paco says they can stay." Paco rested the broom against his erect cock and leaned against the far wall, crossing his arms over his chest. "Paco won't help, but Paco won't send away."

"What...?" Toby's eyebrows arched as Bash sighed, pinching the bridge of his nose.

"What Paco means is that he won't involve himself in this war...on either side. You guys can stay, but he won't aid our cause. But at the same time, he won't help the kings either," Bash translated, still giving his grandfather narrow-eyed looks.

"And you trust him?" I inquired, arching my neck ever so slightly so Jax could continue peppering kisses on the skin there. Toby glanced in our direction, blushed beet-red, and quickly looked away, seemingly uncomfortable with our public display of affection. Honestly, I would've been the exact same way less than a month ago.

It was amazing how death could change a girl.

"We can," Bash said, finally peeling his attention away from the crazy old man. His gaze landed on me, and heat flared to life in his eyes. I couldn't help but remember our...activities from only a few minutes ago, the way he brought us both to completion with both his body and magic. My stomach muscles tightened, lust percolating in my stomach, and if there weren't a bunch of virtual strangers in the shed with us, I would demand that all five of my mates participate in a toe-curling orgy right then and there. But alas, I had to be a mature adult. And mature adults didn't initiate spontaneous orgies on the dirty floors of their mate's grandfather's house.

Shame.

"We'll look after the humans here," Toby told me, gesturing between him and Natalia. "Train them."

"I never asked for an army, guys," I whispered. I felt oddly...flustered, and not in a good way. There was too much responsibility and pressure weighing on my shoulders, pushing me into the ground. I was suffocating under the weight of it all.

"You didn't need to ask for one," Natalia said with a huff, sticking her nose in the air. "They follow you because they believe in you. They're yours, whether you want them or not."

And maybe that was the problem. They saw me as a savior, a liberator, but I was nothing but a scared human girl who fell in love with the monsters under her bed. I didn't even know if I could save myself, let alone an entire species.

"I'll head back with you guys," Axel told us, a frown

pulling at his lips. Turning towards Toby and Natalia, he asked, "And will you—"

"We'll protect Mary-Lynette with our lives," Toby vowed, and something flashed in his eyes, something I couldn't quite put into words. "I know how special that kid is."

I felt my eyebrows climb up my forehead at those cryptic words, and from Natalia's flabbergasted expression, I realized she was just as in the dark as I was.

"What—?" I turned towards Axel, but he immediately shook his head.

"Not now."

"We need to leave, Z," Bash murmured, coming to stand on the other side of me, opposite Jax. He placed his hand on the small of my back and began to lead me towards the door. "We won't make it back to the capital in time if we don't."

I nodded in agreement. "You're right."

"Don't worry about a thing here, Z." Toby flashed me a smile, though it did very little to chase away the chill that had crept up my spine. "Everything will be okay." He began to move towards the door as well, pausing with his hand on the knob to give me one last glance over his shoulder. "By the way, B sends his regards." He winked at me, even as the chill transformed into pure ice. My entire body went numb at the name of my adopted uncle and the leader of the Alphabet Resistance.

"Wait—" Before I could demand answers, demand to know how Toby knew B and where the old man currently was, Toby slipped out of the door, Natalia right on his heels.

Silence descended as we all gaped after the pair, varying expressions of distrust and disbelief in my mates' eyes. Only Paco and Axel appeared unconcerned. The old man now had both hands wrapped around the base of his cock with the handle of the broom tied to the tip. He moved his cock back and forth, forcing the broom to move with it. I was gonna need to bleach my eyes after that sight.

He saved your life, Z. Remember that.

"Welp." Axel rocked back on his heels and blew out a raspberry. When he noticed me looking, he flashed a large smile and wink. "I love plot twists."

"That's not a fucking plot twist," I murmured, facepalming myself.

"No," Axel agreed easily, still flashing that disarming, slightly manic grin. "But I have a feeling that it might end up being one." He easily reached behind him for one of his machetes and twirled it expertly between his hands, whistling. "Let's go, boys and girls. We have a capital to visit, kings to see, and blood to spill. Basically, it's a normal Tuesday evening for me."

TWENTY-SEVEN

Z

We arrived with less than one hour to spare.

When we burst through the doors of the capital, I was panting for breath, my stomach a tumultuous mixture of dread and anxiety and my heart seconds from breaking free of the confines of my chest. I gripped Jax's hand tightly as I moved in the direction of the throne room.

I had to show the kings I'd completed the task, that I saved Jax, before the hour was up. If I didn't...

I'd already faced death once today. I refused to give the Grim Reaper another premature visit.

As my short legs ate up the distance between the throne room and me, a thought occurred to me, and I whipped my head in Dair's direction.

My mermaid prince was once more in his wheelchair, a fact that exacerbated his rage and annoyance. His eyes were tight with strain, and the gentle smile I'd come to love was nowhere to be seen. The spell had worn off while we were in the car on the way here, and Dair hadn't found it necessary to drink more of that strange liquid. As he'd told us, his voice laced with bitterness, his father would just find a way to get him alone and remove his legs once more.

That filthy fucker. When I got him alone—

That thought cut off abruptly, the spell on me prohibiting me from even thinking about inflicting harm on the kings. Dammit. Though...

Though before, I couldn't even think the words 'filthy fucker' without the thought cutting off. I had no idea what that meant, but I didn't dare look at it too closely.

"Dair," I said, addressing my mermaid prince. "Can you find Devlin and Lupe?"

A vague image bombarded me—Lupe in what appeared to be a prison cell...

The thought dissipated before I could grab on to it.

I needed to see my genie and shifter mates more than anything else. I wanted to feel their strong arms around me and bask in their love. The separation...it had been unbearable. Painful, even. I couldn't imagine how it felt from their end, not knowing what had happened with the poison.

At the same time, I wanted Dair as far away from the throne room—and his father—as possible.

"Of course." I leaned down to give Dair a tender kiss before he rolled in the opposite direction, towards the bedrooms. I hoped that he found my lovers and brought them to me. Then I'd show them just how much I missed them.

My body heated thinking of my last sexy times with

both men. Dominating Devlin in bed. Shower fun with Lupe.

Liquid heat pulsed in my core, but I pushed the lustful thoughts away, focusing on the matter at hand.

And to be quite honest, facing the kings was a sure-fire way to kill any lady boner I might've had.

We passed a guard, who instructed us to wait just outside the throne room while he gathered the kings. I could tell my mates were tense, though no one said a word as we waited impatiently. Killian repeatedly scratched at the nape of his neck before running his fingers through his dark red hair. Jax gripped my hand like it was his life preserver and he was adrift at sea, desperate to stay afloat amidst the roiling waves. Bash just stared stonily ahead, his green eyes flashing with his power and his hands curling into fists. And Ryland...he just paced, the shadows tightening around his body in agitation with every passing moment. One second, I could see his beautifully scarred face, and the next, it was completely hidden from view. Of the three of them, I knew he was the most protective of me, so it must've been killing him not to know what the kings had planned.

After only a few minutes, the same guard from before returned, gesturing us through the heavy oak doors.

The moment my foot stepped over the threshold, something sparked to life and then fizzled away inside of my chest. I recognized it as the mage king's spell that tied my life force to the time limit imposed on me by the vampire king. I gasped, rubbing at my heart, and relief washed over Bash's face.

"The spell's gone?" he whispered as we approached the thrones.

"Yes," I replied, though I didn't peel my gaze away from the seven thrones near the far back wall of the room.

I couldn't help but note that the shadow king's throne was empty, and if the tightening in Ryland's face was any indication, he noticed that as well. Neither of us commented, though, as we approached the raised dais and my body automatically lowered into a curtsy.

"Your Majesties," I said with a respect and reverence I didn't feel. Damn the spell.

"You returned!" the shifter king exclaimed, raising his hands in the air like he meant to embrace me before lowering them and guffawing loudly. A shudder rolled through my body at the noise, though I kept my face indifferent.

"And I brought Jax." I turned towards the vampire king, who reclined lazily in his throne, his mouth bright red with blood. He barely spared his son a glance, his eyes intent on me.

"So you did."

Silence descended as I struggled to find the words to say. I knew that the next king would be assigning me a task I needed to complete in order to "prove my loyalty," but I had no idea what that task would be. Would they make me kill an innocent human? Track down the Alphabet Resistance? Something else?

My stomach muscles twisted and tightened, slithering together like a ball of yarn I could never hope to unravel. I tried not to let my unease show on my face as I met each of their eyes, stopping on the shifter king. No one ever said it out loud, but it was obvious to me who wore the pants in this relationship. What the shifter king said, went. No ifs, ands, or buts. If he wanted to set the world on fire, the other kings would eagerly do his bidding with smiles on their faces.

"You've been such a good little assassin, Z. You deserve a reward." The shifter king's smile broadened, revealing two rows of perfectly white teeth. When he smiled like that, I truly *could* see the resemblance between this man and his son. The only difference was their eyes—Lupe's blue orbs radiated passion and love, warmth and kindness. The shadow king's? His were empty voids. It made me wonder if the asshole even had a soul beneath that prickly exterior.

"Reward," Bash repeated in a dry tone, glaring at his father, the mage king. Of course, the mage king was asleep, his head lolling against his shoulder and a steady stream of snores leaving his mouth. Lazy asshole.

"Of course! We're not complete monsters," the mermaid king interjected with a wicked grin, and I was suddenly grateful I'd sent Dair away. That smile...it thirsted for blood. Blood, death, and pain.

"Z, I'm sorry," Axel whispered from beside me, his voice low enough that I doubted anyone but me heard it.

Before I could question him about his cryptic comment, the shifter king gestured the ex-assassin forward with a simple quirk of his finger. Axel obediently moved to stand directly beside the shifter king's throne, his hands clasped behind his back and his face a picture of respect. He looked like a soldier—though not a soldier for my army.

He looked like...the enemy.

Like one of *them.*

"But this is also a reward for our old friend, Axel," the shifter king commented, grinning up at the stoic assassin. "We promised him a reward for helping us with you."

"Helping you with...me?" I repeated dumbly, and Ryland hissed out a breath from beside me.

Axel kept his gaze fixed on something over my shoulder, not meeting any of our gazes as the kings laughed, the sound sharp and taunting. It resembled swords clashing together, sparking with electricity.

I knew that any second, a bomb would drop and detonate, killing us all.

Any.

Damn.

Second.

"If he agreed to help us keep an eye on you, we offered him your hand in marriage," the incubus king explained with a salacious grin, giving me a suggestive once-over. His eyes burned with lust, white-hot and searing.

"What the fuck?" Bash roared, but he was silenced by a wave of the shifter king's hand.

"Z will be married to Axel by the end of this week," he exclaimed with a wide grin. But that grin wasn't aimed at me...it was aimed at the princes.

I realized then that this had never been about me. Not really. Maybe at first it had been, but when news of my mating with the princes reached the kings' ears, they knew they'd finally found leverage over their rebellious sons. Me. This was just another twisted game they were playing, but this time, the prize was my life.

"No fucking way!" Ryland seethed. "Where's my father? He would never allow this."

The kings laughed again, the sound cold and deadly, but didn't respond to the shadow prince.

"D-d-dad," Killian stuttered out, turning towards his father. "Please."

The incubus king's lips peeled away from his teeth in what might've been a sexy smile if it had actually reached his eyes. They remained as cold as ice, not a speck of warmth to be seen.

"By the end of this week, Z will be married to Axel." He propped his chin on his palm and smirked. Rage and disgust burned in my chest, even as a dagger of fear cut me open. How the fuck could Axel do this to me? To us? "And like any wedding, we'll end it with the two of them consummating their marriage."

The kings laughed once more as my rage boiled over, scalding me.

Fuck. Fuck.

Fuck.

The kings just declared checkmate, and our only options were to finish the game...

Or flip the entire table over to start a new one.

I cast a glare at Axel so full of betrayal and rage that he physically flinched, immediately peeling his gaze away from me. I was distantly aware of Bash, Ryland, Killian, and even Jax arguing with the kings, much to the assholes' amusement. But I kept my face perfectly placid, not a flicker of emotion seeping into my hardened gaze.

If the kings wanted a game, they got one.

I would fucking destroy them this time around.

"Perfect." My saccharine sweet voice interrupted the cacophony of noise as all eyes turned towards me. I smiled broadly as I directed my next question at the confused kings. "When can I pick out my wedding dress?"

DAIR

"Devlin? Lupe?" I ducked my head into Lupe's bedroom, fighting off my irritation. His bed was made, a few books sitting on his bedside table, but the lumbering shifter was nowhere to be seen. Frowning, I softly shut the door and wheeled myself down the hall to Devlin's room.

Unlike Lupe's, Devlin's bedroom looked as if it had been plucked straight from a home décor catalogue. It was as immaculate as always, not a piece of clothing out of place and the comforter on the bed smoothed to utter perfection. In the opened closet, I could see Devlin's pressed suits meticulously ironed, not a wrinkle in sight.

Shaking my head in amusement, I shut Devlin's door and checked every bathroom.

Nothing.

My amusement dissolved as true fear replaced it, weighing down my heart.

"Dev! Lupe!" I hurried from room to room, checking

each and every one, including the closets, until one fact became clear—my brothers were no longer in the capital.

My arms ached from the effort I was exuding, and I eventually paused outside my own bedroom, shaking out my fingers. I hated this damn chair more than I hated anything else in my life.

And what I hated even more was the freedom that was dangled enticingly in front of my face like a tasty morsel and then brutally wrenched away. The last few hours, I'd been...free. I hadn't been confined to this prison of a wheelchair, but instead, was capable of venturing on my own two feet. For a man who'd spent the majority of his adult life stuck in this chair, it was a heady, intoxicating sensation, one a person could become addicted to. Maybe that was the aspect of Z that had first captured my attention, before I knew we were mates—the freedom she exhibited. She didn't believe in silly things like fate or destiny, despite it being shoved in her face. Fate was a wind blowing from all directions, never capturing Z because she didn't stay still long enough to let it.

She was, for a lack of better word, free, as I'd always yearned to be.

Shaking my head, I forced myself to roll farther down the hall until I reached the very end.

Were Devlin and Lupe in the throne room with our parents? That would make sense, I supposed, if they wanted to keep an eye on Z.

Despite my resolve strengthening, something didn't feel right. It pricked at my skin repeatedly like thousands of rusty nails. That uncomfortable sensation slid through my veins like poison.

"Prince Dair!" a raspy voice called from behind me, and I swiveled my head over my shoulder to see none other than old Mrs. Grinshaw hurrying towards me, her customary apron firmly in place and her gray hair twisted away from her face.

"Mrs. Grinshaw," I greeted, eyeing her warily. "How are you?"

She released a tired sigh when she finally caught up to me, her wrinkled face creasing with pain.

"The best I can be, considering..." She trailed off and very slowly shook her head from side to side. A strand of white escaped its binding and bounced against her cheek.

"Considering?" Tension reverberated through me, tightening my muscles until they were as stiff as boards.

"You didn't hear?" Her white brows reached her hairline.

"Hear what?"

Had something happened to Z? Fuck, I knew I should've gone with them! If my father laid a hand on her—

"Lupe and Devlin." Mrs. Grinshaw's lips curled downwards as sadness sparked to life in her eyes.

Now I was panicking for a completely different reason.

"What the fuck happened to them?" I demanded, and her eyes narrowed at my curse word. She'd been the one to teach all seven of us etiquette, so I knew that my slip of tongue had her mentally seething.

But then her face distorted once more, the anger transforming into sadness. She lowered her eyes to her hands, where they fisted in the skirt of her dress. "They felt...well...I imagine you felt the same. I'm sorry, dear. I know you must be grieving as well—"

"Grieving?" I interrupted, knowing I was being rude but not giving a damn. There were too many things I needed to focus on.

Her nose wrinkled. "The mating bond?"

"The mating bond," I repeated blankly as pieces to this deformed puzzle finally started to come together. "Devlin and Lupe...felt the mating bond break?"

My heart thumped erratically in my chest, and my hands turned ice-cold. A single bead of sweat slid down my forehead, but I didn't make a move to brush it away.

The feeling of the mating bond snapping in two and then dissolving was unimaginable. It was an agony I wouldn't wish on my worst enemy.

If they felt that...

And if they didn't know that Z was still alive, too lost in their pain and grief to notice the bond reforming...

"Where are they?"

Grinshaw's tongue darted out to lick her lip as she shuffled from foot to foot. I knew whatever she had to tell me was bad, horrible even, and I braced myself, my tongue stuck to the roof of my mouth.

"Lupe went feral," Grinshaw told me sadly. "We had to lock him in the capital's dungeon for fear of what he might do to others...or himself."

Shit.

Panic roared within me for my shifter brother, but I forced myself to push it down and focus on what I did best—fix problems for my family. I may not have been a natural-born leader like Devlin, but I was the problem-solver of our makeshift family. I'd fix this. I had to.

"And Devlin?" My voice was nothing but a raspy whisper, my mind running a mile a minute as I pictured my shifter brother trapped in the capital's dungeon below me, slowly losing his mind to the wrath. Was he at least human, or had he transformed into his bear? Was there anything left of the brother we all loved?

Panic warred in my chest and swallowed the air around me.

And what about Devlin? Where the fuck was he?

Please be okay. Please be okay.

Please, please be okay.

"He left," Grinshaw told me simply, and I could see the underlying fear in her gaze. There was more to the story than what she was telling me.

"Where the fuck did he go?" My hands shook as complete and utter fear consumed me. Annihilated me.

"I tried to stop him." A single tear slid down Mrs. Grinshaw's face as she once more grabbed at her skirt, pulling at a string that had somehow gotten loose.

"Where. Did. He. Go?" I hissed out, though my anger wasn't directed at her.

"He wanted revenge. He said...he said he was going to kill a woman named Aaliyah."

TWENTY-NINE

DEVLIN

There was nothing but pain and darkness.

No light broke through the monotony of my thoughts as I stared out the windshield. Rain splattered the glass, cascading down like teardrops. Fitting, I supposed, with my own tears making salty tracks on my face.

Numb.

I felt numb.

Empty.

Nothing mattered any more—not the kingdoms, not my brothers, not even my own life.

Z was dead.

I'd felt the moment our bond broke, signifying she had left me. And with her went what remained of my heart and sanity.

I'm coming, baby girl.

There were a few things I needed to do before I felt comfortable joining my beloved in the afterlife. When I left her years before, I'd known I would survive it because she was still alive. Still smiling and laughing and *loving*. I would happily live in the dark if it meant she would thrive in the light.

But this? Knowing she was gone for good? It destroyed something fundamental inside of me. Everything ached—from the tips of my feet to my very soul.

I wouldn't be able to save the kingdoms from complete and utter ruin, but I could enact my vengeance.

Aaliyah was going to die for what she did to my mate.

And if death claimed me during the impending fight?

It would just save me a bullet to the skull.

Just a few days, baby. And then I'll be with you.

EPILOGUE

S

"Y ou cannot be fucking serious!" I raged, spinning on my brother. T lifted his hands in the air in a placating manner, though the stubborn glint in his eyes did not cease.

"You can't see her, brother. Not yet."

"Why the fuck not?" I continued to pace the small hotel room, my feet wearing a hole in the carpeting. We'd been here just about two days, and I was going fucking crazy.

When T freed me from my prison, I'd thought I'd be reunited with him and the love of my existence. But instead, I was faced with the cold hard truth—Z was in love with another man. Seven other men, to be exact.

Nightmares.

The crowned princes.

"It's a spell," I seethed, whirling on my brother. "She must be under a spell."

The Z I knew would never sleep with the enemy unless she was forced to or she was undercover. And since T insisted it wasn't either...then that must mean she was under some sort of coercion. Maybe she was being blackmailed? Threatened?

The princes were evil, as were their fathers, and it was my job to save my girl before she fell prey to their wickedness.

"Whatever they're using her for probably isn't good," I continued as T cast me a pitying look. I hated that damn look more than words could describe. He'd told me numerous times before that Z was *in love* with those monsters.

Bullshit.

They must've done something to her.

I stared intently at the picture T had given me, the same picture I'd stared at every damn second for the last day and a half.

It showed Z smiling up at a tall, muscular man with light brown hair and thick glasses. Six other men surrounded her, all staring at her with lovestruck eyes. It was apparent to me that they didn't know the picture was being taken, but that only made me more enraged. Envy swirled in my stomach. I wanted nothing more than to be the man she stared at so...lovingly. Combined with the envy was wrath, white-hot and blistering. How dare these men try to take away my one reason for living? What Z and I had...it was fucking amazing, and these monsters couldn't even try to replicate it.

I was prideful enough to admit that I didn't want Z with anyone else. Not when we could finally be together again. I was gluttonous for more of her—her taste, her laugh, her smile...I wanted it all. At the same time, I was greedy and selfish. I didn't want to share her with those men, not when I knew what it felt like to have her all to myself.

A trickle of lust invaded my senses as I stared at her perfect smile, before dropping my gaze to her smooth collarbone and the swells of her breasts. I traced my finger over her face as emotions bombarded me. We'd been doing nothing all day, and I was feeling pretty damn lazy.

But that was going to change.

Ideas formed in my head the longer I stared at the picture, and with a grunt of determination, I ripped the image in half—eliminating the guys while saving my Z's sweet face. I kissed the picture before gently placing it in my back pocket.

"I'm going after her," I told my brother with a piercing glare. He threw his hands up into the air and released an exasperated scoff.

"And what will you do when you reach her?"

My words were a vow, a promise, a declaration. "I'm going to kill the princes and save my girl."

And they won't even see me coming.

WANT TO KNOW WHAT HAPPENS NEXT? PRE-ORDER book five, Pride, here!

ACKNOWLEDGMENTS

It takes a team to make these books, and fortunately, I have the best one.

Thank you to my alphas Kelly, Ellen, and Ash! I can't even describe with words how amazing your advice and input is.

Thank you to Melody for creating this beautiful cover and to Meghan for editing and polishing this book. You ladies are the best!

And finally, I would like to thank my incredible family. Without you guys...I probably would've finished this book two years earlier. But it's the thought that counts, right?

And finally, I would like to say thank you to my incredible readers. Every day, I am humbled and astounded by your support and encouragement. Thank you for believing in me, my characters, and my stories. I wouldn't be where I am today without all of you.

Katie May is a reverse harem author, a KDP All-Star winner, and an USA Today Bestselling Author. She lives in West Michigan with her family, cat, and adorable puppy. When not writing, she can be found reading a good book, listening to broadway musicals, or playing games. Join Katie's Gang to stay updated on all her releases! And did you know she has a TikTok? Yeah, me neither. Follow her here! But be warned...she's an awkward noodle.

5. Pride

Prodigium Academy (Horror Comedy Academy Reverse Harem)

1. Monsters

2. Roaring

Tory's School for the Trouble (Bully Horror Academy Reverse Harem)

1. Between

2. Beyond (Coming Soon)

Supernaturalette (Interactive Reverse Harem)

1. Introductions

2. First Dates

3. Group Outing

4. Game Night

5. Exes

6. Truth or Dare

Kingdom of Wolves (Shifter Reverse Harem Duet)

1. Torn to Bits

2. Ripped to Shreds

CO-WRITES

Afterworld Academy with Loxley Savage (Academy Fantasy Reverse Harem, COMPLETED)

1. Dearly Departed

2. Darkness Deceives

3. Defying Destiny

Darkest Flames with Ann Denton (Paranormal Reverse Harem, COMPLETED)

1. Demon Kissed

1.5. Demon Stalked

2. Demon Loved

3. Demon Sworn

STAND-ALONES

Toxicity (Contemporary Reverse Harem)

Not All Heroes Wear Capes (Just Dresses) (Short Comedic Reverse Harem)

Charming Devils (Bully/Revenge Reverse Harem)

Goddess of Pain (Fantasy Reverse Harem)

Demon's Joy (Holiday Reverse Harem)

www.ingramcontent.com/pod-product-compliance
Lightning Source LLC
Chambersburg PA
CBHW021226310726
48971CB00006B/1708